A Bookshop Christmas

A Bookshop Christmas

Rachel Burton

An Aria Book

This edition first published in the United Kingdom in 2021 by Aria,
an imprint of Head of Zeus Ltd

A CIP catalogue record for this book is available from the
British Library.

9 7 5 3 1 2 4 6 8

ISBN (PBO): 9781801100571
ISBN (E): 9781801100557

Cover design © The Brewster Project

Typeset by Siliconchips Services Ltd UK

Printed and bound in the UK by
CPI Group (UK) Ltd, Croydon CR0 4YY

Aria
Head of Zeus
5–8 Hardwick Street
London EC1R 4RG

WWW.ARIAFICTION.COM

To my husband

A Bookshop Christmas

"We have entered a contract of mutual agreeableness…"

—Jane Austen, *Northanger Abbey*

Prologue

May 2016

She was watching the weak and almost undrinkable coffee drip into the white plastic cup when her husband died. She wasn't with him because she was waiting by the drinks machine. She hadn't even wanted coffee really, she'd just wanted a moment away from the dimly lit room, the smell of disinfectant and the gentle beep, beep, beep of the machines. She'd wanted a little bit of time on her own and that time made her miss those last moments.

She would never forgive herself for that.

When the nurse met her outside the room and told her, she dropped the cup of coffee and heard a choked, strangled sound that she thought was coming from herself. She pushed past the nurse and into the room, lay down on the bed next to him, took his still-warm hand in hers, and pretended that she'd never left and that his gentle slipping away was still to come.

She didn't know how long she lay there next to him; she didn't know how much time had passed before the nurse came into the room and spoke to her in hushed whispers. It could have been hours or minutes. Slowly she got up and followed the nurse's instructions to go home and get some sleep.

"We can deal with paperwork tomorrow," the nurse said. "Do you have anywhere you can go or someone who could be with you tonight?"

She nodded, pretending. She didn't want to go anywhere but home and she didn't want to be anywhere but alone in bed, the bed she had shared with her husband for so many years.

And she didn't want to think about how she was going to live without him.

1

November 2019

I was hanging the last of the paper chains in the shop window when the phone rang. If it had been my mobile I'd have let it go to voicemail, but it was the shop phone so I let the paper chain drop and walked to the counter to answer the call.

"Taylor's Bookshop, Megan speaking."

"Ah, Ms Taylor, it's Philomena Bloom here," a loud posh female voice boomed down the line and I held the receiver away from my ear a little bit.

"Who?"

"Philomena Bloom," the woman repeated impatiently as though I was meant to know who she was. "Xander Stone's agent," she went on. I could almost hear the woman rolling her eyes.

"Of course," I said. "I'm so sorry – you just caught me at a bad time." You'd think I'd remember a name like that.

A normal person would have asked me if they could call back at a more convenient time, but Philomena Bloom bulldozed on regardless. "I'm checking up on the details for Mr Stone's book launch next week," she said.

"Of course," I said again, cringing inside as I crouched down behind the counter to find the shop diary. I really needed to get more organised and get the diary online, along with the ordering and stock-taking systems. Missy had been nagging me to do it for months but there was something so comforting about a paper diary and I was reluctant to let it go.

"Friday the twenty-ninth," Philomena went on. "Seven for seven-thirty."

"Of…" I managed to stop myself saying 'of course' for the third time. "Yes, everything's organised," I said instead, even though I wasn't sure about that at all.

I was used to organising book launches, author readings and all sorts of other events at the bookshop – how else could we keep it running? – but Xander Stone's launch was the highest profile event we'd ever hosted and I wondered if I'd bitten off more than I could chew. The man who'd self-published a book about the ghosts of North Yorkshire was one thing, but Xander Stone?

"Because Mr Stone is very particular." While my mind had been drifting Philomena had been bellowing so I forced myself to concentrate. "He will want to see the lay of the land for himself, choose the menu and so forth."

"Menu?" I'd thought it was just going to be champagne and nibbles.

"For the nibbles, of course," Philomena said slowly, as though speaking to an inattentive child.

"Well, Mr Stone is very welcome any time at Taylor's

Bookshop," I said forcing a smile that Philomena couldn't see. "Just ask him to come by beforehand and we can discuss all his requirements. Or if he wants to talk sooner he can give me a ring." Over the summer, a new café had opened on the corner by the bookshop – a couple from the coast specialising in artisan teas and unusual cakes and snacks. I'd asked them to cater for Xander Stone's launch and hoped they would be up to his 'very particular' standards.

"I think he's in York at the moment, in fact," Philomena said, and I heard her clicking away on her computer keyboard – she had clearly digitised her diaries. "Yes, here we are. He was due to leave London yesterday."

"Really? The book launch isn't until next week."

"As I said, he's very particular and superstitious."

"Superstitious?" I asked, surprised. Maybe he would fit in with the ghost experts and ufologists who had launched at Taylor's Bookshop after all.

"Yes, he always likes to be out of London when the reviews start to come in and *The Guardian*, *The Times* and *The Telegraph* are all due to review this weekend."

"I see." This raised all sorts of questions which really weren't my business to ask.

"So everything is organised?" Philomena double-checked.

"Everything is organised," I replied, finally opening the diary on the right page and seeing that I had, at least, got the date right. Along with the champagne and nibbles orders I didn't really see what else I could do until the day. "But Mr Stone can pop by any time to let me know what else he might need."

"Excellent, well I'll see you a week tomorrow," Philomena

said before ringing off. So she was coming too then. I wondered if Xander Stone was bringing any more of his entourage with him that I should know about.

It had seemed like such a good idea when Philomena Bloom from Bloom & Cuthbert Literary Agents had first called. There was no Cuthbert apparently, just Philomena herself. "It makes people think there's a man about the place," Philomena had confided in me during that first conversation back in August. "Makes them take me more seriously." I'd agreed noncommittally, not sure what to make of Ms Bloom or the non-existent Mr Cuthbert. I was just excited to be getting our first *Sunday Times* best-selling author launching at Taylor's. Back in the summer it had felt like exactly the sort of publicity the bookshop needed but now, at the end of November with only eight days to go, it felt more than a little overwhelming. Did Xander Stone know that we were just a provincial bookshop? Did he realise that we were hardly Waterstones Piccadilly? He was the current *wunderkind* of postmodern literary fiction and his second novel, *Interim*, had been shortlisted for the Booker Prize. Did he really want his third book to be launched at Taylor's? I suspected that we needed him a lot more than he needed us.

I went back to hanging the paper chains, the last of the Christmas decorations in the shop. I always felt better once the bookshop was ready for Christmas.

It had been Bella's idea to try to get more high-profile authors to lead events at the bookshop.

"You need to start building a relationship with publicists and agents," she'd said with her marketing hat on. "It'll help build up the shop profile."

"I wouldn't know where to start," I'd replied, even though that wasn't strictly true. I did know, I just didn't feel ready to open that part of my life up again.

"Well, I can help if you like," Bella said. She worked in the marketing department of the Jórvik Viking Museum and I'd been so delighted not to have to start making the phone calls to my past life that I'd left her to it. I hadn't expected those calls to end up in booking Xander Stone. I wasn't sure if the bookshop was up to the task.

I'd first met Bella when she had come into Taylor's to do some Christmas shopping. It had been my first Christmas back in York and other than trying to give the bookshop the refurbishment and rebrand it so desperately needed, I'd mostly kept myself to myself, licking my wounds in the upstairs flat where I was living with my mother again, the flat I'd spent the first eighteen years of my life in until I'd moved across the city to the halls of residence at York University.

When I first met Bella, I hadn't really known anyone in York who wasn't directly connected to the bookshop. Bella was Missy's flatmate – Missy came into the shop three days a week to do the accounts and manage our stock-taking systems and payroll ("Missy is short for Artemis," she'd explained when I first met her. "My dad's a Classics professor at Yale.") – and she had invited me to go out with them for a few Christmas drinks.

I'd been reluctant at first, feeling it was still too soon to go out, to enjoy myself, to smile again. But Mum had insisted.

"It's been six months, love," she'd said. "I'm not suggesting you should be anywhere near over it, but I do think it's time you cut yourself some slack. And if you're moving back to York for good, you need some friends your own age."

I'd forced myself to go, ignoring the feelings of anxiety and foreboding in my stomach and armed myself with an excuse to leave as early as possible. I hadn't needed the excuse though because I'd found I'd enjoyed myself and felt distracted enough in Bella and Missy's company to catch a glimpse of who I used to be. Three years later I was still grateful to past me that I'd gone out that night as it had been the beginning of a great friendship. Mum had been right – I had needed to meet people my own age.

"The shop looks fantastic," Mum said as she came down from the upstairs flat, interrupting my thoughts and making me jump. "I was never able to get it to look so beautiful. You've got a real gift for this sort of thing. After you left home the shop always looked a bit like I'd let primary school children run wild every Christmas! You must get it off your dad."

I'd been nearly eighteen when my father left, practically an adult myself. Apart from his ability to decorate bookshops for Christmas – although I personally remember his decorations being from the school of quantity rather than quality – Walter Taylor was also a published poet, who had, over the years, won prizes and slowly started to make a living from his writing. He'd gone to London and left us behind. I think he'd been waiting for me to not need him around anymore, but don't we always need our parents around?

"I need a bigger life," I'd heard him tell Mum before he left, as I stood behind the living room door eavesdropping. "I need to get away from this city, this bookshop. I've been here my whole life." Dad's parents had opened Taylor's Bookshop on a little cobbled street behind York Minster in the early 1960s and Dad, like me, had grown up in the flat above the shop. Mum had let him leave for his 'bigger life' without a word of protest, as though she didn't care where he went, but then she'd cry herself to sleep night after night once he'd gone.

I'd kept in touch with Dad after he'd left, although in the crazy days of A levels, university and meeting Joe I didn't see him again until my wedding day, when I'd asked him to walk me down the aisle. It wasn't until then that I'd realised how angry I was with him for leaving without us or how abandoned I'd felt. It had taken me a long time to get past those feelings enough to have a relationship with my father again and Joe had been pivotal in that. Once we'd moved to London after our wedding he'd insisted we take Dad up on his various invitations out – meals and parties, book launches and openings. Joe and Dad had got on so well, making me laugh with their banter and constant light-hearted bickering, that I'd slowly allowed myself to listen to Dad and to begin to understand why he'd left. After all, hadn't I done exactly the same thing and left York and the bookshop behind at the first possible opportunity, looking for my own version of that bigger life?

But once Joe wasn't there anymore, Dad and I had drifted apart again. He'd moved to France by then, taking up a 'writer in residence' opportunity in Paris. I'd always found some excuse as to why I couldn't visit him or talk to him on the phone for long. I didn't want that bigger life now and I didn't want Dad asking me why.

A small, quiet life was exactly what I needed.

I gazed around the shop – the extent of my life these days – pleased at how festive it was looking now I had all the decorations up.

"It does look good, doesn't it," I said.

"You've excelled yourself," Mum replied.

I wondered what Xander Stone would think when he saw it.

"Have you finished for the day?" I asked. Mum, or Martha Taylor as her readers know her, wrote historical romance serials for magazines and had turned the attic space above the flat into a writing room for herself.

"I've done all I can for now," she replied.

"Do you mind closing the shop for me? I just need to pop out."

The supermarket was heaving. Tinny Christmas music was blaring out of the tannoy system, and it wasn't even December yet. Were people really stocking up for the season already? I pushed my way through the hordes of shoppers towards the wine section, wishing I'd just bought some cheap Cava from the little grocer's shop a few doors down from the bookshop. But I did really want some nice champagne for tonight's book club meeting, because I had something a little bit special to announce.

I'd cooked up the idea of the Die-Hard Romantics Book Club with Bella and Missy two years ago over one too many gin and tonics.

"We don't need to read a certain book each week or anything boring like that," Bella had said, waving her hand in the air tipsily. "It's just a group of women who love romance novels talking about romance novels. We read what we want to read; we recommend to each other…"

"And we drink!" Missy had interrupted, holding her glass aloft.

And just like that, the Die-Hards had come into being. At first it had just been the three of us along with Mum, but after we put some posters up on the bookshop noticeboard more people had been interested. During the book club's first year people had come and gone but now we had formed a steady group that met every week and talked about romance novels, film adaptations and any other gossip we felt like indulging in.

We didn't always agree – there'd been ongoing disagreements about whether or not *Love Story* and *Me Before You* could be classified as romance novels because of their endings.

"You can have *Me Before You*," I'd told them. "But *Love Story* is a romance novel and that's a hill I'm willing to die on."

"There's no point arguing with her," Mum had said. "She's loved that book since she was thirteen – she's never going to back down now."

I smiled at the memory, making a mental note to read *Love Story* again soon and maybe watch the film too. It counted as a Christmas movie ("Of course it's not a Christmas movie," I could hear Bella shouting at me in my head – but Bella refused to accept that *Die Hard* was a Christmas movie, so what did she know), released in December, set predominantly in the winter and those heart-breaking final scenes taking place just before Christmas.

Mum had been right – I had loved both the book and

the film since I was a teenager, but over the last few years I'd found a strange sort of solace in the story. It felt like a blueprint for navigating my life as it was now and it made me feel less alone. Other people, even if they were fictional, had gone through what I had gone through.

I was rudely awoken from my reverie in front of the champagne by a strong and sudden jolt to the back of my legs.

"What the hell?" I exclaimed, turning around.

A tall, dark man in a very expensive-looking wool coat was standing behind me with a trolley full of food, wine and what seemed to be Christmas decorations. He was looking down his slightly crooked nose at me in an irritable manner.

"Did you just hit me with your trolley?" I snapped at him, annoyed at the interruption to my memories.

"You're in my way," he said.

"It's usual," I replied, summoning up my steeliest voice, "to say 'excuse me'."

"I did. You ignored me."

"Well clearly I didn't hear you; perhaps you should speak louder. It's extremely noisy in here."

He didn't say anything for a moment and we stared at each other as Noddy Holder wished everyone a Merry Christmas over the awful supermarket speakers even though there was still over a month to go. He really was very good-looking – the man with the trolley, not Noddy Holder – and I found myself wondering what he might look like if he smiled.

"You're still in my way," the man said after a while without even the merest hint of a smile.

"And you still haven't said 'excuse me' at an audible volume," I replied.

I watched him roll his eyes and look away for a moment. Then he ducked his head and looked straight at me.

"Excuse me," he said slowly and sarcastically.

Reluctantly I stepped sideways, allowing him to pass.

"You're the rudest man I've ever met," I called after him as he walked away. He didn't turn around, he just raised one hand before disappearing into the crowd.

2

When I got back to the bookshop, I took the bottles of champagne that I'd eventually managed to purchase upstairs to put them in the fridge to chill. I felt another wave of embarrassment at the bizarre argument I'd managed to get embroiled in at the supermarket. After the rude man had walked away I'd realised that everyone in the wine aisle had been staring at me and I'd had to pick random bottles of champagne and hasten a retreat as quickly as possible. I didn't really know what had come over me. I wasn't usually the type to engage with strangers, especially ones like that, but there had been something about him…

"Are you all right?" Mum asked as I came into the kitchen. "You look frazzled." I noticed the wrinkle of concern in her forehead – she'd looked at me like that a lot since I'd first moved back to York and I hated how much she worried about me. I was meant to be grown up enough to look after myself these days, even though I wasn't sure I could have got through the last three years without her.

"Oh I'm fine," I replied, trying to sound breezy. "The supermarket was heaving and a man rammed his trolley into the back of my legs and tried to blame it on me. I'm absolutely sure he did it on purpose."

"Ah Christmas," Mum said with a chuckle. "Tis the season to be grumpy."

"It's not even December." I laughed, stacking the bottles in the fridge.

"Have you got everything ready for tonight?"

"As soon as the champagne's chilled we're good to go. Have you chosen a book?" The Die-Hard Romantics had decided to do their Christmas Romance recommendations a little early so we all had time to read each other's favourites and talk (argue) about them through December.

"You know what I'm choosing," Mum said. "How about you? You know you can't have *Love Story* again?"

"I know, I've got something brand new for this year." I paused for a moment, hesitating. "Do you think they'll like my idea for the Christmas party?" I asked.

"I'm sure they will, love," she said, coming over to me and squeezing my shoulder. "I love it and I know Trixie will too. And once Trixie is onside the hard part is over."

Trixie Hendricks was the matriarch of the Die-Hard Romantics – of undisclosed age, but somewhere in her seventies – she had become the fifth permanent member of the group shortly after I'd first put up the posters in the bookshop. A retired librarian with a social life that most women my age could only dream of, and a dating record to match – she particularly loved an unsuspecting widower. She was also a huge Janeite with an almost indefatigable knowledge of Austen and Regency England, and she loved reading historical romances – if only to pick holes in the details. Over the last two years she'd really helped the book group expand its horizons, taking us on trips to Chatsworth, on which Mr Darcy's home of Pemberley had been based, and the Jane Austen festival in Bath when we'd all dressed in Regency costume. The money for these 'field trips' as she called them had come from her own pocket.

"Husband number two left me rather well off," she'd said. There had been three husbands in total, all ancient history now.

I'd loved these Regency outings, but not everyone had been keen.

"Why can't we go on a field trip to meet hot ice hockey players?" Missy, who was more of a sports romance fan, had asked.

I knew Trixie would be a fan of my idea for the big Christmas Eve party but I wasn't sure everyone would be. I was relying on Mum and Trixie to encourage them all to take part.

"Please tell me you haven't chosen *Love Story* again," Missy said, rolling her eyes. The Die-Hards had all arrived early, excited to talk about Christmas romances and my idea for the Christmas party. I'd insisted they do the book talk first, knowing that things would descend into chaos if they didn't get that out of the way, and then nobody would have any reading suggestions for the Christmas period.

"No," I said. "I promised Mum I wouldn't bore you all to death about that for the third year in a row."

"Good, because it's neither a Christmas book nor a romance," Missy said, pouring herself more champagne.

"Well this book is definitely a Christmas book and a romance," I replied, ignoring the jibe. "And it's the prequel to a series so gives me lots to read and discuss with you guys well into the new year."

"Out with it," Bella said. "What is it?"

"It's called *A Christmas Gone Perfectly Wrong* and I think it's the perfect Christmas romance."

"Bold words," Mum said with a smile.

"It's the day before Christmas Eve 1807 and Andrew Blackshear – who is tremendously handsome but rather stuck-up and proper..."

"Of course," Bella interrupted, looking interested. Unlike Missy she loved historical romances.

"He's out in the Suffolk countryside picking up a Christmas present for his sister when he meets a woman in the road. Needless to say that isn't the last time they meet and, due to a series of complicated events, he ends up with her in his carriage, and with a broken carriage wheel on Christmas Eve..."

"And there's nowhere for them to go?" Bella interrupted.

"Exactly." I grinned. "So they have to pretend to be husband and wife to find somewhere to stay for the night..."

"And there's only one bed?" Bella interrupted again. "Please tell me there's only one bed."

"There's only one bed," I confirmed.

"My favourite trope," Bella squealed.

"It does sound wonderful," Trixie said. "I wonder why I haven't heard of it?"

"Your turn, Dot," Bella said. "What's your favourite Christmas romance this year?"

"There hasn't been a new Ruby Bell book this year," Missy said, "So I'm intrigued to see what you've chosen."

Dot Bridges was a lecturer in English at York University, although she hadn't been there when I'd been an English undergraduate. Unlike Trixie, Dot had never married. She'd been a member of the Die-Hards for just over a year – the last permanent member to join – and was Ruby Bell's biggest fan. She always pre-ordered the latest seasonal romance – one in summer, one in winter – from Taylor's Bookshop. Ms Bell had picked up where Jackie Collins had left off, writing sweeping romances set in exotic locations with sex scenes to make a reader blush. But for some reason this winter Ruby Bell hadn't published a new book and there was no real way of finding out why because nobody knew who Ruby Bell was – she had no social media presence, no website, no author headshot on the cover of her books. She was a complete mystery.

"No new Ruby Bell this year," Dot said, pulling a battered paperback out of her handbag. "But I do have this." She held up a copy of *One Day in December*. "It's not strictly a Christmas book but it is so romantic."

"Oh I loved that book!" Mum exclaimed.

"Me too," said Missy and they fell into discussion about the story of Laurie and the boy on the bus.

Mum had chosen *The Lady Most Willing* as I'd guessed she would – a Regency romance about a Christmas trip to Scotland – and Bella had chosen *The Devil in Winter*, another historical romance – early Victorian this time – but one Mum wasn't a fan of.

"I don't know how anyone can forgive Sebastian St Vincent for his actions," she said.

"He's completely swoon-worthy, Martha," Bella replied. "What are you talking about?"

"He kidnapped someone!" Mum replied.

"I'm with Mum," I said. "I just don't see that there's any coming back from the kidnapping."

"The kidnapping was in the previous book," Bella said, trying to defend her hero, who had first appeared in an earlier book in the series. "He's reformed by Evie's love."

Mum made a snorting noise.

"I'm not really convinced by those reformed rake storylines," I said. "Some are OK. I guess it depends what they've done – if they're just rude and arrogant and there's a reason for it I guess we can come back from that." I thought again of the rude man in the supermarket with the dark eyes and the perfect cheekbones. "But kidnapping? I don't think so. Besides, it doesn't even mention Christmas – it's just set in winter."

"We could argue about this forever," Missy said, looking bored. "Who's next?"

Nobody was surprised when Trixie chose a collection of seasonal short stories by Georgette Heyer called *Snowdrift* and Missy chose an ice hockey romance called *Maybe This Christmas*.

"You should read it, Megan," she said. "Ash and Emma are to die for and there's this scene on a physiotherapy couch that is just on fire!"

"I'm not interested in ice hockey," I said.

"You don't need to be. It's just a hot Christmas romance and anyway, it might get you into ice hockey – someone on this grey, wet island must like it!"

Missy had grown up in the Connecticut town of Hartford ("Like Lorelai Gilmore," she'd said, as though Lorelai was a real person), the daughter of two Yale graduates who had had great hopes of their daughter following in their footsteps. She'd disappointed them by getting on a plane to London when she was nineteen instead. She'd been in England ten years now and not many people knew what had brought her here or why she never went back home.

But she'd told me the story one night soon after we'd first met, not long after I'd first told her about Joe, knowing that I would understand how hard it was to go back after something like that had happened. I still wondered if I'd ever be able to go back to London – or if I'd ever want to.

"So now we've all shared our Christmas books, are you going to talk about the party?" Bella asked, topping up everyone's champagne glasses. "You're being very mysterious."

"OK," I said, picking up my glass. "I thought that we could do something a bit different this year rather than just the usual drinks and crisps and standing about kind of party that we've had for the last three Christmases." It had been my idea to have a little gathering after closing on Christmas Eve each year in the first place – something I'd instigated when I'd come back to York and slowly taken over the running of the bookshop from Mum, but it had never been anything very formal. Just drinks with local authors, regular customers and suppliers. "This year I thought we could do a Regency Christmas," I announced to the group.

"I'm intrigued," Trixie said, leaning forward and smiling a red-lipsticked smile. "Go on."

"We could play Regency games, have Regency food and…" I hesitated for a moment, knowing this next announcement might not go down well with everyone in the group "…wear Regency dress. After all, we still have our gowns from when we went to Bath."

Bella groaned. "I was with you until the dressing-up part," she said. "You know I hate that bit." Sometimes Bella's work at the Jorvik Viking Museum meant she had to wear appropriate costume. She hadn't been enthusiastic about the Bath trip, but she'd done it – so I was sure she could be encouraged to do it again.

"Costumes will be optional," Mum said. "After all, we can't expect everyone to have a costume ready with only a month's notice."

"I think it would be nice if we did all dress up, Bella," Dot said. "Especially as we do have the gowns anyway. Lead by example and all that."

"We're all women though," Missy interjected. "It would be better if we had some Regency men in very tight breeches, wouldn't it?" She raised one perfect eyebrow lasciviously.

"Well, I could start by asking Colin to dress up," I suggested, trying not to laugh. Colin was a postgraduate student who worked part-time at the bookshop and, while he was very nice, I wasn't sure he was quite what Missy had in mind.

Missy crinkled her nose. "Hmmmm, I was hoping for someone with more muscular thighs," she said. "But otherwise I'm all for it. Just tell me what I have to do. I can't wait to get that gown on again." Missy had looked particularly good in her gown and her heavily tattooed arms and green diamante glasses had accentuated the look. But then Missy was one of those people who could make a hessian sack look glamorous.

"I think it's a fabulous idea," Trixie said. "But it will take a lot of work to get it right and we don't have much time."

I noticed that she was already scribbling lists in a notebook. "That will have to go," she said, pointing her pen at the Christmas tree that I'd dragged across York that morning and spent most of the afternoon decorating. "Beautiful as it is."

"What? Why?" I asked.

"Because trees weren't brought into the house and decorated in Regency times. Instead greenery – holly, ivy and mistletoe of course – was gathered on Christmas Eve and laid on the mantelpiece, as I'm sure you know from your historical romances."

"Can't we have both?" Mum asked.

"We could take it down on Christmas Eve before the party," Trixie suggested.

"Let's have both," I said. I was the one who'd dragged the tree across town and now it was here it was staying until twelfth night or when all the needles fell off – whichever was sooner. "The Christmas tree stays and we bring greenery in on Christmas Eve as well. We could get everyone who comes to bring a bunch of holly or something."

"OK," Trixie said, making a note. "Now you mentioned games…"

"Snapdragon," Bella interrupted.

"Bella, I don't think a game that involves setting fire to sultanas is a good idea in a shop that is essentially full of paper," I said.

Bella's face fell. "Oh yes, I hadn't thought of that. Still, it sounds like one of the more fun Regency games." I'd never really got to the bottom of the rules of snapdragon, other than that it seemed to involve dried fruit and naked flames, but it had been mentioned in more than one of the Christmas Regency romances that I'd read.

"It is a Regency game," Trixie confirmed. "But I think we'll probably be safer sticking to cards – whist, cribbage and pontoon are all fairly easy to learn."

"You could teach us," Mum suggested. "And we could teach other people on the night."

"And we need to make sure that people only play for matchsticks or something," I said. "No gambling or I'll be closed down!"

"Oooh, we could make it a masked ball," Bella said. "I'd dress up for that."

"But we'd all know each other," Dot said. "It's always the same people who come on Christmas Eve so you wouldn't have to be a genius to work out who was who."

"Besides, we're mostly women," Missy pointed out again. "So there's not much chance of a quickie behind the bookshelves with a masked stranger is there?"

"There's always Colin." Dot laughed.

I held up my hands. "No quickies in the bookshop!" I said. "But dancing sounds fun. Do you know any Regency dances you could teach us, Trixie?"

"A quadrille should be fairly easy to learn—"

"Again," Missy interrupted, "we're all women."

"Well we'll just have to dance with each other then, won't we," I said, feeling as though the Regency night wasn't quite as popular with the Die-Hards as I'd hoped it would be. "Perhaps this wasn't such a great idea after all. We can just go back to what we normally do if you prefer."

"Noooooo," everyone chorused.

"It's a wonderful idea," Bella said, reaching over to squeeze my arm. "I'm sorry I moaned about dressing up."

I smiled. "What about food?" I asked. "What sort of dishes would have been served at a Regency Christmas?"

"Well, I'm assuming you don't want a roast goose and mock-turtle soup," Trixie said with a smile.

"Umm, no, I was thinking more finger food?" Did they have finger food in Regency times? I had no idea. I really hadn't thought this through as thoroughly as I should have done.

"Regency balls usually stopped for a sit-down supper," Trixie said. "But we could do a twenty-first-century take on that – cold meats and pickles, mini Yorkshire puddings, individual pasties, that sort of thing."

After chatting about Regency food for a while and being rather disgusted at things like jugged hare and white soup, everyone agreed to go home, do some research and come back the next week with some ideas.

"I'll bring some playing cards," Trixie said. "And we'll go through a few games. I can bring some music too if you like, Megan, and we could have a dance."

"That would be wonderful," I said, watching Trixie adding more items to the long list she was compiling. "Are you sure you don't mind doing all this?" I asked.

Trixie grinned. "Don't be silly, dear," she said. "I love this sort of thing, happy to help. But I must be off now," she went on, putting the list in her huge black handbag. "I must see how Stan is."

Bella and Missy exchanged a glance. "Stan?" Bella asked.

"My latest flame, my dear. If he's still around at Christmas I might see if he'll don some tight breeches. I think he'd look rather dashing. A bit like Colonel Brandon."

3

Everybody left the bookshop that night hooting with laughter at the fact Trixie had yet another new boyfriend.

"I wonder how long this one will last," Bella said.

"I wonder how young he is," Missy replied.

"Come on, you two," Dot said, ushering the women out of the door. "Leave Trixie alone." And with a flurry of goodbyes they were gone.

"You go up, Mum," I said as I locked the door behind them. "I'll finish off down here."

"Are you sure?" she asked, and I noticed the flash of worry across her brow.

I smiled. "I'm fine, Mum, really." I was fine, wasn't I? At least a lot closer to fine than I'd been in a long time. I wanted my mother to stop worrying about me; I wanted to stop hearing the note of concern in my father's voice every time he called. I knew why they worried. I knew what a mess I'd been after Joe died, and Mum and I had always been close, so she was bound to be concerned. But recently their concern had started to make me feel claustrophobic and I'd taken that as a good sign, another step forward, as though I was managing to finally get away from the cotton wool haze of grief I'd been living in for so long.

I listened to my mother's footsteps on the stairs as she made her way up to the flat above the shop and I sat down for a minute under the lights of the Christmas tree and thought about how much my life had changed in the last three years. I still missed Joe so much and there were times when feelings of guilt and emptiness still completely overtook me, but the times when I didn't think about him, when I didn't feel empty and alone, were starting to be more frequent.

When Mum suggested I come back to York for a while I'd been concerned that the memories here would be as bad as the ones in London, but they were different, more distant somehow, less immediate – and I found myself able to remember the time I'd spent with Joe in York in a more gentle way, a way that didn't feel like a punch in the stomach every time I woke up.

Besides, Taylor's Bookshop had needed me, or at the very least it had needed me to give it some TLC.

"I don't know what happened," Mum had said when I'd been back a few weeks and had started examining the state of the bookshop, and – more importantly – the bookshop's accounts, in more detail. "I knew something needed doing but time just got away from me somehow."

But I'd known it wasn't time that was the problem. When Dad had left for his 'bigger life' in London, not only had he abandoned his wife and daughter but the bookshop he'd inherited from his parents as well. Mum had never had very much to do with the bookshop when I was growing up – she'd spent her days in her writing room, so when Dad left she didn't have any idea what to do to keep the business running and a roof over our heads.

I'd been working part-time in the shop since I was a teenager so I was able to help Mum out, and between me and Fred Bishop – Dad's friend who'd worked in the bookshop for years – we were able to keep things ticking over. When it had come to choosing a university, I'd chosen York so that I could be nearby and continue to help out at the weekends. But when Joe and I had moved to London, even though Mum and I had spoken on the phone several times a week, I'd stopped thinking about the bookshop every day for the first time in my life and I hadn't really realised how much it had been spiralling downhill.

The first thing I'd decided to do when I returned from London was to spruce the whole place up. I had money in the bank from the sale of our flat and, despite Mum's protests, I'd used a little of it to give the shop a thorough makeover. I'd polished the wooden floors and painted the walls white. I'd painted the wooden counters and bookshelves sage green with teal accents and added a little reading nook with a couple of comfy chairs so that shoppers could sit down and browse through books. I'd had the outside of the building repainted as well, in similar colours, and had the logo redesigned by a local artist.

The bookshop stood in a row of shops on one of York's pedestrianised streets near the Minster and had lots of passing trade, but the nicer the shop looked from the outside, the more customers we'd attract. Then I'd moved the dusty second-hand books, which had always seemed to take over the whole shop, into a section of their own, and divided the rest of the shop into more sections – classics, crime, non-fiction, horror, sci-fi, fantasy and, my favourite and most well looked-after and thoroughly dusted section, romance.

Once all that was done, I'd realised just how big the bookshop was. It had become so overcrowded with old books and too-big bookcases that I'd forgotten that we had the space to host bookish events and I became determined to turn the shop into a community space as well – hence the book club and the author launch parties, the latter of which were usually held in a section towards the back of the shop and set up in whatever way the author in question saw fit.

And then I'd set about finding a bookkeeper.

"We need a decent ordering and stock-taking system as well," I'd said when Missy-short-for-Artemis had come for her interview. "I'll be ordering a lot of new stock over the next few months and I need to make sure it's catalogued properly."

"No problem," she'd replied, outlining different systems that we could use. "It's one of my favourite things to do." She'd grinned, and then she'd perused the romance section, introduced me to sports romances after we'd had a short but passionate discussion about whether or not *Persuasion* was a better book than *Pride and Prejudice*, and a friendship was born.

The shop was unrecognisable now to what it had been when I'd first moved back to York from London. As I looked around it, the Christmas lights twinkling, a sense of warmth and pride started to fill the empty hole I felt whenever I thought of Joe. My life would never be what it was and, despite what the ladies of the Die-Hard Romantics Book Club might think, I knew I was never going to meet anyone like him again, but I had the next best things. Friendship and books.

A loud and angry banging on the bookshop door

interrupted my thoughts and I stood up to see who was outside at this time of night. It was very dark in the doorway of the shop and it took me a moment to recognise the shadowy figure on the doorstep. All my seasonal goodwill dissolved as my hackles rose again at the very sight of him.

"What on earth do you want?" I asked as I pulled the door open to the man from the supermarket.

"Megan Taylor," he snapped, without greeting or explanation.

"Yes, that's me."

A startled look passed over his face, as though he'd just realised who I was. "You're Megan Taylor?" he asked, trying to regain his composure.

"Yes and the bookshop closed hours ago so unless this is some sort of life-or-death emergency then can I ask you to come back tomorrow please?"

"But I want to see the inside of the shop," the man said calmly, as though a stranger trying to get into a shop at nearly 10 p.m. was perfectly normal.

"Why?" I asked. I should have shut the door in his face but curiosity was offsetting my anger a little. "Who are you? And why do you keep bothering me wherever I go?"

"I'm Xander Stone," the man said.

I felt my stomach drop as I looked away from him. *Of course you are*, I thought.

"You'll have to excuse the mess," I said as Xander stepped through the door, although quite why I felt I needed to justify the state of my bookshop to the rudest man on earth I didn't know. "We have a book club meeting here on Thursday nights." I'd decided not to turn him away – after all, I did still want him to launch his book at Taylor's and I had promised Philomena he could come by any time. I had expected it to be during opening hours though.

Xander glanced at the empty champagne glasses and shrugged, his hands thrust deep into his coat pockets, before beginning to circumnavigate the shop floor. I watched him, not really knowing what to say. I presumed this was what Philomena Bloom had meant about him wanting to get the 'lay of the land'.

"It's very cluttered in here," he said after a while. "Can we move that?" He waved his hand irritably at the Christmas tree before thrusting it back into his coat pocket.

"No," I said. "As I explained to Ms Bloom when she first booked the venue, it's the month before Christmas, it's our busiest time of year and the shop will be Christmas focused. She said you wouldn't mind."

"Did she?" Xander replied, his back to me as he looked at the bookshelves. "You certainly seem to sell a lot of romance novels." He said the words 'romance novels' in the same sort of tone that one would say 'cat sick'.

Xander Stone he might be, but he was still the rudest man I'd ever met and I felt myself jumping to the defence of my beloved romance novels.

"Romance is one of the most popular and top-selling genres," I said, trying not to sound quite as rude as him. The truth was the bookshop had barely been breaking even this year and I was desperate to turn things around this Christmas. If I was rude to Xander Stone he could just walk away and never come back and I needed his book launch to get people through the doors and buying books if we were to have even the slightest chance of surviving.

"Oh I've heard it all before," Xander said irritably. He was standing so close to me that I had to tilt my head back to look him in the eye and my heart did a strange flutter in my chest. He really was very good-looking. I'd noticed that much in the supermarket – the way his dark hair fell across his forehead, those big brown eyes. He was, in fact, even better looking in the flesh than the author headshot on the back of his books suggested and I was surprised I hadn't recognised who he was earlier. I suppose I hadn't been expecting to see Xander Stone in a supermarket.

"Heard what before?" I asked.

"How romance keeps the industry going so that publishers can take a chance on people like me. But it's just so…" He paused, waving that impatient hand at the shelves as though he was searching for the right word. "Formulaic!" he went on triumphantly. "Boy meets girl, girl either despises boy or finds a ridiculous reason for them not to be together, but they get together anyway and have eye-watering sex at around page 150 followed by a ridiculous misunderstanding at page 225 and then still manage to get a happily-ever-after no matter how nasty they've been to each other."

"But those happy endings are important," I insisted. "When a reader picks up a romance novel they know that happy ending exists. They don't have to worry about *what* will happen and they can just get totally immersed in *how* it happens. Sometimes when life deals you a few blows that kind of thing is important."

"Pure escapism," he replied scathingly, as though wanting to escape from real life every now and then was a bad thing.

"You seem to know an awful lot about romance novels for someone who professes to hate them."

He smiled a sort of half-smile that was full of smugness and shrugged. "Now when did I ever say that I hated them?" he asked. "Besides, I've always thought it was crime that kept the industry going."

Xander turned his back on me again as he continued to peruse the bookshop. He moved over to the counter and started picking up things from the gift section – bookmarks, scented candles, mugs. Each time he picked something up and put it back again he flicked his fingers as though they were unclean.

"It's rather elitist, don't you think," I said as I tried to lead him away from the gift section and back towards the centre of the shop before he smashed a mug.

"What's elitist?" he asked, looking at me as though he didn't quite know who I was or what he was doing in the shop. Was he drunk? Was that why he turned up so late? I tried to surreptitiously smell his breath.

"It's elitist to be so snobby about books," I said. "Just because somebody loves to read romance or crime novels doesn't mean they don't also love to read Ovid or Shakespeare or Dickens or McEwan – who all write about love by the way – or even you."

Xander leaned against the wall and crossed one long leg over the other. And then he smiled a proper smile, not sneery or smug – and what a smile it was, even better than I'd expected. His grumpy, arrogant face lit up if only for moment. It almost made me shiver. Almost.

"And what about you, Ms Taylor," he said. "Have you read any of my books?"

"I've read the first one," I said, looking away from him. That smile was quite disarming.

"And what did you think?"

"Well I thought it was brilliant, obviously," I replied. I wasn't going to lie to him, even though it seemed to make him smile even more. *Boxed* had been one of the greatest postmodern novels I'd ever read – up there with Paul Auster and Jennifer Egan. I hadn't thought it would be my sort of thing at all as it was about a young man growing up in the boxing clubs of East London and was supposedly semi-autobiographical, but I'd surprised myself by how much I'd loved it. "It's a wonderful book," I went on, hoping I didn't sound as though I was gushing. "But just because you wrote that doesn't give you the right to be snobby about genre fiction. Reading is completely subjective and most readers read all kinds of different books. Being a snob about genre is like pretending that reading on e-readers or listening to audiobooks is somehow not proper reading. It's ridiculous." I stopped, realising that I'd said far more than I'd intended and that Xander was still smiling at me.

"I wouldn't have thought a bookseller would be advocating digital reading," he said.

"It's important to open reading up to as many people as possible. E-readers and audiobooks have made reading so accessible." I thought suddenly of Joe's mum, whose eyesight was fading. She had been embarrassed to borrow the large-print editions from the library so Joe had bought her an e-reader and shown her how to change the size of the font. How long had it been since I'd last spoken to Joe's parents? I should call them more often.

"Well anyway," Xander said, waving his hand impatiently in my face to get my attention. "This book launch. Whereabouts are we having it among all this clutter?" I presumed by clutter he meant the Christmas decorations as, since I'd been back, I'd always tried to make sure that the bookshop was spacious and airy. He should have seen what it was like when Mum was in charge.

I stifled a yawn. "Do you think you could come back another time for all this?" I asked. I was tired and wanted to be on my own with the Christmas lights and my memories again, as I had been before Xander Stone had marched into the shop uninvited. "Perhaps during opening hours."

I watched Xander hesitate as though, just for a split second, he was unsure of himself, as though he'd suddenly realised how rude it was to turn up and start demanding things at ten o'clock at night. He rubbed a hand over his face and turned away from me again.

"Fine," he said. "I'll come back in the morning."

4

I sat on a bench – the one I used to think of as 'my bench' – outside York Minster and closed the book I'd been reading. It was still early and, even bundled up in multiple layers, I was cold.

I hadn't slept well after Xander Stone's impromptu visit. Something about him had unnerved me and made me feel as though there was a crack in the armour that I had taken to wearing after Joe, a crack that let a sliver of light in, light I wasn't sure I was ready to look at. I'd tossed and turned all night thinking about Joe, about the life we'd planned together. What would he think if he could see me now, living in my childhood home, barely leaving the bookshop, being unnerved by the smiles of strange men?

If things had been the other way around, what would Joe be doing now?

I'd first started sitting on this bench with a book just after my dad announced he was leaving to embark upon his bigger life. I'd left the shop, and my parents' arguments, which I didn't understand, behind one Saturday afternoon still clutching the book I'd been shelving – a copy of *Don Quixote* – and walked around the Minster until I'd found the empty bench. With nothing else to do, and not wanting to go back to the shop, I'd sat down and started reading. I couldn't remember how long I'd sat there on that Saturday afternoon but somehow, after that, the bench became my refuge, the place I went to when I needed to be alone.

I'd been sitting on this very bench reading *The Moonstone* when I'd first met Joe. It had been a cold day in November, just like this one, and even in my first term of studying English literature I had managed to get behind on my reading list because I'd been prioritising the Christmas romances that Mum had been ordering at the bookshop since the autumn over my university texts. Joe had sat down next to me, asked me what I was reading and if I remembered him.

"Sorry no," I'd said, a little annoyed at having my quiet time on my bench interrupted. "I'm Megan though."

"I know," he'd said. "And I'm Joe." He'd held out his gloved hand and I'd taken it briefly. "We have a history of art class together."

He'd smiled as he'd said it and I'd noticed the freckles on his nose and the way the corners of his hazel eyes crinkled. "It's freezing," he'd said. "Can I buy you a hot chocolate?"

I'd been surprised and even a little envious of the easy way he'd chatted to a virtual stranger. I'd felt so anxious as he'd been speaking to me, scared of stumbling over my words. I'd spent so much of my teens immersed in the books I'd 'borrowed' from the shelves of Taylor's Bookshop that I'd almost forgotten how to socialise with real people. The weekends had been the highlight of my first term at university – not for the big nights out that everyone else seemed to enjoy, but because I got to escape and to return to the familiar surroundings of the bookshop.

But once Joe had persuaded me to go for a drink with him, once we were stirring marshmallows into our oversized Christmas-themed mugs, I'd felt myself relax in his easy company as we'd talked about books and films (*"You've Got Mail* is my favourite," he'd said when I told him I'd grown up in a bookshop. "And I don't care what anyone thinks") and life at university. He was studying law but, like me, was taking advantage of the opportunity to study other modules in the first year – hence the history of art class.

When he'd asked if he could take me out for dinner on the Saturday night, I'd found myself saying yes without even thinking of an excuse or a reason to refuse.

After that the bench had stopped being 'my bench' and had become 'our bench' and these days it was where I always came when I wanted to feel close to Joe.

I went back to my book, trying to shake away the painful memories. I'd picked up a copy of *The Devil in Winter* from the bookshop on my way out. I'd decided to give it another go after Bella had chosen it for book group the previous evening, but I still didn't think much of Sebastian St Vincent, even though I knew most of the romance reading world would disagree with me. However, despite Sebastian being described as fair with blue eyes, in my head he now had dark brown eyes, perfect cheekbones and a lock of hair that kept falling into his face...

"Hello," said a gruff voice next to me. I turned around to find a tall, dark-haired man sitting where Joe should be. I hadn't even noticed him sit down.

"Are you stalking me?" I asked. "Or is it just chance that has you turning up wherever I am?"

"I prefer to think of it as a happy coincidence," Xander

said. He looked far from happy and was staring straight ahead across the Minster precinct, his hands thrust deeply into his coat pockets again. "It's beautiful, isn't it?" he said quietly, nodding towards the Minster.

"Something we can agree on," I replied. "I think it's the most beautiful building in the world. I always miss it when I'm not here."

"Is that why you're sitting here in the freezing cold? Admiring the architecture?"

"Sort of. What's your excuse?"

"I was coming to see you," he said, finally turning towards me. He wasn't smiling this morning, but he was still very good-looking. The watery winter sunlight lit up his face, enhancing the shadows of his cheekbones. "To pick up where we left off last night, as it were."

"It's eight-thirty in the morning," I said. "I told you to come back during opening hours."

"Well we're both here now. I'll come back to the shop with you." It felt like more of a demand than a request and I wondered why he was so eager to see the shop again, to talk about the event. I remembered that moment the previous night when he'd hesitated, as though he wasn't as sure of himself as he would have me believe. Did he come across as rude because he was protecting himself from something? And if so, from what?

"Come on then," I said, standing up reluctantly. "As you're here."

I began to walk back to the bookshop. As he walked beside me, instead of asking me what I was reading like a normal person would do – like Joe had done on that first day we met on the bench – he snatched the book from my hand and snorted with derision.

"*The Devil in Winter*," he sneered, looking at the cover that depicted a forlorn-looking woman standing in the snow, but at least it wasn't one of the many romances that depicted a bare-chested duke on the front. I didn't think I could bear a lecture about objectification in romance novels this early in the morning.

"You might like that one," I said, snatching the book back. "I think you might discover an affinity with the hero – he's extremely rude to everyone as well."

Xander cleared his throat and looked away. "I owe you an apology I think, Ms Taylor," he said.

"Please stop calling me 'Ms Taylor', it's Megan."

"Well, Megan, I owe you an apology. I'll admit that I was rather rude to you in the supermarket yesterday afternoon and I shouldn't have descended on your bookshop at ten at night demanding to be seen. I probably shouldn't have interrupted your reading this morning either. Will you see fit to forgive me?"

He spoke in a very formal manner, very like a duke from a historical romance novel in fact, and I couldn't work out if he was being serious or not.

"I'll forgive you if you stop waving impatiently at me and saying that my shop is full of clutter."

He nodded once. "OK," he said.

"OK," I replied as we arrived at the bookshop and I led him through the front door and towards the back of the shop, past Colin who was on the early shift and getting the shop ready for opening, and to the space in which we held the book launches. "It's up to you how we set things up," I said. "Your agent said you'd be doing a reading and then a Q&A session."

He nodded again without looking at me.

"And she'll be asking the questions?"

"That's what usually happens," he said flatly. "And then we let the audience ask questions too." He pulled a face that made me think the last thing he wanted to do was to let the audience ask him anything.

"Then you'll probably want rows of chairs rather than people standing about," I said, noticing Colin waving at me from behind Xander's shoulder. I tried to ignore him.

Colin was only twenty-two but dressed like somebody three times that age – a style that I'd always suspected he thought made him look like a serious academic. He tended to hang around the history or non-fiction sections and categorically refused to help anyone out in the romance section. Missy suspected he was a little bit scared of romance. Today he was wearing a tatty tweed jacket with leather patches on the elbow and, not for the first time, I thought about making the staff wear a uniform.

"Xander Stone?" Colin asked in an awed whisper as he approached.

Xander turned towards him.

"I'm such a huge fan," Colin gushed, holding out a hand that Xander took rather reluctantly. "I think *Boxed* is the greatest postmodern novel ever written. In fact, it forms the basis of my master's dissertation and I was wondering if I could ask some questions…"

"Xander," I interrupted, noticing a strange look of discomfort on his face at the threat of Colin's questions.

"Can you excuse us for a moment while we get the shop ready for opening?" I looked pointedly at Colin, whose face fell as he realised I wanted him to come with me.

"I genuinely didn't think you'd pull it off," Colin said as he followed me towards the till.

"Thanks very much, Colin."

"What's wrong with him?" Colin asked. "You'd think he'd be pleased that someone is writing a thesis on his work."

"I'm not sure," I replied, glancing back at Xander, who was pacing back and forth. "Maybe just leave him alone for now and get the shop ready for opening. You can ask him questions at the launch if you like."

Colin sighed and rolled his eyes and I left him to it.

"Sorry about that," I said as I went back to where Xander was pacing and frowning at the floor. He looked up at me and shrugged. "You're the first Booker nominee we've had in the shop so it's bound to cause a little excitement."

"Hmmmm…" he muttered, and started pacing again.

"Are you all right?" I asked again. He didn't look all right. He looked… well, he looked nervous. Was it possible that Xander Stone was nervous about a provincial book launch?

"It just…" He waved impatiently towards where Colin was setting up the till for the day. "I wasn't expecting anyone else to be here so early." He paused and took a breath and I watched his face harden again. "I'm not quite caffeinated enough for gushing fanboys just yet," he said, with that smug smile playing on his lips. He was back to being rude again, but I'd noticed that something about Colin's gushing had definitely unnerved him.

"Yes well, I'm sorry about Colin," I said. "He can be rather overenthusiastic about some things. Shall we just get this book launch sorted out so we can both get on with our days?"

He looked at me then and when his eyes met mine, I felt myself shiver. I thought he was going to say something but instead he just nodded again and rubbed a hand over his unshaven jaw.

Over the next half an hour we sorted out the details of the launch – from the sort of space he would need, to the precise descriptions of the 'nibbles' that had been ordered, to the number of people that were expected.

"I have a limit on how many people I'm allowed in the shop for events like this," I said. "And all the tickets are sold out so—"

"Are they?" Xander interrupted, that nervous look passing over his face again. "No pressure then." I waited a moment to see if he'd expand on that, but he didn't.

"Anyway, as all the tickets are sold out," I said, filling the silence, "I only have ten free spots, so if you're inviting anyone you'll…"

"Don't worry, only my agent is coming from London."

I nodded. "OK, well, I think that's everything then. I'll finalise the food with the café owners later in the week and if you think of anything else then you know where I am."

He reached into the inside pocket of his coat and pulled out his wallet, from which he took a thick piece of cream card. "My number's on there," he said. "If you need me or…" He hesitated.

"Or what?" I asked.

"Nothing," he said. "I'll leave you to enjoy your romance novel," he said, his lips curving into that half-smile again.

As he turned away towards the door, I called him back. "You know, you shouldn't be so derogatory about a genre of fiction that you've clearly never read."

"And what makes you think I don't read romance?"

"You should come to our book club," I heard myself saying. What on earth was I doing, inviting a man into the hallowed female-only space of the Die-Hards? Mum was going to kill me. "We meet on Thursdays at seven-thirty."

He looked at me for a moment and I was sure he was going say that he had better things to do. But then he smiled again.

"Now that, Ms Taylor, is an offer I cannot refuse," he said.

"We all try to bring a book to recommend," I went on, still quite surprised at the words that were coming out of my mouth. Surely I wasn't going to land the rudest man I'd ever met on my friends? "So maybe you should read this." I handed him the copy of *The Devil in Winter* that I was still clutching. "Like I said, I think you'll quite like the hero."

He took it from me, turning it over to glance at the blurb on the back cover.

"I'll see you next Thursday then," he said, before leaving the shop, book in hand.

5

"Is it true that you've invited a man to book club?" Bella asked, her face a perfect mask of fake horror. "Men never come to book club, not even Colin."

"According to Missy, Colin is terrified of romance novels," I said. "What would be the point in asking him?"

"While Xander Stone is, of course, known for his love of romance," Missy said sarcastically.

The three of us were in the new tearoom on the corner, ostensibly for lunch but today lunch consisted of Christmas spiced tea and mince pies. We'd started frequenting this particular café when it opened in the summer and hadn't looked back. It played classical music, served every tea imaginable and the most delicious baked goods and Ellie, its owner, was a frequent visitor to the bookshop – although I hadn't managed to convince her to join the Die-Hards yet. ("I'm more of a fan of thrillers to be honest," she'd said.) I liked it here because it was new and contained no memories of Joe or any of the other things that I was trying not to think about.

"Have you run mad, Meg?" Bella asked dramatically. "You've avoided men for as long as I've known you and now, when you finally speak to one, it's the man you described as the rudest person on earth."

"I've explained that," I said. "I think there's more to him."

"Well I suppose there's more to everyone than the way they present themselves to the world," Bella mused. "He is a brilliant writer after all, but who cares really? He'll be gone next week and then..." She paused, narrowing her eyes at me. "Unless of course you've..."

"I just think that beneath the surface he's not as confident about his work as you'd think," I interrupted, knowing exactly where Bella was going and not wanting to have to admit to the fluttering feeling I experienced whenever I was near Xander Stone. "He reacted quite strangely to Colin."

"Everyone reacts strangely to Colin," Missy said, mouth full of mince pie.

"This was different," I said and explained what had happened. "And when I told him that all the tickets to the launch had sold out he seemed, well... he seemed nervous."

"Really?" Missy looked sceptical.

"It was only for a split second, but it just made me wonder."

"He never seems nervous in his interviews," Bella said. "He always just seems a bit full of himself."

Missy nodded in agreement. "There's a lot of rude people out there, Megan, and most of them are just plain rude. Why should he be any different just because he writes books?" Missy had a very cynical attitude towards her fellow humans. It was, she claimed, the reason she read books where the people could be trusted to act in a certain way. I'd always suspected that Missy's cynicism was also an act and after what she'd been through at such a young age it was hardly surprising. It protected her from having to deal with that again. But was it healthy? I suspected not, but I also suspected that hiding myself away from the world and refusing to talk to men was equally unhealthy, so I didn't dwell on it too much. We were both just trying to stop ourselves getting hurt again.

"I don't know," I said, breaking the crust of my mince pie into crumbs and not looking at either of them. "I was just intrigued I guess, plus he was so rude about romance novels that I thought he should come to book club to be brought down a peg or two."

"Maybe he's a Darcy," Missy said thoughtfully, leaning her chin on her hand as she stared dreamily into the distance. Missy might love an ice hockey romance but her heart would always lie with Fitzwilliam Darcy. ("Imagine if Darcy had played ice hockey," she'd said one night after too many cocktails. "You're drunk, Missy, go home," Bella had responded.) "You know, all dark and brooding and socially awkward. He doesn't mean to be rude but he just doesn't know how not to be."

"Rubbish," I replied. "Besides, I've never bought into the whole Darcy myth – you know that. Rude is rude and I'm not saying Xander Stone isn't rude, I'm just saying that there's more to him."

"I'll never understand how you can prefer Bingley over Darcy," Missy said.

"Bingley is kind and sweet and funny and he'd do anything for Jane," I replied. *Just like Joe*, I thought to myself. "Not everyone wants a Darcy. They aren't as attractive in real life as they appear on paper. Darcys are difficult and you'd have to spend your whole life—"

"You're both veering off the topic and I have to go back to work soon," Bella interrupted the almost-daily Darcy versus Bingley discussion.

"What is the topic?" I asked.

"That you've invited Xander Stone to book club and I want to know why."

"Because he's been very derogatory about romance novels and I want us to show him how important they are."

"And that's the only reason, is it?" Missy asked, draining her mug and raising her eyebrows.

"Of course it is."

"It's got nothing to do with you having a big old crush on him?"

"What?" I replied, horrified. "Of course I don't have a crush on him." I tried not to remember the way his smile had made me feel or how, whenever I thought about that smile, my stomach fizzed a little in a way it hadn't done for years.

"Oh my God," Bella said. "Look at you. You do have a crush on him!"

"Don't be so ridiculous."

"You're blushing, Megan, which means you're lying."

"I saw you with him in the bookshop the other day," Missy said. "Cosied up in the corner, whispering to each other."

"We were planning the book launch – as well you know."

"And you've been constantly checking his Wikipedia page."

I sighed and held up my hands. "OK, that I'll admit to." I had spent a little too much time researching Xander Stone online since I'd accidentally invited him to the book club. Not that my research had told me much that I hadn't already known, but I could now recite most of his Wikipedia page off by heart thanks to my almost constant virtual stalking. He was born Alexander Daniel Stone in 1987 in East London, the eldest of five siblings. His father had died when he was a teenager and he'd dropped out of school when he was sixteen to try to earn money for the family. He'd been boxing since he was a kid and turned semi-professional not long after leaving school, combining it with whatever other work he could pick up. At some point he also found time to go back to school to complete his abandoned A levels and then an English degree as well. It was while he was doing his degree that he'd started writing the book that had become *Boxed* and which had catapulted him to seemingly overnight fame, fortune and success, and had secured him one of the biggest advances for a debut novel that had been seen in years.

"It's not because I have a crush on him though, I'm just interested in him as a writer, particularly as I am counting on his book launch to be a success for the shop."

"Yeah right." Bella laughed.

"It's time to go back to work," I said, standing up. "I have to talk to Ellie about the food for the book launch anyway."

"Megan, it's OK to have feelings for someone else you know," Bella said as she put her coat on. "Whether or not that someone else is Xander Stone. It's been three and a half years."

I nodded, not meeting her eyes. "I know you both worry,"

I said quietly. "Mum does too. But I'm fine, I promise. Now both of you go back to work. I'll settle up here and talk to Ellie."

I walked the long way back to the bookshop afterwards. As I walked past the Minster I noticed that my bench was free and I took the opportunity to sit down. It was a crisp, cold afternoon with a clear blue sky and the Minster looked magnificent in the watery sunshine. I took a breath and leaned back, thinking about the conversation I'd just had with Bella and Missy.

While I wouldn't exactly call it a crush, there was no denying that there was a definite attraction. But stronger than the fizzing, popping feeling I got in my stomach whenever Xander was in the vicinity, I felt an overwhelming sense of guilt. I never thought I'd notice another man again after Joe and I'd been quite happy to disappear into a quiet spinsterhood, safe in the knowledge that nobody could ever measure up to my husband.

The last time I'd spoken to Joe's mum she'd told me that if it was the other way around Joe wouldn't have spent his whole life living like a monk and he wouldn't have expected me to be joining a convent. But Joe's mum didn't know the truth; she didn't know that I hadn't been there when Joe died like I'd promised him I would be. Even thinking about Xander's smile felt like a betrayal, and when he had sat down on the bench next to me the day I'd invited him to come to book club, it had felt as though Xander had been pushing the very memory of Joe to one side, as though he was pushing him off the bench.

This was our bench, mine and Joe's. We'd even had our wedding photos taken here. It wasn't Xander's bench.

What would you do, Joe? I asked silently. Was his mother right? Joe had always grabbed life with both hands and everybody loved him. Would he have spent three years shut away in a bookshop?

I absolutely didn't have a crush on Xander Stone but perhaps that fluttery feeling I got whenever he smiled was a wake-up call, a reminder that I was still here even if Joe wasn't and maybe, just maybe, I needed to start living again.

When I got back to the bookshop Missy was standing in the romance section, shelving books.

"This is an unusual sight," I said. Missy rarely ventured out of the back office. ("I'm a self-employed accountant," she'd say. "Not a bookseller.")

"I was waiting for you," she replied. "Come with me."

I followed Missy into the office, which was a converted storeroom at the back of the shop. Everyone could use it whenever they needed to but it was Missy and me who spent the most time in here as we were the ones who ordered the stock and balanced the accounts (as much as that was possible – some months the accounts didn't balance no matter how hard we tried). It was warm and cosy in the office and I sat down on the wing-backed chair that I'd bought on eBay but which had turned out to be too large for the shop's reading nook. There was just about room for it in the office if one didn't stretch one's legs out too much.

"Bella and I," Missy began. "We didn't mean to make you feel uncomfortable before when we were teasing you about Xander. I'm sorry, I know how hard you find all this."

I leaned against the back of the chair. "It's OK," I said. "I know I need to get on with my life. I know I can't hide out in the bookshop forever. I know Joe wouldn't have wanted that."

"Would you have wanted that for him, if it had been you?"

"Of course not," I said. "It's just hard sometimes. You should know that more than anyone."

"I know that," Missy said quietly. "And I know that sense of loss never truly goes away. But eventually it just becomes part of you, part of the baggage that you carry with you – like other people carry divorces or redundancies. It gets easier; life gets easier. I promise."

"How long was it for you?" I asked. "Before you started dating again?"

"Oh I started dating as soon as my plane landed in London," Missy replied with a wry smile. "But we're all different, and to be honest I wasn't ready and I wouldn't really recommend doing what I did."

Missy had arrived in London just before her twentieth birthday, ten years ago, running away from a heartbreak that no nineteen-year-old should have had to deal with. She'd given up a place at Yale, much to her parents' disapproval, to move to Boston with her high school sweetheart, until he'd died in a motorbike accident a year later. Unable to face her parents, Missy had set out on a grand tour of Europe but, after several months in London dating unsuitable men, she'd moved to York and never got any further than that. I didn't know much more about Missy's past and Missy hardly ever talked about it. What she was saying this afternoon in the little office at the back of the bookshop was almost more than she'd ever said before.

"But you're comfortable dating now," I confirmed.

"I am, although it's been a while since I met someone who I preferred to spend time with over you and Bella," she said. "But that doesn't mean we should tease you. I am sorry, Megan."

"You weren't wrong though," I admitted quietly.

"What?" Missy's eyebrows shot up. "You mean you do have a crush on him?"

"Shhh," I said, pressing my finger to my lips. "The whole shop doesn't need to know and it's not a crush, it's just…" I trailed off.

"If his author photograph is anything to go by, he is very good-looking," Missy said. "I've only seen the back of his head so far but I presume those cheekbones aren't photoshopped."

"They are not photoshopped," I confirmed.

"Well, I'm looking forward to meeting our Mr Stone properly in that case – a romantic hero at our book club. Imagine…" She sighed dramatically. "Although I promise to only look. I'll leave any touching to you."

"I have no intention of touching him." I laughed. "I've told you, it's not a crush. It's just the first time I've really acknowledged that another man is attractive since Joe and it feels strange to acknowledge that, as though I'm cheating on his memory."

"Grief is such a peculiar thing," Missy said. "But take it from me, it's perfectly normal to find other men attractive or even to have crushes on them."

"You said you'd stop."

Missy held up her hands. "I know, I know," she said. "But not even a little crush?"

"He's extremely rude."

"I thought you said that was shyness."

"When he smiles it does make me do a bit of a double take," I admitted, trying not to think about that fizzing feeling in my stomach again.

"Aha!" Missy squealed. "Bella was right."

"Bella was not right," I said, but I did wonder if Bella was a little bit right. "And even if she was, Xander will be gone by the weekend. I don't even know why she's so obsessed with me finding love again when she's so perpetually single."

"About that," Missy said.

"What? Has Bella met somebody?"

Missy nodded slowly. "A six-foot-four Viking called Norm with a PhD and who currently works with her at the Jorvik Centre."

"Norm?"

"Short for Norman."

"Six-foot-four? But Bella's only five-foot-one!"

"I know! Opposites attract."

"But why didn't she tell me?" I asked, feeling disappointed that my friends didn't feel they could confide in me. "Do you both feel that you can't talk about dating in front of me?"

Missy screwed up her face. "I guess," she said in a small voice. "A little bit."

"God I'm so sorry," I said. "I really do need to stop playing the unmerry widow, don't I."

"You don't have to be merry if you don't feel like it, but..."

"I need to learn to live a little bit again."

Missy nodded and held up her finger and thumb. "Just a little bit," she said.

"I know I've been really self-absorbed," I began.

"Grief does that to you. It's perfectly normal."

"Maybe, but I hate the idea that you and Bella can't tell me stuff."

Missy didn't say anything for a moment and then she sighed and opened her laptop.

"Well, if you're in the mood for being told stuff," she said. "We really need to talk about the bookshop accounts."

I groaned internally.

It was time to face the music.

6

"I don't understand why I can't come to your book club now men are allowed," Colin complained as I ushered him out of the shop at closing time the next evening.

"Colin, you don't even like romance novels," I said. "Why on earth would you want to come to book club?"

"Well it's always good to broaden one's horizons," he began.

"Up until you found out Xander Stone was coming you had zero interest in romance novels at all. Missy thinks you're scared of them."

"Ridiculous, I—"

"You can come if you can name one iconic romance novel that you've read," I interrupted.

Colin opened his mouth and then closed it again.

"I do have quite a lot of study to do I suppose," he said eventually.

"And you can pick Xander's brains at the book launch tomorrow."

Colin turned up his collar and set off into the cold evening and I turned back into the shop. I was seriously beginning to regret the rash decision to invite Xander to join the Die-Hards that night. Was he just going to be rude to them all, and sneer at romance novels as he'd sneered at the romance shelves in the shop last week? I knew that Dot and Trixie, and maybe even Mum, just wouldn't stand for it and the last thing I wanted was for there to be an argument. It was Christmas after all, and I was determined to at least try to live a little as Missy had suggested. I wanted to have some fun this Christmas, not that I thought any of that fun would involve Xander Stone, or any other man for that matter, but having fun, in my opinion, did not include refereeing arguments.

I needn't have worried because as soon as Trixie arrived, she took charge completely.

"Open the wine, Megan," she said as she swept in, bringing a waft of cold air with her. "And everyone gather around. We're learning pontoon and whist tonight."

"Not everyone is here yet," I pointed out, as neither Dot nor Xander had arrived. I was still hoping that Xander wasn't coming; I hadn't heard a word from him since the previous week when I'd first invited him, and all preparations for the book launch had been made by daily phone calls from the formidable Philomena Bloom.

"I'll be there at 3 p.m. tomorrow," she'd told me earlier today. "To oversee everything."

Another thing to look forward to, I thought. This surely wasn't what Missy had in mind when it came to living a little. But while I was quite relieved that Xander was a no-show, it was unlike Dot to be late for book club.

"No Xander," Missy whispered, nudging me.

"No chatting, Artemis, please," Trixie said before I had a chance to reply. For some reason Trixie always insisted on calling Missy by her full name, which was a bit rich I thought coming from someone called Trixie, which had to be short for something – although if it was none of us knew what. Nobody had ever dared to ask her.

"We've got a lot to get through tonight," Trixie went on, handing out an agenda to everyone gathered around the table.

"I'm beginning to wish I'd never asked Trixie for her help now," I said quietly to Mum, who was sitting on the other side of me. "Or come up with this Regency Christmas party idea at all."

"Shhh…" Mum whispered, nudging me and suppressing a smile. When I looked up Trixie was giving me a hard stare.

"If you're quite ready, we'll begin," Trixie said as she put everyone into pairs and started dealing out cards.

"Aren't we going to wait for Dot?" Bella asked.

"She'll have to catch up."

"Are you going to tell us the rules?" Mum asked.

"You'll pick them up as we go," Trixie said. "Now…"

But she was interrupted by the front door of the bookshop opening, bringing with it another gust of cold air as Dot and Xander arrived together. My heart did something peculiar and I couldn't work out if I was pleased to see him or disappointed that he'd come. Xander said something to Dot as he closed the door firmly and Dot laughed as though they were sharing a personal joke. Did they know each other? I racked my brains but couldn't think of anything Dot had ever said about Xander. In fact, of every member of the Die-Hards, she'd been the only one who hadn't had an opinion about him when his agent had first booked his launch back in August.

"Hello, everyone," Dot said. "Sorry I'm—"

"Sit down, sit down," Trixie interrupted. "As I was telling everyone else, we've got a lot to get through."

"This is Xander Stone," Dot went on, ignoring Trixie.

"Megan invited me," he said. "She seems to think that my knowledge of romance novels is somewhat lacking. I hope that's OK with everyone." He smiled and looked over at me and I felt my heart do that strange thing again. This rather charming side of him was one I'd barely even glimpsed before – just a hint of it the very first time he'd ever smiled at me – and although it was preferable to him sneering at our choice in reading material, I wasn't sure if my heart was going to cope with it very well.

All the Die-Hards except for Trixie and me stood up and swarmed around Xander, asking him a million questions at once, and I watched his smile turn to a grimace not unlike the expression on his face when Colin had threatened to bombard him with questions last week. There was definitely more to Xander Stone than our initial meetings had suggested, and I couldn't help being interested in what that was.

He looked so uncomfortable I thought I should say something and make everyone sit down but Trixie beat me to it and demanded we start the whist lesson immediately before we wasted any more time.

"Dot, you can partner with Xander as everyone else is paired up already," she said.

"Do you and Dot know each other?" I asked Xander as he picked up his cards.

"Actually," Xander said, "Dot and I go way back."

"Really? How?"

I was shocked and, if what Xander said was true, a little hurt. Why hadn't Dot ever said anything? Why hadn't Xander mentioned that he knew Dot? And if they really did go way back then he must already have known about the book club when I first mentioned it to him. Perhaps that's why he agreed to come so easily, because he knew Dot would be there. Judging by the way the rest of the Die-Hards had cast their playing cards aside and were staring open-mouthed at Dot and Xander, it seemed they were as surprised as I was.

"Why did you never tell us you knew famous authors?" my mother asked.

Xander turned to Dot. "Sorry," he said. "Would you rather I hadn't said anything?"

Dot laughed. "It's a bit late now," she said.

Xander pulled a face and apologised again, which seemed unlike him. He seemed to be acting very out of character tonight. Perhaps it was Dot's influence.

"Do you want to tell them or should I?" he asked Dot.

"Well you're the storyteller, not me," Dot replied.

"Without you, Dorothy Bridges, there wouldn't be any stories." Xander smiled at Dot so tenderly it almost impossible to equate him with the man who'd been waving impatiently at me and snapping about how cluttered the shop was and how dreadful romance novels were the week before. I felt a twinge of jealousy. Were they flirting with each other? What was going on?

"Before Xander tells you, I'd really rather it stayed among ourselves if that's OK?" Dot asked. "It's not something I want the whole world to know about."

Everyone was very intrigued now, focusing on Xander and Dot and wondering how this story would end. Everyone except Trixie, who was tapping her scarlet fingernails on the table impatiently. Perhaps she already knew.

"You know you can trust us," Missy said. "What happens at Die-Hards stays at Die-Hards, right?" She looked around the table and everyone nodded and murmured assent.

"I never finished school," Xander began. "My father died and—"

"You left school to be a boxer," Bella interrupted. "Sorry, I read your author bio before I came tonight and…" She trailed off, looking suitably embarrassed. We'd all read his author bio and Wikipedia page far too many times than was healthy but there was no need to admit it to his face.

"My author bio is rather selective," Xander said mysteriously. "But that's the gist of it. Anyway, after a few years I took my A levels at night school and then I started studying literature part-time at the University of London. I'd always loved reading and I wanted to learn everything I could about it – a fact I had to keep secret from the other lads at the boxing clubs of course."

"Before I moved to York I used to teach postmodernism at Birkbeck," Dot said.

"You were his tutor?" Bella asked.

"Oh my God, were you *the* tutor, Dot?" Missy squealed, realisation dawning. "The one he claims to owe everything to? The one in the dedication of his first book?"

"Absolutely she is," Xander said as Dot blushed and looked away.

Missy jumped up and fetched a copy of *Boxed* off the bookshop shelf. "To the university professor who saw in me that which I never saw in myself, with eternal gratitude," she read from the dedication page.

That was Dot? Why had she never said anything? I'd be shouting it from the rooftops! When I looked over at Xander he was staring at me and I felt something unravel inside me. He looked away and for a fleeting moment he seemed either embarrassed or nervous, just as he had when I told him that the book launch was sold out.

"Xander gives me far too much credit," Dot said. "All I did was encourage him to send it out to agents."

"Why did you never say anything?" Bella asked the question that we must all be thinking.

Dot shrugged. "It never seemed very important; I never felt I'd done very much. Besides, I didn't think Xander would want people to know."

"Without Dot, I'd never have sent any work out to anyone," Xander said, although I did wonder if this was true. He seemed to know exactly how good he was. Surely he'd have sent the book that became *Boxed* out to agents without Dot's encouragement eventually. "And the only reason I didn't tell anyone is I was worried Dot would be bothered by the press. I hadn't really been expecting my first book to be quite so popular."

"So is Dot the reason you're holding your book launch here at Taylor's?" I asked. It was all starting to make sense now. I'd always thought it was amazingly good luck that we'd managed to nab Xander Stone for a book launch. I'd hoped the good luck would spread to other areas, like the shop's finances. One could dream.

"Partly," Xander replied. "My agent heard about you and she knows that I come up to York to see Dot from time to time, so she suggested it and I asked Dot what she thought. I was looking for a small, intimate venue for this book, something a bit different."

"And I said that Taylor's was the best bookshop in town." Dot smiled.

"Well thank you, both of you," I said. "I'm hoping the launch tomorrow will really help with publicity." I didn't add how much we needed it. I'd been hoping we'd be doing better than we were one month before Christmas.

"That and the Regency Christmas." Missy grinned. "I for one am very much looking forward to a night of men in breeches." She turned to Xander. "You should come." She smiled suggestively.

"What's this?" Xander asked, his brow furrowing.

I explained my idea for Christmas Eve at the bookshop.

"And tonight Trixie is going to be teaching us Regency card games," I said.

"Well hopefully we'll get around to it," Trixie huffed impatiently.

"Hang on," Xander protested. "I feel like I've been duped. I thought we were talking about romance novels, not playing cards."

"I'm sure you can manage to talk and play," I said. "But we have to stick to historical romances tonight."

Xander snorted. "Historical romance," he muttered. This sounded more like the Xander I was expecting to turn up tonight. He looked over at me again and I noticed the corners of his mouth twitching. "That's the worst of it all, so much bodice-ripping and inaccuracy..."

"Xander," Dot interrupted, tapping him on the arm.

"You did promise to be polite. It is a romance book club, after all!"

"OK, OK," he said, holding up his hands. "You all love historical romance novels, I get it."

"He can be rather snobbish sometimes," Dot said.

"And that's exactly why I invited him!" I said. "He needs to understand the importance of romance novels, how powerful they can be, how they can pick you up when you're feeling at your lowest."

"After all, what is a novel without love," Mum said defensively – she believed all books were essentially about love.

"I think crime writers might have something to say about that," Xander retorted.

"I disagree," Mum replied, quietly. "I read a lot of crime as well – you might be surprised to learn that we are all quite eclectic readers – and so many of those books are about crimes of love, of passion, of marriages gone wrong. Love, or the lack of it, is central to all literature, I think."

Xander looked as though he was about to say something else rather condescending when Trixie finally snapped.

"Can we please get on?" she said. "If you want this Regency event to be as authentic as possible, as historically accurate as possible…" she paused to give Xander one of her hard stares "…then we have a lot to get through."

She collected the cards up and started dealing them out again. "Regency whist is very different to the modern versions of whist that you might be used to."

"So nothing like the game we used to play in the students'

union then?" I asked, slightly disappointed that I wouldn't have a head start on the game.

"No, nothing like that," Trixie replied. "It's played in pairs so it's more like bridge. It should be played two against two so we're one person short tonight. I'll play two hands."

Everyone concentrated for a surprising amount of time considering how disruptive the early part of the meeting had been. Missy and Bella were getting quite competitive, winning trick after trick.

"I think we're quite good at this," Bella said. "We should start placing a wager on each game."

"No gambling in the bookshop," I reminded them.

"What other games can we learn, Trixie?" Bella asked.

"I thought pontoon would be a good one. Most of you will know that one already – it's just *vingt-un*."

"And are we supposed to teach other people on the night?" Dot asked.

"That's the plan," I said. "I think I'm going to type up the rules on laminated cards for everyone though."

"That's not very historically accurate," Trixie sniffed.

"Come on, Trixie, we can't expect everyone to know how to play Regency whist, and as for the dancing—"

"Dancing!" Xander said, clearly unable to keep his cynicism under control any longer. "You didn't tell me there was going to be dancing."

"We're learning a quadrille apparently," I replied. The way he was looking at me was making my voice sound a little strangled. Did he have to be quite so good-looking?

"And we need more men to dance with us," Missy said.

Xander shook his head. "Also in Regency dress, I suppose?" he said.

"Absolutely," Missy replied. "I'm only doing this for the men in breeches."

"I feel as though you aren't taking this very seriously, Artemis," Trixie said.

"Oh come on, Trixie," I said. "We are taking it seriously, but we're having a bit of fun too."

"So you'll all be dressed as Regency ladies?" Xander asked. His question was to the whole group but he was looking at me again.

"We all got gowns go to the Jane Austen weekend in Bath last summer," Dot replied. "It was a fun few days."

"And what about waltzes?" Xander went on. He leaned back in his chair and steepled his fingers in front of him, that smug smile playing on his lips again. "According to those Regency romances you all love, dancing a waltz with someone was the Regency equivalent of sex in a public place."

"Do you have to be so crude?" Trixie sniffed. "Not to mention historically inaccurate. No waltzes."

"Oh that's a shame," Xander said. "I was looking forward to a waltz." He looked at me again and I felt as though my face had been set on fire. I avoided all eye contact with everyone.

"However," Trixie went on, "Artemis is right that we do need some more men to learn the quadrille with us. So if you are still around next Thursday you'd be very welcome to join us to make up numbers."

There was no way Xander Stone would hang around any longer than he had to. By the end of the weekend the book launch would be over and most of the reviews of his new book would be published and he'd be back in London. I'd never have to see his smug face or his disarming smile again.

"I have to say, I'm very tempted to join you again," Xander said, surprising us all. I turned in my chair to stare at him. "I'll have to check my schedule and let you know." He stood up and started putting on his coat. "But for now, if we're finished with card games for the night, I'm afraid I have to go as I've got a big day tomorrow." He glanced towards the back of the shop where his book launch would be taking place the next day. "Although I don't feel I've learned as much about romance novels as I should have done."

"Well, just see how you get on with the one I gave you to read," I said. "We can take it from there next week if you insist on coming back."

"Oh I insist," he said.

"You didn't tell me you'd lent him a book," Missy said. "Which one?"

"*The Devil in Winter*," I replied. "I was giving it a second chance after last week's book club and Xander interrupted me when I was reading it – I thought he might find a soul mate in Sebastian." I saw Mum supress a giggle.

"Oh I love that book," Bella said dreamily. "Although Megan isn't a fan."

"I have to say…" Xander replied, smiling his disarming smile again and making my stomach do whatever it was that it kept doing when he smiled "…that so far I'm rather enamoured of the hero. He seems like my sort of fellow."

"Rude and obnoxious, you mean?" I said.

"Exactly that." He was still smiling, and I could feel my cheeks getting hot again. What was wrong with me? I'd spent all these years mourning Joe, living in my own past and not even looking at anyone else, and the first person I find attractive is an arrogant snob like Xander Stone.

Regardless of what Dot might think of him and that small glimpse at his more charming side, I was still struggling to find many redeeming features – except for that smile of course, and those cheekbones, and the way that lock of dark hair fell over his forehead…

"Come on, Dot," Xander said as he buttoned up his coat.

"Is Xander staying with you, Dot?" Mum asked.

"He always stays with me when he's in York."

"She'd kill me if I booked a hotel," Xander said before turning his attention back to me again. "But I need to go because I've got a book to read."

"Don't force yourself to finish it on my account," I replied.

"Don't forget to bring a man with you next week, Dot," Trixie called after them. "For the quadrille."

Dot turned around. "I'll bring Xander," she said. "If he's free."

"Xander will be dancing with Megan."

"Well I don't know if I'm going to be dancing at all," I said. "I'll have a lot to do on the night…"

"Nonsense," Trixie interrupted. "The dancing will be the best bit." I felt as though everyone was ganging up on me, forcing me to have crush on Xander even though I didn't want one.

"Can't I just dance with you, Trixie?" Dot asked.

"No, I'll be dancing with Stan, but I'll see if he has a friend he can bring along for you."

After Dot and Xander had left, I tried to talk to Trixie.

"I really appreciate all you're doing to help," I said. "But this Regency Christmas idea was only meant to be a bit of fun and…"

"If something's worth doing, it's worth doing properly," Trixie interrupted as she started to pack up all her lists and agendas into her large handbag. "We need to talk about food and music but I'll send you an email over the weekend. I have to get back to Stan now." And with a parting wave she was gone, following Xander and Dot out into the cold winter evening.

"Let her organise it," Mum said, giving my arm a squeeze. "Give yourself a break. You've worked flat out on this bookshop for the last three years. Enjoy yourself for once."

"That's what I keep telling her," Missy said. "It's time she had some fun, don't you think?"

"I do think," Mum said quietly.

"And you get to dance with Xander Stone," Bella said.

"Are you bringing the Viking to dance with you?" I asked to take the attention away from who I would or wouldn't be dancing with.

"You told her?" Bella asked Missy.

"Yes she told me," I said. "I can't believe you didn't tell me."

"I'm sorry, I was only trying..."

"You don't have to walk on eggshells around me when you meet someone," I interrupted. "I'm happy for you and I'm looking forward to meeting him." I still felt terrible that Bella hadn't felt she was able to tell me about Norm the Viking. I had to start paying more attention to my friends and family, to my life.

"I haven't actually told him about dancing a quadrille yet. I'm not sure how he'll take it."

"But you will bring him?"

Bella nodded. "And I'll get him to bring a Viking friend for Missy."

"I can find my own men," Missy protested.

"Who?"

Missy didn't say anything for a moment.

"See," Bella said. "You can dance with Norm's friend. It's either that or Colin."

Missy pulled a face. "Norm's friend will be fine," she said.

"Mum can dance with Colin." I laughed.

"Lucky me," Mum muttered.

"Xander seems nice," Mum said as she put a mug of herbal tea on the table in front of me later that night.

"Does he?" I replied, surprised. "You didn't seem to agree with him very much!"

Mun sat down, curling her fingers around her own mug. "Well I'm not sure I agree with him about romance novels, but he's clearly very well read, clever, funny…"

"You sound like you're trying to challenge Colin for the role of head of the Xander Stone fan club." I laughed. "He's also quite rude and condescending, don't you think?"

She shrugged. "I think we both know there's more to him than that and he seems to really like you."

My stomach turned over. "No he doesn't," I protested. "He's just…"

"And I'm fairly certain the feeling is mutual," Mum interrupted, ignoring my protests.

I rested my chin in my hands. Mum knew me better than anyone so there was no point denying it. "A little bit mutual," I admitted quietly. "He is very attractive, but how do I know I'm ready to... well... you know."

"You won't know until you try," she replied.

"He'll probably go back to London next week."

"Maybe, but that's no reason to not stay in touch with him. Besides, I've got a feeling he'll be joining us for the quadrille, even if it's just to spend time with you again."

I didn't say anything for a moment. Perhaps she was right, perhaps there would never be a right time to move on, perhaps I just had to do it and see. But there was something else I needed to talk to Mum about before we went to bed, something I'd been trying not to think about too much all evening.

"Mum," I began. "Missy and I went through the accounts this afternoon."

Mum put her mug down carefully and sighed. "Yes," she said. "She showed me the other day. It's not looking good is it?"

"It's looking terrible. What are we going to do?" Whenever I thought about it I felt a wave of panic. The truth was, if things carried on at this rate we were going to lose the bookshop and our home in a matter of months and no number of rude literary fiction novelists launching their books were going to save us from that.

I'd known for a while that we couldn't possibly go on the way we were. While we'd been able to carry on paying both Colin and Missy for now, it had been nearly a year since Mum or I had taken any sort of salary from the shop. Luckily we didn't have many outgoings due to the fact that my grandparents had owned the building outright so we had no rent or mortgage payments to make, and between

Mum's income from her writing and my savings we'd been making do. But my savings wouldn't last forever.

"We're going to have to talk to your father," Mum said. "It's his shop really, his name on the deeds. He needs to make the decision."

Mum and Dad's break-up was complicated. After Dad left they hadn't seen each other until my wedding, but something had happened that day – I'd been too caught up in my own happiness to know exactly what – and they'd had a tentative friendship ever since. I wasn't sure if they kept in touch just for business matters or if there was more to it. I suspected the latter.

"What do you think he'll decide?" I asked. I already had a feeling there would be only one outcome to this situation.

"I won't know until I ask him, love," Mum said. "I'll call him soon."

7

Philomena Bloom burst into the bookshop at exactly three o'clock the next afternoon, leaving a wave of expensive perfume in her wake. The handful of customers browsing the shelves all looked up at the same time like meerkats.

"Darlings," she boomed at Mum and me as we stood behind the counter. "Delighted to be here at last. Bloody trains take forever and leave one feeling positively unclean." She screwed up her nose. "Megan darling, how are you?"

"Um, hi…" I began before I was drawn into an effusive embrace and my words were muffled against Philomena's ample bosom. "I don't mean to be rude," I went on when I'd been released. "But have we met before?" From Xander's agent's overly familiar welcome it felt as though we must have done, but if we had I couldn't remember.

"You know I don't think we have, but I know all about you!" Philomena wagged a bejewelled finger in my direction before turning to Mum.

"And you must be Martha Taylor," she said. "Wife of Walter."

Mum opened her mouth to say something but Philomena was talking to me again. "I was so sorry to hear of your husband's passing and that you decided to leave publishing. Such a loss."

"I'm sorry," I said, really rather perturbed now by Philomena's attitude – she was as rude as Xander in her own way. "But if we've never met, I don't understand how you know…"

"Well I did my research, of course," Philomena said, waving her hands in the air and causing a collection of bracelets to jangle noisily. "I had to know who I was up against, and what do I find? That the bookshop is owned by the poet Walter Taylor and run by his daughter – who used to be one of the commissioning editors for Rogers & Hudson. I knew Xander was in good hands as soon as I found that out." She began to walk around the shop, running her fingers along the shelves and not letting me get a word in edgewise. "A tragedy about your husband though, my dear, a tragedy. Do you think you'll come back to London, back to publishing?"

"I don't think so," I said. "And I don't really understand how you know about my husband." Mum and I began to follow Philomena as she moved slowly up and down the shelves until she stopped abruptly in the cookery section and turned around.

"Do you see your father often?" she asked.

I felt that pang of guilt again when I remembered all my excuses about why I couldn't go to Paris and how I hadn't seen him since Joe's funeral. "Not for a while," I replied. "But…"

"Is he still in Paris?"

"Thinks he's bloody Hemingway," Mum muttered under her breath.

Luckily for Mum a customer needed some help and she scuttled off with him, leaving me to cope with Philomena.

"Let's talk about the book launch, shall we?" I said as decisively as I could manage before Philomena could reveal any more of the personal information she seemed to have dug up on me. I'd always known publishing was a small world but this was ridiculous. I'd been gone for over three years.

It had been Joe who'd encouraged me to apply for the internship. We'd married in York in the August after we graduated and moved almost immediately to London so he could start law school in the autumn. We'd rented a tiny flat near the Thames between Kingston and Surbiton, and I'd spent the first six months working as a bookseller in the Kingston branch of Waterstones. I wanted something more, though – I didn't just want to sell books, I wanted to help make them.

"It's an internship with one of the big publishers," Joe had said, showing me the advertisement. "You should apply."

I'd made up all sorts of excuses as to why I shouldn't – the pay was terrible, there would be thousands of other people applying – but Joe wouldn't listen to excuses.

"You're scared to rock the boat," he said. "And I get that. But this could be your dream job."

"And what if it isn't?" I'd replied.

"Then you quit and go back to bookselling and you've lost nothing." Joe, like most lawyers, had an answer for everything.

Somehow I'd got the internship – the woman who'd interviewed me spent more time asking me about growing up in a bookshop than telling me about the job – and Joe and I had celebrated with a bottle of cheap fizz on a bench by the river.

"It's not our bench," he'd said. "But it'll do." He'd been so happy for me and a few days later we had cause to celebrate again when he found out he'd been accepted on a training contract at one of the big City law firms.

Two years later he'd been offered a permanent job in the litigation department and I'd commissioned my first novel – a historical romance that had gone on to be a huge best-seller in America. I'd felt as though between us we could take on the world. We moved out of our tiny rented flat and bought a bigger flat just down the road. Our life had felt as though it was perfect... but Joe's white blood cells had probably already started to misbehave by then, even though we didn't know it at the time.

Philomena Bloom was waving a thick wodge of papers in my face, which snapped me out of my memories. She plucked a glasses case out of her huge Liberty tote bag and perched a pair of half-moon glasses on the end of her nose. "Xander tells me you have an area where launches take place," she said, peering at me over the top of the glasses. "Where is that?"

"This way," I replied, leading her out of the cookery section and towards the area that I'd had Colin set up that morning in preparation.

"Hmmm..." Philomena pondered. "This will have to do, I suppose." She looked around. "It's not very big in here, is it?"

"No, well, I did tell you that..." The bookshop was plenty big enough and she must have known it wasn't going to be the size of some of the big London chains.

"And Xander has OK'd all of this?" she checked.

"Yes, he said it would be fine."

"He hates this sort of thing, you know," Philomena said quietly.

"Really?" I replied, thinking again of that fleeting look of nervousness on Xander's face the week before.

She nodded, earrings jangling. "Oh yes. I know he comes across as terribly brash and forthright but deep down he's a kitten." She grinned at me, showing a lot of very white teeth.

"Brash and forthright is one way of putting it," I said. It was also a good way of describing Philomena herself, but I didn't say that out loud.

She laughed then, a strange braying noise that sounded a little bit like a donkey. "Ah, I see he's left an impression," she said. "But like I say, he's such a softie underneath all that bravado."

"So it is bravado, then?" I wasn't sure if Xander would thank Philomena for telling me this.

"Oh yes, he's quite shy really and terribly sensitive. He gets quite het up before these things." She waved her hand towards the rows of chairs.

"Is there anything we can do to make tonight easier for him?" I asked. I hated the thought of any writer not feeling at home in Taylor's Bookshop. It was meant to be a haven for everybody who loved books – even though Xander was quite derogatory about some of them!

"Make sure he gets a glass of champagne before he does his reading," Philomena said. "Try to stop the fans swarming around him asking questions – we'll have a Q&A session afterwards – and make sure you're very complimentary about him when you introduce him."

"Noted," I replied. "That shouldn't be a problem, although I'm afraid I haven't had a chance to read the new book yet." I picked up a copy of *Mists of Our Waters* from the pile I'd set up in preparation for selling signed copies tonight. "I hear it's very good." Most of the early reviews had been glowing. "Seeing as I haven't read it though, what's the best way to introduce him?" It suddenly felt very important that I get this right, and not just because of the publicity for the bookshop.

"It is a very good book," Philomena replied, tapping a navy blue fingernail on top of one of the piles of Xander's books. "It's about an academic who is writing a history of British waterways when he comes across the disappearance of a woman in the nineteenth century and gets obsessed with solving the mystery."

"So it's a crime novel?" I asked.

"Not really, it's an investigation into human beings' relationship with the world around them. A sort of homage to how oblivious we are to both nature and one another." I took a breath when she said that, remembering how oblivious I'd been to everyone around me recently, to the point where my friends were barely telling me their news. "It's a bit..." Philomena paused for a moment as though searching for the right word "...different to his other books but it's excellent. The best so far, in my opinion."

She still hadn't helped me decide how to introduce Xander though. "I'll just say something general, shall I?" I asked. "Introduce him and the book, quote from a good review, that sort of thing?"

Philomena waved a hand in the air. "Yes, yes," she said.

"That sort of thing. Now surely it's time for a G&T? The sun will be over the yardarm somewhere."

Somehow Xander's agent managed to talk me into going for a drink with her, although I only had tonic as I wanted to keep a clear head for the book launch. She talked almost non-stop about her journey to York, how much colder it was here than in London, and name-dropped a few famous authors that she 'looked after' – all of which I already knew. Philomena Bloom wasn't the only one who'd done her research. I still couldn't work out if she'd known me when I was a commissioning editor though, or if everything she knew about me and Joe was just general publishing gossip she'd picked up.

I managed to stop her from ordering a fourth double gin and steer her back to the bookshop before seven o'clock. People were already starting to arrive when we got back and I left Philomena to introduce herself while I nipped upstairs to change into a dress and brush my hair.

When I came back downstairs Mum was manning the champagne table.

"Ben from the tearoom has been and gone," she said, nodding at the buffet table she'd set up earlier when I'd been trying to stop Philomena Bloom from drinking the pub dry of gin. "The nibbles look amazing but are already going quickly. If you want to try any of them you'll need to get in quick."

"Any sign of Xander?" I asked.

"Not that I've seen. Maybe his agent is taking over." She pointed to where Philomena Bloom was holding forth to a small crowd that had gathered around her – champagne glass in one hand, cheese-and-onion tartlet in the other.

I checked my watch. "There's still plenty of time," I said. "I'll go and see if our Ms Bloom has heard from him."

"You've got his number, haven't you?" Mum replied. "Why don't you call him and see where he is?"

"Because I don't want to hassle him. He's not actually late yet."

"Why did he give you his number then I wonder?" Mum asked with a gleam in her eye. "Maybe it was because…"

"He's here," I said, interrupting her before she started telling me all about how it was time I started dating again.

"Here he is!" Philomena boomed, arms aloft, as she greeted Xander. "The man of the hour."

I watched as Xander ducked his head away from everybody's inquisitive gaze and made his way towards the back of the bookshop and Philomena picked up whatever thread of conversation she had dropped to welcome Xander.

Remembering what she had said earlier about making sure he had a drink before he did his reading, I picked a glass of champagne up off the table and took it over to him.

"I thought you might like this," I said, handing it to him.

"Thanks," he said, taking the glass from me and downing half of it in one gulp.

"Your agent mentioned that you might need a drink before you started."

He smiled his disarming smile and I felt my stomach flip. *Pull yourself together, Megan*, I thought, reminding myself that at least Xander and his formidable agent would be gone by the end of the evening – never to be seen again.

And then I remembered Dot's relationship with Xander.

Perhaps he wouldn't just disappear into the ether after all. I couldn't work out if that was a good thing or not.

"You've still got a bit of time before we begin," I went on. "Do you want to sit in the back office for a few minutes, just to be on your own for a while?"

"That would be great, actually," he replied.

"No problem." I led him through to the little room that Missy and I had turned into an office space. He put his champagne glass down on the table and pressed the heel of his hand to his forehead. "I really hate these things," he said.

"So your agent was telling me," I replied. He looked different to usual – not quite the shy, sensitive kitten that Philomena had described – but worried, vulnerable.

"Was she now?" he said, his brow furrowing. I knew he wouldn't be happy about Philomena blabbing away to me.

"I'd sort of guessed though. You didn't exactly seem enthusiastic last week."

I watched him take a breath. "You've gone to all this trouble and all I've done is be rude to you."

"So you aren't rude to everybody?" I asked. "Just me."

He shook his head, not meeting my eye. "When I have a new book coming out everything feels a little out of my control and I can end up coming across a bit…"

"Brash and forthright?" I asked, using Philomena's words.

"Hmmm… I guess."

"Can I ask you something?"

"Sure." He ran a hand through his hair.

"Why do you do launches if you hate them so much? I

mean, it's great for the shop that you're here but surely your books will fly off the shelves regardless?"

"Maybe, but I'm told this sort of thing helps – it makes me seem more human or something. Plus, like you say, it helps bookshops and that's important to me." He cocked his head on one side and smiled at me. "But don't worry, Ms Taylor, I won't show you or your bookshop up." A look passed over his face then as though he was putting on a mask and I realised that the rude, arrogant persona was a cover for something else, as I'd suspected, and for some reason tonight he'd briefly let me see the vulnerable part of him that lay underneath.

As I was leaving him alone he called me back. "Megan," he said. "Can I ask a favour?"

"Sure."

"Keep Philomena away from me for a few minutes, will you. I just need to practise the section I'm reading one more time."

"She is quite overwhelming, isn't she?"

He nodded. "She's a brilliant agent, exactly what I need to get me off my arse a lot of the time, but..." He trailed off and held his hands up.

"Leave Philomena to me," I said as I walked back into the bookshop, shutting the office door behind me.

Philomena accosted me as soon as I came back into view.

"What have you done with him?" she asked with a chuckle.

"He's just having five minutes before we start."

"Ah yes, he does love his quiet time does Xander," she said loudly, broadcasting Xander's personal preferences across the shop. "It's very frustrating. I could get him on TV panel shows, on the radio, so much more publicity if he didn't need so much *quiet time*." She made air quotes around the last two words and I smiled foolishly at her, not really knowing what to say. I needed 'quiet time' from Philomena and I'd only known her for a few hours.

We were thankfully distracted by the arrival of Missy, Bella, Dot and Colin, who bustled into the bookshop together removing hats, scarves and coats and greeting people they knew. I could see Colin looking around for Xander and was glad that I'd thought to let him use the office. He didn't need to be bothered by Colin's overenthusiastic questions before the event had even begun. I saw Mum beckoning me from the champagne table.

"Excuse me, Philomena," I said, but she had already started talking to a tall man in glasses. I left her to it and went over to see Mum.

"I think everyone's here," she said. "I'm going to wander around and see if anyone needs a top-up of fizz and then we'll start, shall we?"

"I'll go and see if Xander's ready," I replied.

I had never seen the bookshop so full or so quiet as it was while Xander read the opening paragraphs from *Mists of Our Waters*. The words – about rivers meandering through the countryside to converge at the ocean's edge, taking their stories with them – were so beautiful that they gave me goose bumps and made me desperate to keep reading, to find out what happened next. When Xander's eyes met mine just before he sat down to be interviewed by Philomena the goose bumps turned to a shiver and I had to look away. I'd known he had been feeling nervous beforehand and probably still was, but none of it showed and he had nothing to be worried about – his writing was beautiful, breath-taking, and I knew *Mists of Our Waters* was going to be just as successful as *Boxed* and *Interim*.

I watched quietly from the back of the room as Xander and Philomena chatted about the initial ideas for his new book, which he said came to him while walking his dog along the River Thames. I found it hard to imagine him with a dog and wondered what breed it was. Then, as he answered a plethora of questions from the audience (not all of them from Colin), I set up the table for him to sign people's books. He'd already requested a black Sharpie for the signing, and I made sure there was a spare just in case, before going to help Missy at the till.

She rubbed her hands together as people started to queue up to pay for their books before taking them over to Xander to be signed. "It's going to be a good night," she said with a grin. She was talking about the money, but in my mind it had already been a great night – the best launch Taylor's had ever hosted.

Lots of people seemed to be doing a bit of Christmas shopping – buying other books besides Xander's as well as mugs and candles – while one woman bought four copies of *Mists of Our Waters*.

"For my friends," she said to me as she took the pile of books over to Xander to get them signed. "They couldn't get tickets for tonight."

"We did sell out really quickly," I said apologetically.

"I promised them a signed copy," she went on. "But it's

not the same as being here, is it?" She cast a dreamy look in Xander's direction. "He is ever so good-looking, isn't he? What a coup for your bookshop to get Xander Stone to launch here!"

I smiled and nodded politely as she went to join the queue of people waiting to have their books signed. I watched Xander as he carefully signed each book. That lock of hair fell into his face every time he bent over a book to sign his name. The customer was right – he was very good-looking. I felt my cheeks burn again and turned away, walking around the shop collecting the empty champagne glasses and clearing the empty plates from the buffet table. I never did get a chance to try any of the delicious-looking nibbles.

Over the course of the next hour people started to leave, clutching their bags of purchases, and Missy cashed up.

"We've done brilliantly," she said, telling me how much we'd taken. "We need to do this more often."

While I was delighted with how well the launch had gone and hoped that it would bring new customers to the shop, we'd need to host a lot more launches than this with writers even more famous than Xander to make any real difference. I wasn't sure how much longer we could keep paying Colin's wages.

"I admire your positivity," I said quietly to Missy. "But we both know…"

She held up a hand, stopping me. "Yeah," she said. "We both know, but it's Christmas so let's pray for a miracle, OK?"

"Megan darling," Philomena interrupted then. "I sadly must away." She pressed me to her bosom once again before pushing me away so that she could hunt something out from her tote bag. "Here's my card," she said, thrusting a brightly printed and larger-than-normal business card into my hand. "I want you to have a long hard think over the next few weeks about your future. And if that future lies in publishing, which I suspect it will, I want you to call me."

"OK," I said, smiling nervously and wondering where all this was coming from.

"Life goes on," she said. "The living are left behind to forge their own way."

"OK," I said again as Missy suppressed a giggle behind me. "You have to go, you said," I hinted, guiding Philomena towards the door.

"Yes, I have to get back to London tonight. I've another launch in Piccadilly tomorrow."

"Your taxi's here, Ms Bloom," Mum called from the doorway and I'd never been so pleased to hear five words in my life.

"Call me," Philomena repeated as she left.

I leaned against the shop counter in relief.

"Sorry about that. She can be a bit much." Xander was standing next to me.

"She's exhausting." I laughed. "How do you put up with her?"

"By hiding from her most of the time. As I said, she's a very good agent. I'd never have got as far as I have without her and, surprisingly, she can be very discreet."

"Does that mean you have secrets that you need keeping?" I asked. It was meant to be a joke but I watched as his brow furrowed and he looked away.

"Everybody wants to keep a modicum of privacy," he said.

"Well, thank you so much for doing this launch here. It was a really wonderful night and I can't wait to read the new book."

"I hope it helped," he said quietly.

"It really did," Missy said as she finished cashing up.

When Missy had gone, practically skipping with the takings towards the safe in the office, Xander turned to me again. "Megan," he said in a voice that sent a shiver up my spine. "I still owe you an apology."

"For what?"

"For last week, for the supermarket and for barging in here late at night. I…"

"Oh all's forgiven after tonight," I said.

"Still, I'd like to make it up to you. Will you at least have coffee with me tomorrow before I go back to London?"

So he was going back to London after all? I ignored the sense of sinking disappointment I felt.

"Saturday is our busiest day in the bookshop," I said. "I'm not sure I'll be able to get away."

"She'll be free in the afternoon," Mum said, popping up suddenly from behind the counter. How long had she been hiding there? The last I'd seen of her she'd been ushering Philomena towards her taxi. "Pick her up about three o'clock?"

Xander smiled at my mother and then turned back to me.

"Until tomorrow," he said, as he shrugged on his coat.

"I told you he liked you." Mum grinned at me as Xander left. "And judging by the colour of your cheeks, I was right about you liking him too. It's about time."

8

"Let's go to the Christmas Market," Xander said as we stepped out of the bookshop the next afternoon.

"That would be great," I replied, almost too enthusiastically.

Even though I knew Mum and Missy were right and it was time to start broadening my horizons again, there was a big difference between agreeing in theory and going on a date in practice. Was it even a date? Or was it just a thank you before he disappeared back to London and I never saw him again? And did it have to be coffee? Or worse, at this time of year, hot chocolate? The thought of going for coffee with Xander just reminded me of meeting Joe all over again, of him sitting on my bench and taking me for hot chocolate. He always insisted that day was our first date, whereas I thought of our first date as the evening he took me out for pizza and walked me back to the bookshop afterwards and kissed me in the porch. The porch I was now standing in with Xander.

So I jumped a little too enthusiastically at the chance to go to the Christmas Market instead of sitting in a café.

"Hopefully I can get some ideas for Christmas presents while I'm there," I said. "Before the bookshop gets too busy and I forget and everyone ends up getting books, which is great but not very original." I paused and looked out of the corner of my eye at him. "What about you? You don't strike me as a very Christmassy person."

He laughed then, a deep chuckle that I realised I hadn't heard before. I wondered again why he held on to himself so tightly, as though he was trying to hold off a storm.

"Is this because I criticised your Christmas tree the first time I came to the bookshop?" he asked. "I thought you'd forgiven me for that night."

"It's not just that." I shrugged. "I think the world is divided into people who have held on to their childish excitement about Christmas and people who haven't."

"And you think I fall into that second category?"

"Well… yeah."

He blew out a breath, which steamed in front of him in the cold afternoon air. "You're not far off the mark, to be fair," he said. "I'm not much of a Christmas person. Certainly not since my divorce and my mother's death."

"Oh," I said, my heart flipping suddenly. "I hadn't realised. I knew your father had…"

"I don't really talk about Mum or my ex-wife," he interrupted. "Mum died just after my second book came out, my divorce was finalised not long after – that's why this latest novel has taken so long."

I did some quick maths in my head. Xander Stone's second book had come out while Joe was in hospital for the final time. It was why I'd never gotten around to reading it. It sounded as though 2016 had been an awful year for both of us. Was he still hurting as much as I was? Was he still trying to pick up the pieces? It would explain the strange mix of rudeness and vulnerability that I'd witnessed this week if so.

"I'm sorry," I said, knowing from bitter experience how utterly useless other people's sympathy was in the face of grief.

We were approaching the Christmas Market, which saved us from any more of this depressing and awkward conversation.

"Let's get some mulled wine and have a wander around," I suggested.

"Good idea, even a Grinch like me can't say no to mulled wine. I did wonder if we should have served it last night, made the whole evening a bit more seasonal. Late November seems a strange time to have a new book out but I was so late handing it in that I felt I shouldn't complain."

"I have a feeling it's going to sell extremely well even in late November without mulled wine," I said.

"I don't know if Philomena told you, but I'm a bit superstitious when it comes to these things – I like to always serve the same food and drink…"

"And get out of London when the reviews start coming in," I finished.

"She did tell you then!"

After we got our mulled wines we looked at the stalls and while I made some mental notes about things I could come back to buy for Mum, Missy and Bella, Xander talked about his childhood Christmases.

"We never had any money growing up," he said. "But Mum always went all out at Christmas and our family was huge – seven of us and then countless aunts, uncles and cousins. It was hectic to say the least." I watched him smile to himself at the memory and found myself wondering what his life was like now. Did he keep in touch with all those cousins? Did he live alone? I remembered the dog he'd mentioned at the book launch.

"Did you like it?" I asked. "I'm not sure I'd have coped very well with all those people around. Our Christmases were always very quiet – just the three of us until Dad left and then…"

"Sorry," he replied. "I didn't mean…"

I held up a hand. "No, it's fine. I've just always been fascinated by huge families and never known how I'd have coped if I'd been part of one."

"It can be exhausting." He smiled. "But you get a lot of presents."

We passed some tables and chairs outside one of the market stalls and Xander gestured for me to sit down. "Let me get you another drink," he said.

When he came back with two more steaming cups of mulled wine I asked him if he'd finished reading *The Devil in Winter*.

"One chapter left," he said. "I'll finish it before I get the train tonight and leave it with Dot."

"Keep it," I said, making a mental note to put the money for it into the till at the bookshop or else Missy would lecture me on proper record-keeping again. "Think of it as a memento of your time in York and your honorary membership to the Die-Hard Romantics Book Club."

"Is that what you call yourselves?" he asked, shaking his head. "Dot never mentioned that!"

"So what did you think of the book?"

"Hmmm…" he said, taking a drink of his wine.

"I can see that you're desperately trying not to be rude."
I laughed.

"I didn't hate it," he said, which was quite diplomatic for
him when it came to romance novels.

"But…"

"But it's one of your friend's favourites, isn't it? The
woman who works at the Viking Centre?"

"Bella? Yes, she loves that book. I can't get past my
dislike of the hero."

"Ah yes, the rude, arrogant hero." Xander smiled at me. I
bet Sebastian St Vincent didn't smile like that. A lot can be
forgiven for a good smile. "I don't want to read one of your
friend's favourite books," Xander went on. "I want to read
your favourite books."

His eyes locked on mine with such intensity that it
knocked the breath out of me. He leaned closer.

"And I want to know," he said quietly, almost a whisper.
"Why it is that whenever you get uncomfortable you fiddle
with the third finger of your left hand as though you are
playing with a ring that used to be there?"

I looked away from him, towards my hands, thinking
of the three rings I used to wear – the cheap engagement
ring that Joe had bought just before our finals, the plain
wedding band and the exquisite eternity ring that he'd
bought on our third wedding anniversary to make up for
the cheap engagement ring. I'd taken all three rings off a
year ago and hidden them in a jewellery box in my first,
failed attempt to get on with my life.

"Shall we talk about my favourite books first?" I
asked, so many emotions fighting inside me – guilt, worry,
excitement… attraction.

He nodded, moving slightly away but not taking his eyes from me.

"Have you read *Love Story*?" I asked.

"I've seen the film," he replied. "Don't tell anyone but I quite liked it."

"Then read the book and read the sequel too. You could watch *Oliver's Story* but the book is better. Also try reading *One Day in December* – Dot's got a copy that I'm sure she'd lend you before you leave, and if you can stand another historical romance then try *A Christmas Gone Perfectly Wrong*."

"And what about Austen?" he asked. "Dot tells me you all spend a lot of time talking about Austen."

"Well even a snob like you must have read Austen!"

"A little, for my degree. Which is your favourite?"

"Impossible to answer," I replied. "All her books are perfect, but they are all very different. *Persuasion* is her only real romance novel in my opinion, but I'm a big fan of *Northanger Abbey* as well. It's Austen at her best – witty and clever and rather scathing of the popular literature of her time..." I paused. "Not unlike you, really!"

He was tapping something into his phone. "Noted," he said. "I'll read them all and report back."

"Really?" I was surprised. I thought he was just making conversation.

"If you tell me why you don't wear a ring on that finger anymore."

I looked away then and an uncomfortable silence descended. Why was he being so pushy about this? Why was he so interested? I felt cold all of a sudden and I must have shivered because I felt his hand on my arm and the shiver turned into a sensation of electricity.

"Are you OK?" he asked.

"Let's walk," I said. "Sometimes I find it easier to talk when I'm moving." Joe used to call it our 'walk and talks'. Whenever I had something I wanted to discuss with him, or an important decision to make, I preferred to talk about it while walking. When I felt Xander's hand on my arm, I knew I had to tell him about Joe but I couldn't do it sitting at a very public table while he looked straight at me.

"How much did Philomena tell you about me?" I asked. I knew Dot wouldn't have told Xander about Joe, but his agent had known an awful lot about my past and I had no idea how much of that she might have passed on.

"She told me you used to work in publishing – that you used to be an editor for Rogers & Hudson," he replied. "I think she wanted to assure me that you knew what you were doing."

I didn't say anything for a moment, not sure where to start, not knowing how he would react.

"Look, I know divorce is really hard," he began, perhaps trying to make it easier for me.

"I'm not divorced," I said.

"Separated then?"

"Sort of," I replied, taking a breath. "Permanently separated. I'm a widow."

I felt his energy change and his steps slow down. I didn't want to stop walking so I crossed the road to put my empty mulled wine cup in a nearby bin.

"I'm so sorry," Xander said when I returned. "I know

that's completely inadequate..." He paused, rubbing his hand across his face. "How old was... what...?" He trailed off and looked away.

"Leukaemia," I replied. "He was twenty-eight. He died waiting for a stem cell donor."

"My mother died of leukaemia," Xander said quietly. "I know how devastating it can be."

"I'm sorry you had to go through that too." My voice sounded oddly formal and I realised we were standing in the middle of the street staring at each other, Christmas shoppers bustling past. We stood so close I could feel the warmth of his body and I had an inexplicable desire to rest my head against him, for him to wrap his arms around me.

After a moment Xander blinked and shook his head. "Let me walk you back to the bookshop," he said. He offered me his elbow and I held lightly on to his coat sleeve. It wasn't even remotely intimate, but I felt a sudden surge of emotion.

"Thank you for telling me," Xander said as we walked along.

"I'm sorry I was so reluctant to go for a coffee with you and I'm sorry about my mother being so pushy but I guess now, at least, you know why."

"And I completely understand."

"I haven't really done anything except work in the bookshop and go out for a drink with Bella and Missy in the last three years. Mum and my friends think I should be moving on by now... and I know they're right, I just haven't felt able to. I've felt sort of stuck."

"Then I'm honoured you accepted my invitation," Xander said.

"I'm glad I came," I said quietly.

We turned the corner past the new tearoom and walked towards the bookshop. Xander paused just before the window and turned towards me.

"I'm so sorry for everything you've been through," he said softly. "I'm assuming that's why you left publishing?"

"I left my job to look after Joe," I said. "After he died I couldn't bear to stay in London and so I came home." I looked over my shoulder at the bookshop. "It was meant to be temporary but..." I stopped, shrugged.

"Grief is different for everyone," he said quietly, and I thought about what he'd said before, about how he didn't really enjoy Christmas anymore now that his mum had died. "I'd like to see you again, Megan," he went on. "But I completely understand if you would prefer us to just say goodbye here and..."

"No," I said decisively. Missy was right – I had to start living again and Xander Stone was a lot more understanding than I'd previously given him credit for. He was someone who at least had some idea of what I was going through, of how hard this was for me. "I'd like to stay in touch. Let me know when you're next in York."

He smiled. "Well in that case I'll see you on Thursday," he said.

"Thursday?"

"We're learning to dance the quadrille, I understand."

I laughed. "Oh my God, you really don't have to come. Don't let Trixie push you into it."

"I want to come," he said.

"Well, on your head be it," I said. "Don't say I didn't warn you."

"I'll see you on Thursday then, Ms Taylor," he said, before he walked away and my stomach flipped over.

For three years I had hidden away in the bookshop because I never wanted to feel the pain that I'd felt after Joe died again. But by trying to avoid pain and grief and suffering, which were all part of life anyway, I'd also shut myself away from joy and adventure and love. Running the bookshop had been my way of finding some sort of control in my life after the unthinkable had happened, but I knew now that I had no control over anything, not even over the survival of the bookshop.

The thought of seeing Xander again made me feel nervous but in a good way, the way you're meant to feel when you first start dating someone. The truth was that I did really like him – Mum had been right about that – and I needed to move on. I tried to ignore the memories of the cheap coffee dripping into the plastic cup as my husband lay dying. My crippling guilt wasn't going to change the fact that Joe was dead any more than my not having gone to get that coffee in the first place would have stopped him from dying.

It was time to live my life again.

9

I didn't hear from Xander again all week, but he said he'd be there on Thursday and Dot said he'd be there on Thursday so I had no reason to think he wouldn't be. But I was still surprised when he arrived before anyone else with what appeared to be a wriggling lump under his coat.

"I'm a little early," he said.

"No problem, come in." It was absolutely freezing outside. "Um..." I looked at the lump under his coat again. "Your coat seems to be moving."

"Ah yes," he said, as a snuffly wet nose appeared out of the front of his coat, followed by two big brown eyes and two floppy ears. "This is Gus." He placed a small sausage dog on the floor and took his coat off. When I'd wondered about what breed of dog Xander Stone walked along the River Thames I hadn't thought it would be a sausage dog. Gus trotted off into the bookshop and disappeared into the cookery section, just as Philomena had done the week before.

"I'm not sure..." I began. We didn't usually allow dogs in the bookshop unless they were service dogs. I started to walk towards the cookery section myself to see what Gus was up to. "We don't usually let dogs into..." I paused again, looking over my shoulder at Xander. "He is house-trained, isn't he?"

Xander laughed. "He is definitely house-trained," he confirmed. "He's just quite curious. Here, let me fetch him." He strode past me into the cookery section and returned a few seconds later with Gus in his arms.

"He didn't come with you last week, though," I said.

"No, my brother was looking after him last week, but I don't like to leave him with other people for too long."

My discomfort about having a dog in the bookshop must have shown on my face because Xander offered to take him back to Dot's.

"Dot said you wouldn't mind but I can see she's not mentioned it to you and that you're not very comfortable. I'm sure he'll be OK on his own for an hour or two."

Xander was wearing a dark blue cashmere roll-neck sweater and dark jeans. He'd rolled the sleeves of his sweater up, exposing muscular forearms, and Gus had settled down into the crook of his elbow. As I looked at him, my stomach flipped over and I had to look away before he saw me blushing yet again.

"Of course he can stay," I said as I walked over to the table I'd already prepared for the book club meeting and started to move the wine glasses around unnecessarily. "Just maybe if he didn't wander around on his own?"

"He'll probably fall asleep soon anyway. He's had a very exciting day of travel and being spoiled by Dot and I've just given him a long walk."

"Do sausage dogs need such long walks?" I asked. "They have such little legs."

"And a lot of energy."

My cheeks had cooled down enough to be able to turn around and look at Xander again. "You don't really strike me as the sausage dog type," I said.

"And what sort of type do you think I am?" he asked, smiling wolfishly at me.

I shrugged. "Something bigger," I said.

"I see." He smirked and raised an eyebrow. I felt my cheeks flame again.

"Like a wolfhound or a German shepherd," I went on. They were the only big dogs I could think of off the top of my head.

"Wolfhounds and German shepherds are not the best dogs to keep in central London apartments."

"No, I suppose not," I replied, looking at Gus, who was staring back at me with big doleful eyes.

"That's the look he gave me when he saw me at the shelter," Xander said. "I'm embarrassed to admit that look was all it took for me to be smitten."

Gus barked as if to confirm the story.

"What would your adoring public think if they knew that Xander Stone was such a softie?"

"I don't know what you mean." He smiled at me again then and my stomach did that thing that it seemed to do whenever Xander was around. There was something about him standing there cuddling a small dog that was bringing up all sorts of feelings that I hadn't felt in years.

"As you're here early," I said, breaking eye contact and trying to get those feelings back under control. "Can you help me move this bookcase? I need to make space for our dance lesson and I can't do it on my own and I don't want to disturb Mum while she's writing."

"Your mum's a writer too?" Xander asked as he put Gus down on one of the chairs, where he promptly curled up and went to sleep.

"She writes historical romance serials for magazines," I replied. "I can't imagine why she didn't tell you, what with you being such a fan of historical romance!"

"Yes, well…" he said as he picked up one end of the bookcase and the muscles in his forearms flexed in a way that almost made me drop my end on my toe.

"Megan," he said softly as we pushed the bookcase against the wall. "I came here early to see if you were OK. I really appreciated what you shared with me on Saturday and I wanted to ask…" But as he spoke the bookshop door opened and two of the tallest, broadest men I'd ever seen in my life squeezed through, closely followed by Bella and Missy.

"Maybe later," Xander said quietly.

"The Vikings are ready for their dancing lesson," Missy called out as Bella giggled beside her. Then they saw us, standing close together.

"Oooh, are we interrupting something?" Bella cooed.

"No, nothing," I snapped, stepping away from Xander. Why did I feel so embarrassed? As though we'd been caught doing something we shouldn't have been doing. "I'm just going to pop upstairs to get Mum. As soon as Trixie gets here with the music we can start."

Colin was the last to arrive. He slid into the bookshop at the last minute just as I'd given up on him coming at all.

He had been very reluctant when I'd asked him.

"You only want me to come to make up the numbers for the dancing," he'd said.

"Last week I had to force you to stay away," I'd replied.

"Last week I wanted to meet Xander Stone and you know it."

"Xander will be here this week too," I'd said, even though at that point I still hadn't been sure if he would come or not.

Colin's brow had furrowed in what looked like disgust and disbelief. "He's doing this ridiculous dancing?" he'd asked.

"It's not ridiculous."

"Well I've met Xander now anyway," Colin had said dismissively. I had a feeling that Colin had been disappointed by Xander.

"How do you know about the dancing anyway?" I'd asked.

"It's all Bella and Missy have been talking about all week," he'd replied. "You act as though I'm not there half the time but I can hear everything you say so…" He'd shrugged.

I knew that Missy didn't think particularly highly of Colin and I was just as guilty as she was when it came to ignoring him. As for Bella, she didn't even work here!

"I'm sorry," I'd said. "You're a valuable member of Taylor's Bookshop too and I want you to be there for the Christmas Eve party and I'd love it if you learned to dance the quadrille with the rest of us."

He'd folded his arms across his chest. "And partner your mother no doubt," he'd said.

"You can have an extra day off over Christmas," I'd

replied, rather rashly as it would be me who'd be working instead.

It must have worked though, because here he was, and Xander must have noticed Colin looking uncomfortable because he raised a hand in greeting. Colin seemed to relax a little then.

"Can we all concentrate please," Trixie shouted, banging a walking cane that she had acquired from somewhere on my beautiful wooden floors. She looked like a geriatric version of that dance teacher from *The Kids From 'Fame'*.

We all listened again as she explained, with the use of diagrams, the dance steps involved.

The quadrille, Trixie told us, is danced in sets of two couples standing in a rectangle and is similar to American square dancing. None of us really knew what that was either so it wasn't much help.

"No, Artemis, it's nothing like line dancing," Trixie scolded when Missy tried to show us all a grapevine with heel dig and pivot turn.

"I didn't know you did line dancing," I whispered.

"There's a lot you don't know about me," Missy replied mysteriously.

"Stan and I will demonstrate," Trixie said. Stan was a tall, well-dressed man in a dapper three-piece suit and I wondered if he was the owner of the walking cane. I hadn't noticed when he'd arrived. He seemed to be around the same age as Trixie – which was unusual in itself as she had a preference for younger men. He was also less susceptible to being bossed around than her previous boyfriends. From what little I'd seen of him so far, he seemed lovely. "As the name suggests, and as I've set out here," Trixie went on, pointing her cane at one of the diagrams, "the quadrille is danced in a group of four couples – so, Megan, you and Xander can dance with us."

I tried to resist, pretending I had to get another bottle of wine out of the fridge and that Bella and her Viking Norm could do it instead but, surprisingly, Xander had already stepped into the space we had cleared earlier for the dancing. He seemed very keen and turned towards me holding out his hand, which unnerved me slightly. It wasn't so much that I didn't want to acknowledge how I felt about him. It was just that after all these years I didn't really know what to do with those feelings.

I felt Missy give me a gentle shove in the lower back and I staggered into the middle of the room, reluctantly taking Xander's hand. And there was that tingly feeling again.

"Right," Trixie said as she arranged Bella and Norm and Missy and Norm's friend, who nobody had been introduced to yet, so that each couple was standing on one of the four sides of a square looking into the centre. Everyone else looked on. "Let's begin."

Trixie pressed 'play' on the portable CD player she'd brought with her and what I think was harpsichord music filled the shop. It did feel for a moment as though we were in a Jane Austen adaptation. This would be brilliant when we were all in costume. Suddenly my head was full of images of Xander in breeches and...

"Concentrate, Megan," Trixie snapped at me. I was very aware of the heat in my cheeks again and Xander's hand in mine. "What did I just say?"

"I... that... um..." I stammered.

"I said that you, me, Stan and Xander are the head couples."

"Which means?"

"We dance first."

"But how...?"

"Follow me," Trixie said. I felt Xander squeeze my hand and then let go as he stepped into the centre to take Trixie's arm. He must have been paying attention when I was daydreaming about him in breeches. I took Stan's arm and he twirled me around and back to Xander. At least someone knew what they were doing.

After we'd practised the first part of the dance a few times it was our turn to be 'side couples' as Bella, Missy and the Vikings took a turn. Trixie did a lot of sighing and eye rolling as they danced but I thought they did very well considering this was their first time.

"You seem to have taken to this very easily," I whispered to Xander as the others danced. "Have you done it before?"

"I don't like to go into things blind," he replied. "So I may have watched some YouTube videos over the last few days."

"But why?" I asked. "Why are you so interested in this anyway?"

He looked down at me for a moment. "I'd have thought that was obvious," he said and my breath caught in my throat.

Before he could say anything else Trixie was issuing instructions again.

"Artemis, can you please try to keep your head up and dance on the balls of your feet." She sighed. I've no idea why she and Missy always managed to rub each other up the wrong way but they did. "You look like a baby elephant."

That was it for Missy and she collapsed into giggles, which set Bella off too. Norm and his friend looked bewildered. I wondered how much Bella had told them about dancing quadrilles before they'd come tonight. I suspected not very much.

"Let's swap you four out," Trixie said and Bella, Missy and the Vikings were replaced by Mum, Colin, Dot and Stan's friend John who had come along to be Dot's dance partner. He was short and bald and wore round gold-rimmed glasses and seemed to be making Dot laugh a lot.

"Is he flirting with her?" Xander asked me.

"I do hope so." I smiled. "Dot deserves some fun." I'd only known Dot about a year but I'd never once known her to date or even to go to dinner with anyone who wasn't a colleague at the university. She was a bone fide introvert and very happy in her own company, just like Mum. But it was nice to see someone making her laugh.

As one of the 'head couples' I was expected to dance the quadrille again with our new 'side couples' rather than go and talk to Norm and his friend, which is what I wanted to do. Over the course of the next hour Xander and I must have danced the first parts of the quadrille about three hundred times with the other couples being swapped out at Trixie's whim. Meanwhile Gus, who had been sleeping under a chair for a while, woke up and became very excited at seeing his master dance. He somehow got up onto the table, despite his small legs, and started to bark in time with the music.

"Whose dog is this?" Trixie shouted in disgust over the noise.

Xander rushed over to try to calm Gus down. "This is Gus. I didn't get a chance to introduce him to you all." Nobody had had a chance to be introduced and everyone took this as a cue to wind things down and make a fuss of Gus, who was clearly in his element. Trixie, however, had other ideas.

"Enough," I said firmly when Trixie wanted us to go through it again. "Can we please have a break? My feet are killing me."

"Yeah come on, Trixie," Missy said as she tickled Gus's chin. "I think we've all got the hang of it now. We are only doing a fun demonstration at the party – it's not like we're entering a competition."

"And this is meant to be a book club," Dot interjected.

"OK, OK," Trixie said reluctantly. "We can break for wine and snacks if you like."

"Has anyone read anything fun this week?" Dot asked as I poured wine for everyone, knowing full well this wouldn't be just a break and that nobody was going to be doing any more dancing tonight.

"I want to know what Xander thought of *The Devil in Winter*," Bella said, raising her eyebrows in Xander's direction. "And be polite please, it's one of my absolute favourites."

"Well…" Xander began carefully, sitting down next to me and placing Gus on his knee. "I didn't hate it…" He repeated what he'd said to me at the Christmas Market. It was clearly his stock line in diplomacy.

"Ha!" Bella interrupted triumphantly. "Snobby, arrogant Xander Stone likes my favourite romance novel."

"Bella!" I said and Gus barked at her.

"Sorry, I didn't mean it like that."

"Before you get too triumphant about it," Xander said, holding up his hand, "I haven't finished. It was a lot of fun but I'm inclined to agree with Megan and Martha that the hero leaves a lot to be desired."

"You read a romance novel?" Colin asked quietly from the corner he was sulking in. He had most definitely not enjoyed dancing the quadrille and probably should have watched a few YouTube videos before joining us. Perhaps we all should have done though, to be fair.

Xander nodded. "Megan quite rightly pulled me up for being a snob about genre fiction."

"Well he clearly only read it because Megan asked him to and he wants to…" Mercifully Colin stopped there when Mum tapped him on the shoulder but I could feel my cheeks burning again. Why did everyone seem to think that Xander and I were a done deal? We hadn't even been on a proper date yet and I didn't know if we would do. I was surprised that he kept turning up to book club, to be honest. Was that really just to spend time with me? Was that what he meant earlier, before Trixie interrupted us?

"I've also read *One Day in December*, *Love Story* and half of *Northanger Abbey*," Xander went on and Colin's eyebrows shot right up into his fringe. I felt a bit sorry for him, as though his hero was being torn to pieces in front of his very eyes.

"You read *One Day in December*." Dot beamed at him. "What did you think?"

"I loved it, Dot, you were right. I need to read with more of an open mind."

"I'll get you to read Ruby Bell yet." Dot laughed.

I watched a strange look pass over Xander's face as though he was slightly repulsed at the thought of reading Ruby Bell. I'd have thought he'd think more highly than that of one of Dot's favourite writers. We had a long way to go to turn Xander into a romance reader.

"*Love Story* isn't a romance though," Missy said. "Just to be clear."

"Why not?" Xander asked. "It's ridiculously romantic." He looked at me for a moment as he said it and my breath caught in my throat.

"I'll admit it's romantic," Missy said. "But it's not a romance because they don't get their HEA."

"HEA?" Norm asked.

"Happy Ever After!" we all chorused at him.

Everybody started talking at once, mostly trying to recommend books for Xander to read next, and I thought it would be a good opportunity for Bella to introduce me to Norm, who shook my hand in bone-crushing way.

"He's got a PhD in chemistry from Bristol," Bella said proudly.

"Is that a qualification needed to dress up as a Viking at a novelty museum in York?" I laughed.

Norm's eyes crinkled at the corners when he smiled. "Yeah I know," he said. "My mum said the same thing, but I've always loved doing Viking re-enactments and when I heard about the job I thought it would be a good way to spend some time while I apply for the funding for my post-doctorate." He paused, pulling Bella towards him. "And then I met this one," he said.

"How long have you been together now?" I asked.

"Three months," Bella said in a small voice.

"Best three months I've had in a long time." Norm grinned.

I smiled back at them but inside I felt terrible. They'd been dating for three months and Bella hadn't felt able to tell me. I really had been wrapped up in myself for far too long and I absolutely had to start living my life – if only so my friends could start living theirs without worrying about me.

Norm introduced me to his friend, Bryn.

"Do you dress up as a Viking too?" I asked. He looked very like Norm except that he was dark rather than blonde.

"I do actually," he said. "But just for fun. Unlike Norm here, I have a proper job teaching science at a school in Fulford."

As we were talking, which mostly consisted of us all teasing Bryn as he tried a myriad of ways to get Missy to go on a date with him and she refused all of them, I felt a touch on my arm and that familiar tingle.

"I should go," Xander said. "I need to take Gus out before he gets too excited and pees on your floor."

"You did promise me he wouldn't do that." I smiled.

"I was wondering…" he began.

"Yes?"

"Would you like to have lunch with me this weekend?"

I didn't reply for a moment. My immediate reaction was to say 'no', to find some excuse as to why I would be busy all weekend. And then I remembered that Bella hadn't told me about Norm for three months and that Missy was right about me needing to get out more.

"Are you staying in York for a while?" I asked, buying myself some time.

"I need a break from London…" He paused as he

crouched down to clip Gus's lead on to his harness and I wondered why he needed a break and whether he was still staying with Dot.

"Sunday would be better for me," I heard myself saying. Was I ready to have lunch with Xander? Walking side by side through the Christmas Market was one thing, but lunch?

"I know this great place," he said. "I'll call you."

And before I could protest or change my mind, he and Gus had gone.

IO

"Lunch at Graydon Hall!" Mum exclaimed. "Very fancy."

"Too fancy maybe?" I asked. It was closing time on Saturday evening and Xander had phoned to let me know where we were going for lunch the next day and when he'd pick me up.

"Of course not," Mum replied dismissively as she poured hot water over our teabags. "It's a date isn't it? He should be taking you somewhere fancy. It'll give you an excuse to dress up. You've got that lovely dark red dress that I don't think you've worn since the Christmas party last year. That will be perfect." She sighed happily, bringing our tea mugs over to the table. "I've been wanting to go to Graydon Hall myself for a while," she went on. Her excitement over my lunch date with Xander was infectious, and I found myself looking forward to it. "They sent us some vouchers earlier this year and I was going to take you for afternoon tea but..." She trailed off and the silence that she left in her wake was almost palpable.

"But I never want to go anywhere except the pub or the tearoom with Missy and Bella." I finished her sentence for her.

Mum put her mug down and reached over for my hand, giving it a little squeeze, but what I'd said was true. I hadn't been anywhere outside of York's city walls in over three years. Before Joe died, Mum and I used to love exploring old houses and gardens together and we'd meet up all over the country to do so. Since I'd been back in York, I hadn't so much as gone inside the Minster with her and I suddenly felt an overwhelming sensation of sadness – one that wasn't just about losing Joe but about all the other aspects of my life I'd lost since he'd died.

"It's understandable, Megan," Mum said now.

"Is it?" I replied. "I've been so wrapped up in myself, so selfish. Did you know that Bella has been dating that guy she brought to book club for three months? Three months and she didn't tell me because she thought she'd hurt my feelings?"

Mum nodded.

"So even you knew she'd been with Norm for three months?"

"None of us blame you, Megan."

"I blame me," I replied. Because I did. I wasn't sure what had triggered it, perhaps it was meeting Xander, but I felt as though my eyes had suddenly been opened to just how self-absorbed I'd become. At first it was understandable, grief is destructive and complicated, but I'd had so much support and gentle coaxing from my friends and family, even from Joe's family, and I'd ignored it all.

"You've done a lot of good work in the bookshop."

"Have I? I've given it a lick of paint and moved some shelves around but it's hardly been a roaring success, has it?

Most weeks we're not even breaking even and it's supposed to be our busiest time of the year."

"You can't blame yourself for that either…" Mum began.

"When I came back I thought this was my purpose, my life now. That it was up to me to make the bookshop a success again, but recently I've started to realise that I want something more than this." I paused. "Don't take that the wrong way, Mum," I said. "I've loved being here with you over the last three years and I don't know what I'd have done without you." I thought about that first Christmas after Joe died, the Christmas I first met Bella and first went out with her and Missy. Everything had been so raw then and I'd felt so vulnerable and exposed, as though a layer of my skin had been stripped. I spent so much time thinking about him and what I'd be doing if he was still here, if he'd recovered, if the leukaemia hadn't come back, if I'd been with him when he died.

How I felt now, three years later, was very different. Joe wasn't front and centre of my every waking hour anymore. He was always there in the back of my mind and I knew he always would be, but I also knew he wasn't coming back. I had to get on with my life without him – whatever that might mean.

"And it's been wonderful to have you here, but we both know you need more than this, a life outside of these four walls. You can't live with your old mum forever. I'm pleased, to be honest."

"Pleased to be getting rid of me?" I joked.

"No, Megan," Mum replied, "I'm pleased that you're finally feeling ready to move on, to try new things, to see where life takes you. I've been worried about you. We all have."

"All?" I asked.

"Me, Bella, Missy and your dad of course. He's probably been the most worried as he hasn't even seen you."

I wondered how much my parents had been in touch, how much time they'd spent talking about me. "Dad could always have visited," I said quietly.

Mum shrugged. "I know," she replied. "But you know what he's like."

Sometimes I wondered if I did know what he was like. When I was young we used to be so close – I was close to both my parents. They had felt like my best friends, people who were always there to talk about books and stories and I knew how lucky I was to have them. When Dad left I tried not to take sides but it was hard, especially when I heard Mum crying, and it was inevitable that I'd grow closer to Mum and subconsciously taken her side. Even when I'd started seeing Dad regularly in London I'd never felt as close to him as I had to Mum, and neither of my parents ever really talked about each other. I knew they kept in touch; I knew they saw one another once in a while but other than that their relationship was a mystery to me.

"Have you spoken to Dad about the shop?" I asked now.

Mum nodded. "I asked Missy to email through the accounts to him. He said he'll mull it over and let us know."

"Let's hope he has some genius plan to save the day then."

"He'll come up with something," Mum said. "But I don't want you to worry about that today. You've got a hot date tomorrow and I want you to enjoy it."

"It's not a hot…" I began.

"Isn't it?" Mum interrupted with a twinkle in her eye. "It sounds like one to me. He's keen as mustard, why else would he be subjecting himself to Trixie's dancing lessons, do you think? Watching YouTube videos so he doesn't show himself up?"

"I don't know."

"You're just a bit out of practice and you don't notice these things anymore. Trust your mother."

"I don't even know how to date anymore," I said. "Do you think there are new rules?"

"Don't ask me." Mum laughed. "It's been decades since anyone took me out for a fancy lunch."

This would have been a good time to pursue a line of enquiry into my mother's dating life, or lack of, but she had gathered up the mugs and disappeared to her writing room before I got a chance.

"What a beautiful building," I said as Xander drove his gunmetal-grey Porsche up the sweeping gravel driveway towards Graydon Hall.

"This place serves the best Sunday lunches I've ever had," he replied as he reversed the car into a parking space in a spray of gravel and I realised that I'd been gripping on to the edges of the passenger seat for quite a while. "And they're dog-friendly if we eat in the bar." Gus barked from the back seat as though he knew what we were talking about. "It's an old Jacobean manor house," he went on. "Just wait until you see inside." The hotel was just outside of the village of Graydondale in North Yorkshire and the drive out had been stunning (if a bit fast).

"I feel as though I recognise it," I said, as I got out of the car. "But I don't think I've ever been here before." I wrapped my coat around me. It was absolutely freezing now we were out of the city and there was an icy bite in the wind.

"They filmed an adaptation of *Mansfield Park* here a few years ago, just before it reopened as a hotel," Xander said as he picked Gus up out of the back seat, locked the car and led me towards the hotel entrance. Gus was sporting a natty red bandana for the occasion.

The reception area was a huge open space with a sweeping wooden staircase leading to the floors above and one of the biggest Christmas trees I'd ever seen sitting in the middle.

"Wow," I whispered.

"I know," Xander replied as he walked towards the bar, which was equally beautiful. I'd worried that I was a little overdressed for Sunday lunch but now we were here in this rather glamorous setting, certainly more glamorous than anywhere I'd been in a long time, I was glad I'd let Mum persuade me to wear the red dress. Xander always seemed to look as though he'd just stepped off the pages of a designer magazine whatever he was wearing, so I didn't feel out of place.

"Let me take your coat," he said, when we'd been shown to our table and Gus had settled himself under one of the chairs. He stood behind me to help slide the coat off my shoulders and I felt his breath on the back of my neck. It made me shiver and I closed my eyes for a moment and took a breath. This was what dating was like these days then. *Just go with it*, I told myself.

"Would you like something to drink?" the waiter asked as he handed us menus.

"Well I'm driving," Xander replied. "So just a sparkling water for me and a bowl of water for Gus." He looked over at me. "Megan?"

I was about to ask for water too but then I thought a small glass of something might calm the anxious butterflies that were dancing around in my stomach. "A glass of red please," I said. "A merlot if you have it."

"I feel as though we didn't get much of a chance to talk on Thursday," Xander said, when the waiter had left.

"I'm sorry, Trixie can be very domineering. When I planned this Regency-themed Christmas party I hadn't intended for Trixie to completely take it over like this. And I certainly hadn't intended for her to rope you into it."

"Oh don't worry about me," he said, leaning back in his chair. "I can handle Trixie." He paused and I thought again about why he'd want to handle Trixie or learn to dance the quadrille. Was what Mum suggested true? Was he doing this for me?

I'd have thought that was obvious.

I swallowed down the nerves. It had been a long time since I'd been on a date and back then Joe had been a lot easier to read than Xander Stone was.

"So tell me about Gus," I said, looking for a neutral topic of conversation. "You said you first found him in a shelter?"

"Well I think we found each other," he said, leaning down to scratch Gus's head. "I know it sounds trite but this little ball of energy changed my life." He paused, his eyes flicking away from me for a moment. "After the divorce and my mother's death I got very depressed and sort of reclusive. I think my family started to worry about me because they staged an intervention – except instead of going to rehab I was taken to Battersea Dogs Home."

The waiter returned then with our drinks and we both ordered the Sunday roast. Xander promised I wouldn't be disappointed. "Although you might need a doggy bag," he'd said, at which Gus's ears pricked up.

"So Battersea is where you met Gus?" I asked, picking up where we'd left off.

"Yup," he replied. "I thought the whole thing was ridiculous. I didn't want a dog but I went along with the charade in the hope that when it became clear that I was not a dog person my brother would leave me alone to wallow again. However, Gus had other ideas."

"He chose you."

Xander nodded. "The thing about rescue animals is that I think they are the ones who do the rescuing. I was so determined not to get a dog that day – I just wanted to go home and go back to bed but this little one just kept barking at me. Then he looked at me with those doleful eyes and the next thing I knew I was filling in the paperwork."

"And the rest is history?" I asked. He suddenly seemed very different to the man who'd rammed his trolley into my legs (I hadn't had the nerve yet to ask if that was on purpose or not) or who bickered about romance novels. When he spoke about Gus or the days after his mother's death I felt as though I was getting a glimpse of the real Xander and the vulnerability that he almost revealed to me in the bookshop office just before his book launch. Now I knew what he'd been through – losing his mother and getting a divorce – I was beginning to understand the striking dichotomy of his personality. We all find our own way of dealing with trauma; goodness knows I knew that as well as anyone.

"Well we had some troublesome days first." Xander laughed. "You'd be surprised by how much damage one small dog can do and you may have noticed he has a very loud bark, which didn't go down very well with the neighbours at first, although they've all fallen in love with him since and are always arguing about whose turn it is to look after him if I have to go away for the day. But you can't lie in bed moping and drinking vodka all the time when you've got a dog that needs feeding and walking and playing with, so I had to get up and get dressed. After a while I started showering regularly again and eating proper meals and then, one day, Gus decided I was ready to start writing again."

"Gus decided?" I wasn't much of an animal person and I always felt a bit cynical when people anthropomorphised their pets.

"I'd closed up my office when Mum died, locked the door on it all and didn't write a word for nearly a year. Gus had never shown any interest in what was behind that closed door until one morning when he started barking at it and scratching on it. I thought that perhaps a mouse or something had got in, so I went to check it out. There wasn't anything there, but as I started tidying the room up an idea for a book started to form in my head."

"Was that the idea for *Mists of Our Waters*?" I asked.

He nodded vaguely as the waiter arrived with our food. The way he described his life after his mother died was something I easily understood. My life had been very similar after Joe's funeral. For weeks I'd wandered around in my bathrobe, eating peanut butter straight out of the jar, watching our wedding video over and over and drinking too much cheap wine. I knew what it felt like to think you'd lost everything and I knew what it felt like to have people who cared about you enough to intervene. In my case it had been my mother, who'd forced her way into my home, helped me pack up Joe's things and called the estate agent. She'd dealt with the sale of the flat while I moved back to York and painted the front door of the bookshop.

"So we've got Gus to thank then," I said as I stabbed my fork into a fluffy roast potato. "Without him we'd never have had a Xander Stone book launch at Taylor's Bookshop!"

"Gus and a lot of long walks along the Thames," he replied, smiling softly. "And it's just been me and him ever since, hasn't it, buddy?" He sneaked a piece of beef under the table to his dog.

"Just you and Gus?" I asked tentatively. "Nobody else?"

"Is that your way of asking me if I'm dating anyone?" He laughed. I looked down to concentrate very hard on my lunch.

"I'm not," he went on. "Dating anyone, that is. I wouldn't have asked you to lunch or spent so much time studying the quadrille if I was. And for what it's worth, I haven't dated anyone since my divorce."

I looked up at him, surprised. "Really?"

"Are you dating?" he asked.

"Obviously not, but that's different."

"Is it? Grief is grief and dating hasn't been top of my agenda for the last couple of years."

"You really are nothing like I imagined," I said.

"If you'd prefer to bicker about romance novels for the rest of the afternoon, I'm game."

I held up a hand. "It's OK." I laughed. "We don't have to do that every time we meet. I'm just surprised, that's all."

"About what in particular?"

"Well, I mean, look at you! You must have women swarming all over you..." The words were out before I could stop them and I could feel my whole face burning. Hopefully Xander would think it was just the open fire that was blazing in the fireplace on the opposite wall. "Oh God," I said. "I totally didn't mean that, I..."

"The thing is," he interrupted, completely deadpan. "I have this habit of being appallingly rude to women whenever I meet them and you're the first one I've managed to wear down to go on a date." Just as I thought I'd really offended him and ruined our afternoon his face broke into that beautiful smile again. "Don't worry, no offence taken and thank you for the somewhat back-handed compliment. But without wishing to destroy the image you have of me, I'm not actually Sebastian St Vincent and I've never kidnapped an heiress."

"Your car is definitely something St Vincent would have owned if he'd been a twenty-first-century rake though," I said, trying to compose myself again.

"Ah yes, the car. Do you like it?"

"I guess." I shrugged. "I never really think about cars to be honest. I've always lived in a city so I've never really needed one. I'm surprised you do."

"Owning a Porsche is a bit of a childhood dream, to be honest." He laughed. "Mum always told me it was a total waste of money but we all have our Achilles heel."

From Sebastian St Vincent we moved on to the books that he'd been reading from my recommendations.

"I've finished *Northanger Abbey*," he said. "And I'm about halfway through *Persuasion*."

"That's my Desert Island Discs book," I said. "I take it everywhere with me. What do you think?"

"I'm actually enjoying it a lot more than I thought I would," he admitted. "I've got to admit never really reading much Austen. I had to read *Mansfield Park* for my degree but I didn't enjoy it much. I might be changing my mind about her though."

"Whatever you do, do not tell Trixie that you don't love Jane. You'll rapidly fall out of favour."

He grinned as he wiped up the gravy on his plate with his last potato.

"So what are your favourite books, Xander Stone?" I asked. "What should I read next?"

"You're an English graduate too so I'm guessing you've read a lot of my favourites," he said. "*Great Expectations, The Life and Opinions of Tristram Shandy*, McEwan's *Enduring Love*, Paul Auster's *New York Trilogy*." He paused. "More recently I've loved *The Luminaries*."

"Oh me too," I said. "But I've never read *Tristram Shandy* and I've always meant to."

"Do – it's a lot more fun than you'd think it would be."

The waiter came over again then to clear our plates and ask us if we'd like desserts or coffee.

"No dessert for me," I said. "I'm stuffed. But I wouldn't mind a coffee."

"Shall we sit by the fire?" Xander gestured to the opposite

side of the room where the armchairs either side of the fireplace had just become free.

I agreed and took the opportunity for a quick trip to the loo. I was on my way back to the bar when I noticed the big fluffy white flakes falling from the sky and the ever-deepening blanket of snow on the ground. When had that happened? How had we not noticed? And, more importantly, how on earth was a Porsche 911 Carrera possibly going to make it back down the drive in this, let alone back to York?

11

"All the roads between here and the dual carriageway are closed," Xander said. "And it's unlikely the snowploughs are going to come out before the morning."

I groaned and buried my face in my hands. "What are we going to do?" I asked. The snow hadn't been forecast as far as either of us could see, but none of the staff seemed surprised.

"Comes down unexpected, love," the barman told me, as though it was quite normal to get snowed in. "No such thing as bad weather, just unsuitable cars," he'd gone on unhelpfully.

And Xander's car was completely unsuitable. There was no way it was going anywhere in this, and the snow was still coming down.

"I've got good news and bad news," Xander said. "Which would you like first?" He'd gone to talk to the manager as soon as I'd pointed out the snow to him and the unlikelihood of us being able to get back to York.

"The good news," I replied, grasping at straws. "Always the good news!"

"We can stay here tonight."

"At the hotel?"

He nodded. "Yup, and Gus can stay as well."

"Well I suppose that's better than trying to sleep in your car," I said.

"They can provide toothbrushes, shampoo, shower gel, bathrobes, everything we need, even dog food," he went on. "The only thing is…"

"Here comes the bad news," I said.

"There's only one room."

I stared at him and felt my stomach drop. This suddenly felt like too much. I knew that Missy and Mum had both been right about my needing to get on with my life and I even agreed with them about this lunch date with Xander. I'd been enjoying myself so much that I hadn't had time to feel guilty and I knew that was a good thing, I knew it didn't mean that I'd forgotten Joe or loved him any less. But lunch had suddenly turned into sharing a room with a man who wasn't Joe and I didn't know if I was ready for that.

"Please tell me it's a twin room," I said. My voice sounded small and faraway.

"OK," he said slowly. "It's a twin room."

"Is it?"

"I have no idea, Megan." He paused and looked away. "I'm really sorry about this." He rubbed a hand over his face. "I shouldn't have let this happen; I should have checked the forecast."

"There wasn't any snow forecast until tomorrow, according to the barman," I said. "Apparently this happens out here a lot though."

"I've only ever been here in the summer before."

I took a breath and looked out of the window again. The snow was coming down faster than ever and there was absolutely nothing I could do about it. I should be grateful that we had somewhere safe and warm to stay. Joe would have found this to be a glorious adventure and would already have made friends with some of the locals.

But Joe wasn't here.

"Let's go and look at this room then, shall we," I said.

"Oh you have got to be kidding me!" I said as I looked at the room that had been allocated to us. Xander stood behind me carrying our coats and Gus, who barked in disgust at the whole situation.

The room was beautiful, with a huge bay window overlooking the gardens of the hotel. A dusky rose-coloured sofa sat in the window with a pile of vintage Penguin books on a table next to it that I was already itching to sort through, and there was a large en-suite bathroom with a free-standing bath. It was the perfect hotel room for a romantic getaway – particularly as right in the middle stood a huge brass bed.

Just the one bed.

Xander cleared his throat behind me and I could see him shift from foot to foot uncomfortably, out of the corner of my eye.

"Only one bed," I said. "This is Bella's favourite romantic trope."

"What?" Xander stared at me.

"Come on, Xander, you're a writer," I said. "You know about tropes."

He shrugged, looking more and more uncomfortable by the minute.

"Romance novels are full of tropes. It's how the writer gets the hero and heroine together. You can force them to work together, or to go on a road trip. Then there's the fake engagement or marriage of convenience trope…"

"Like Sebastian and Evie in *The Devil in Winter*?"

I nodded. "Or," I said, gesturing at the bed, "you can abandon them in the middle of nowhere with only one bed to sleep in."

"So we're living in our very own romance novel." Xander smirked. He seemed to relax a little then. He stepped a little closer to me. His hand gently brushed my arm. I felt the familiar tingle. There were worse people to be stuck in the middle of nowhere with. "I can sleep on the sofa," he said.

I looked at the sofa and then back at him.

"The only way you could sleep on that sofa is by folding yourself in half," I replied. I walked away from him towards the bed. "It's quite a big bed. We can probably both manage to sleep in it and keep our dignity intact." As soon as the words were out of my mouth I regretted them.

"Dignity intact?" he asked, but I could hear the smile in his voice and hazarded a look over at him. "I don't know what romance novels you've been reading, Ms Taylor, but keeping one's dignity intact has never seemed to be top of anyone's agenda in any of the ones I've read."

"Well in this romance novel our dignities remain intact," I replied primly. I could see that he was trying not to laugh and then something else he'd said clicked in my brain.

"Hang on," I said. "What do you mean by 'any of the ones I've read'? You've only read *A Devil in Winter*, haven't you?"

"I never said I hadn't read romance novels. You just presumed I hadn't."

"Rubbish," I began, but he was right. He'd never actually said he hadn't read any, but he'd made it quite clear that he wasn't a fan.

When I looked at him he was grinning at me. "Don't worry though," he said. "I'll make sure your dignity stays intact. For tonight at least."

I felt my face burning again and I pressed the palms of my hands over my eyes.

"Oh God," I groaned. "I'm sorry, I wasn't suggesting that…"

"As I'm not driving anywhere tonight," he said, looking as though he was trying not to laugh in my face, "I might go and get a glass of wine. Would you like to join me?"

"I need to call Mum first and let her know what's going on so she doesn't worry."

"Shall I meet you downstairs in half an hour?"

"Sure."

He draped our coats over the back of a chair and walked towards the door, taking Gus with him.

Xander and Gus were sitting in front of two glasses of red wine at a quiet table in the corner of the bar when I came back downstairs.

"So tell me more about these romantic tropes," he said as I sat down. "Which one is your favourite?"

The bar and restaurant area were quiet and I wondered if anyone else who had been eating Sunday lunch here had got stranded or if they had known the snow was coming.

It was dark outside now and the snow sparkled under the hotel's outside lighting. Inside it was cosy and festive, soft Christmas music played and there were twinkly lights everywhere. It really was terribly romantic if you chose to look at it like that – which my mother had, of course.

"It's like living in your very own romance novel," she'd cackled when I'd told her what had happened and about the one massive bed in the middle of the room.

"Don't you start," I'd said. "Xander's already said that."

"Has he now? I have a feeling Xander Stone knows more about romance novels than he lets on."

"Yes well, that's as may be," I'd replied, remembering his comment about how I'd assumed he didn't read romance. "Can we focus on the problem at hand, please?"

"I don't see a problem, love," Mum said. "You're snowed in at a beautiful hotel with a handsome man. What more could anyone want?"

"Mum, you know it's not as simple as that." I'd felt myself starting to get a little bit panicky. "It's the first time…"

"I know, my darling." Mum's tone had been softer, the laughter gone from her voice. "I know. But you have to spend a night away from the bookshop at some point. This way it's like ripping off a plaster. And I know he can be a bit brusque—"

"Is that code for rude?"

Mum had laughed. "Yes, I suppose it is."

"He's actually been quite nice this afternoon."

"Well that's good. How does he feel about the whole sharing a room thing?"

"I don't know," I'd replied. "He's hard to read, but I think he's a bit embarrassed." I thought again about how he hadn't dated for the last few years. This was probably the first time he'd had to share a room with anybody since his divorce.

"I'm sure he is. I've always thought those 'only one bed' scenarios were more mortifying than romantic, whatever Bella might think. But promise me you'll have fun at least."

"I promise to try," I'd replied.

I picked up my wine glass now and looked into it. "Well," I replied slowly. "I do love a marriage of convenience." I looked up at him again. "Ruby Bell is great at those."

"Hmmm," Xander replied with a disgusted look on his face. He really did seem to hate Ruby Bell.

"But my absolute favourite is the sickbed trope," I went on. "When one character has to look after another who is ill or has been injured, usually under duress or out of necessity – that one was in *The Devil in Winter* as well. Love blossoms in the sick room obviously."

He looked at me over his wine glass. "Obviously," he said. "And what about your least favourite trope?"

"Oh that's easy," I replied. "Enemies to lovers. I hate it when the characters just snipe at each other for the whole book and then we're supposed to believe they live happily ever after."

"But isn't that the format of many literary greats? Elizabeth and Darcy in *Pride and Prejudice*, Beatrice and Benedict in *Much Ado About Nothing*."

"I am no fan of Fitzwilliam Darcy. He always seemed more trouble than he was worth, and much as I love Shakespeare, I really hate *Much Ado About Nothing*."

"Bold statements."

I grinned at him. "You don't have the monopoly on strong opinions."

He put his wine glass down on the table between us. "And what is your opinion on pantomimes?" he asked.

"That's a weird question," I said, surprised at the sudden change of subject. "Where's that come from?"

"I just wondered if you'd like to go to one tonight," he said. "Apparently it's opening night at the village hall and we've been invited. We can get a lift down on a tractor."

I stared at him. "A tractor? I'm not exactly dressed for a tractor." I glanced over at his extremely expensive-looking trousers. "And neither are you."

"I've got some boots in the car that I use for walking Gus sometimes," he said. "And apparently they have quite the collection of boots at the hotel for guests to borrow. As the barman said, this happens a lot." He pointed to the snow outside.

"And what about Gus?" I asked.

"Some of the staff are stuck here for the night and are very keen to look after him. He makes friends wherever he goes." Gus gave a little snuffly growl as though he knew we were talking about him. "I thought it might be fun." He shrugged, leaning back in his chair and crossing one ankle over the other.

"I didn't say I didn't want to go," I replied. I sounded scratchy and irritable which, to be fair, I was. But I was trying very hard not to be. I suddenly felt horribly awkward anywhere near Xander and kept thinking about tonight when I'd have to lie in that big double bed with him all night. A pantomime might take my mind off that at least.

"Relax, will you," he said. "It's just some snow and a shared room. What do I have to do to convince you I'm not Sebastian St Vincent?"

"What?"

"I promise to keep all my body parts on my half of the bed and my offer to sleep on the sofa remains."

"What pantomime is it anyway?" I asked, trying to distract myself from the thought of Xander's body parts.

"*Beauty and the Beast*," he replied.

Of course it was.

12

The tractor ride turned out to be a lot more fun than the pantomime itself. We arrived at the village hall exhilarated from the bumpy ride across the snow, our cheeks glowing from the cold, and were introduced to everyone.

"He drove out here in December in a Porsche, can you believe it?" the barman from the hotel, who was playing some minor character or other in the pantomime, told anyone who would listen. Xander pretended to laugh at his own apparent incompetence, but his smile looked increasingly like a grimace and I led him away to sit down before he reverted to the rude, arrogant version of himself.

The village hall was freezing cold and smelled strongly of disinfectant, as though somebody was trying to cover up a more sinister aroma. Hard, plastic chairs were set out in rows facing a high stage surrounded by faded red velvet curtains.

"Are you OK?" I asked Xander as he sat down, folding his long legs under the chair. Typically, the boots he had in his car were navy blue Hunters and he still looked like he belonged on a designer photoshoot. I, on the other hand, had to borrow bright pink wellies with yellow flowers on them. The cold air had made my hair static and I was generally feeling a bit of a mess.

"This is going to be awful, isn't it?" he replied. "What was I thinking?"

"I did wonder."

"I thought it would be interesting, you know. People-watching."

I looked around at the other people in the audience – a mix of families, older couples and what appeared to be a Brownie pack – and wondered where they'd all come from and how they'd got through the snow.

Once the show started I realised we were in for a bit of an ordeal. I don't think anything could have prepared us for how utterly dreadful the pantomime was. The man playing the Pantomime Dame was also the director (and the chairman of a group that was rather ambitiously known as 'The Graydon Players') and kept giving stage directions while in character so that nobody could tell which lines were part of the play and which weren't. Other than the Dame, nobody knew their lines at all, which resulted in long and uncomfortable silences. Some people seemed to be playing more than two roles at once and I couldn't work out if that was intended or because some of the actors (a word used very loosely) had been snowed in somewhere.

Just as I was beginning to think the first half of the pantomime would never end, the curtains were suddenly drawn.

"Thank Christ for that," Xander said, standing up and stretching his legs.

"Shall we get a cup of tea?" I asked. "They're selling them for 50p over there." I pointed towards the back of the hall.

Everyone was staring at us as we queued for the tea. I felt ridiculously overdressed despite the electric hair and vibrant boots. Xander, meanwhile, stood head and shoulders above almost everyone else and his clothes couldn't scream 'I come from London' more if they'd tried. Everyone already seemed to know he was the hapless Porsche driver but then he doubled down by asking if they had any green tea.

The women who were serving the tea muttered among themselves for a moment.

"Now you've thrown the cat among the pigeons," I whispered to Xander.

After some commotion, it was concluded that there was only PG Tips.

"But we've got hot orange squash if you like, love," one of the women said.

"Never mind," I said, trying to be as friendly as possible. I put a pound in their collection jar and led Xander away from people before he said something rude and obnoxious and had us exiled from the village forever.

"Green tea," I heard someone saying as we walked away. "First a Porsche and now green tea." I could feel Xander tensing up beside me.

"Shall we go outside?" I asked and he nodded.

It was freezing outside but the snow looked beautiful and the sky was completely clear. Xander puffed out a breath that steamed in the cold night air.

"Well, this was a truly terrible idea of mine," he said.

"Green tea though?" I asked, nudging him gently.

"It's not like I asked for Lapsang Souchong," he snapped.

"You should meet Ben," I said. "He and his girlfriend run the tearoom near the bookshop – it's called The Two

Teas – and he's a fan of tea that tastes like bonfires." I heard Xander exhale beside me. "They did the catering for your book launch actually. I can introduce you when we get back to York."

"If we ever get back," he sighed despondently. He turned to me. "Today has been a disaster."

"Has it?" I asked. "I think it's been fun."

"You do?" He seemed startled. "With the snow and the pantomime and the bed situation?"

"Well the pantomime was a disastrous idea, admittedly, and the bed situation was... unexpected, but the snow is very pretty, the food and wine were lovely and the company was OK too."

"Well I stand corrected." He smiled. "But I don't know if I can bear to go back in there for the second act."

"Don't we have to wait for our tractor ride home?"

"We could walk. It wasn't that far and it's straight up the road."

I looked at the snow doubtfully.

"I could carry you, Ms Taylor," Xander said. "Like one of your romantic heroes."

"No need for that," I said as I started to walk in what I hoped was the direction of the hotel.

"It's this way," Xander called after me, pointing in the other direction. I turned around and started walking back towards him when my slightly-too-large boot hit an icy patch and the next thing I knew I was flat on my back in the snow.

"At the very least take my arm," Xander said, hauling me up onto my feet again. "Unless you want to re-enact one of those sickbed scenes you're so fond of."

He offered me his elbow and I reluctantly slipped my

hand into the crook of his arm, feeling my stomach tip at little at his proximity, even through all the layers of wool. We walked along in silence for a while, the only sound the crunch of our boots in the snow.

"Can I ask you something?" I said after a few minutes. "Tell me to shut up if you think I'm prying though."

"OK," he replied slowly.

"Did your life really used to be like you describe it in *Boxed*? It's just… well…" I hesitated. "You seem quite different to how I imagined, what with the clothes and the car and the taste for fancy tea."

"Aren't we all a little bit different to the image we put out into the world?" he replied. "Don't we all have a tendency to eclectic tastes and hypocritical opinions? People tend to have this ridiculous idea that because of my background, I should behave in a certain way, but none of us really fit into preconceived pigeonholes, do we?"

"You don't really look like a boxer though."

He chuckled. "And what should a boxer look like?"

"OK, fair point on the pigeonholes."

"I didn't box heavyweight, you know," he said.

"I don't know what that means."

"Boxers fight at a certain weight that depends on their own bodyweight. The famous boxers that you've probably seen on TV are heavyweights. I was a welterweight, which is much lighter."

"I see," I said, not really seeing and not really wanting to ask him how much he weighed.

"And to answer your question," he went on. "*Boxed* isn't as autobiographical as my publishers might have made it out to be."

"So you didn't fight for a living?"

"I did for nearly three years, but I wasn't as successful as the main character in *Boxed*. Plus I was much more vain than him. I gave up after I broke my nose for the third time and the doctor couldn't set it straight." He touched his nose subconsciously. I'd noticed it was crooked the first time I'd met him in the supermarket – I thought it suited him, adding to his rakish good looks.

"And so you just stopped boxing completely?" I asked.

"No," he replied. "I quit boxing competitively just before I got married and I took over the management of one of the gyms I used to fight at. I'd gone back to school by that point and it freed up a little bit of brain space. But I carried on training there too. I still do, but just to keep fit really. I don't fight anymore but I find the discipline of the training really helps me keep in shape – physically and mentally." I tried not to think about the 'physically' part that would be lying next to me in bed in the not-too-distant future.

"Did you keep working at the gym until you had your first book published?" I asked.

"Yes…" He hesitated and I wondered if I'd pushed too hard into an area of his life he didn't really want to talk about. I didn't say anything else or ask any more questions. I just listened to the crunch of our boots in the snow and waited.

"How old were you when you got married?" he asked eventually.

"Twenty-one. We met in our first year of university and married the summer after we graduated."

"Did you ever feel you were too young? Or that you grew apart too quickly?"

"We never really got a chance to grow apart," I replied quietly.

"Oh God I'm sorry, Megan, I—"

"Don't worry about it. I know what you were trying to ask. Joe and I never got much of a chance to dig deep into whether or not we married too young, whether or not we'd changed. We'd been married less than five years when he was first diagnosed and suddenly my entire life revolved around him and his treatments and his hospital appointments. But I'm guessing that's what happened to you?"

"I married the sister of one of the guys I used to box with. We'd been dating since we were fifteen and got married just after we both turned twenty, mostly because it seemed the logical thing to do. Except..." He puffed out a sigh, his breath fogging in the air. "I went back to school and then I got into Birkbeck to study English. April, my wife, started to think I was leaving her behind, she kept telling me I thought I was too good for her and our old friends. I never meant to hurt her or make her feel inadequate; I just felt as though I was changing, going in a different direction to everyone else I knew. To be honest, it was as much a surprise to me as it was to her."

"You never imagined yourself becoming a writer?" I asked.

"Not in a million years." He laughed. "People like me didn't grow up to be writers, no matter how much we secretly loved books."

"But you did it anyway," I said.

"And trust me, nobody was as surprised as me when that happened." He paused again. "The book deal was the last straw for April. She moved out just before my first book was published and our divorce was finalised eighteen months later."

"She couldn't handle you being a writer?" I asked. It seemed a strange thing to get divorced over.

"She just wanted a different life from the one I was heading towards. She wanted to settle down and have children and I was being invited to publishing parties and talk shows. But it seemed to be the name change that was the final straw for her."

"Name change?" I asked, even though I knew Xander Stone wasn't strictly his real name.

He turned to me. "April always just knew me as Alex Stone. Xander was Philomena's idea, but you must already know that." He smiled at me. "I doubt you'd have booked me to launch at your shop without doing some research on me."

"I may remember something about it on your Wikipedia page," I replied, pretending to sound vague. "Which might I say is otherwise very much lacking in detail."

"Philomena manages all that," he said. "I make her keep it as impersonal as possible." He paused. "Anyway, I don't know why, but the name thing seemed to be the final straw for April – the confirmation that I'd changed too much to ever go back to who I used to be."

I didn't say anything for a moment, waiting for him to go on if he needed to.

"I'm sorry," I said eventually, when it was clear he'd finished.

"You have nothing to be sorry about. Plenty of people go through a divorce and in the grand scheme of things ours was fairly amicable. I still see April's brother from time to time and I know that she's happy, married again now with their second kid on the way, living in Bermondsey. If it hadn't been for Mum dying at the same time as my decree absolute arriving I'd probably have come through it all fairly unscathed, but…"

"Grief is a bitch, right?" I said. It was a heavy, maudlin thing to say but I figured he'd understand.

"How did you cope?" he asked. "How did you manage after your husband…" He hesitated again. "You don't have to talk about this if you don't want to."

"At first I coped because I had to." I looked down at my brightly coloured boots in the snow. "Like I said, from the moment Joe was diagnosed my life revolved around him – his appointments, his treatment, giving him the best chance of surviving. Work were amazing and let me take as much time off as I needed but when Joe's leukaemia returned, a few months after we thought he'd gone into remission, I knew I had to take a sabbatical. Until that point everything had been about getting Joe better, but after that a part of me knew he might never get better and I just wanted to spend as much time with him as I possibly could, that work could wait, that Joe needed me."

"And afterwards?" Xander asked, so quietly I almost didn't hear him.

"I remember walking out of the church after Joe's funeral service and my boss was there. It was so kind of her to come, to support me, but I knew as soon as I saw her that I'd never go back to my job. But you asked me how I coped and the answer is, that after Joe died I didn't. It was easier to cope when he was ill because he needed me to be strong, but afterwards…"

"Everything fell apart," Xander said in the voice of someone who knew.

"Let's just say that the story you were telling me earlier about before you got Gus…"

"The story about lying in bed drinking vodka that made me sound so incredibly attractive," he said, half-smiling.

"That one," I replied. "Well it was familiar – except I lay on the sofa in my dressing gown eating peanut butter out of the jar until my mother came down from York and told me it was time to pack up Joe's things and make a decision about the flat."

"How did you know when it was time?" Xander asked.

"To move out of London and sell the flat?"

He nodded.

"I don't think you do know, do you? And I know for many people packing up their loved one's belongings is the hardest part, but it wasn't like that for me. I actually wanted to do it but couldn't find the energy. I spent months living in a cloud of inertia and guilt." I took a shaky breath as I remembered that feeling of being stuck on the sofa, unable to move or make a decision. Sometimes it was only when I looked back that I could see how far I'd come. "How about you?"

"Having four very noisy siblings makes even the hardest tasks a little bit easier." He smiled.

"Tell me about them."

"I'm the oldest, my brother is eighteen months younger than me, then come the three girls – whose sole purpose is to make my life a misery." He laughed. "I don't know how my parents managed. There's only seven years between me and my youngest sister. By the time Mum was my age she had five kids under ten. I can't even imagine that." I watched his face soften as he talked.

"I can't even imagine having siblings," I said. "Family's important to you, isn't it?" I asked.

"I've always felt a bit responsible for them, even now they're all grown up and everyone except me and Ivy have kids of their own."

"Which sister is Ivy?"

"The youngest – she's the only other one who went to university. She studied textile design at Central St Martins and works for a big fashion retailer now. Her ambition is to work for Chanel."

"Wow."

"She's pretty amazing – they all are really, even though I complain about them." He paused. "Was it lonely growing up an only child?" he asked.

"I never thought about it really. Besides, I had a bookshop full of books!"

Ahead of us we could see the hotel now and the glowing lights in its windows felt like a beacon of warmth and hope after our cold walk and rather depressing conversation. But at the same time I felt reluctant for the walk to end, and not just because it meant that sharing a room with Xander loomed ever closer. As we'd walked from the village I'd felt able to talk to him about Joe in a way I'd never talked to anyone before, and part of me didn't want to step back into the hotel or for the conversation to end.

"Can I ask you one other question?" Xander said as we approached the steps leading up to the hotel entrance. He turned to me, his eyes locking on mine.

I nodded, my mouth feeling dry.

"You said you felt guilty about your husband's death, but why?" he asked. "It's been, what, three years?"

"Three and a half," I corrected quietly.

"So why do you still feel guilty?"

How on earth could I answer that? I looked away from him, tears burning the backs of my eyes as I thought about watching that horrible hospital coffee drip into the plastic cup. I was back in the hospital, standing in front of the drinks vending machine while my husband died alone. As I thought about it I took a step away from Xander, letting go of his arm, his proximity suddenly feeling as though it was too much. Because while I knew it was time to move on with my life, the guilt was still there and I didn't know what to do about that. I felt as though I was stuck on a carousel, going round and round for evermore, never able to get off, never able to catch my breath.

I opened my mouth to try to say something, anything, but I was interrupted by a riot of barking. When I looked up Gus was standing in the hotel entrance looking for all the world like he owned the place.

"Hey, buddy," Xander said, running up the steps to pick up his dog. "What are you doing here?"

One of the girls we'd left Gus with appeared then. "Sorry, Mr Stone," she said. "I think he must have heard your voice."

"I hope he's behaved himself," Xander said.

"Good as gold!"

Xander turned to me. "I could do with a brandy to warm up. What do you reckon?"

"Brandy sounds great," I replied, following him and Gus into the bar.

Gus and I sat down on a sofa near the bar and Xander

came back with two glasses of brandy a few minutes later. We sipped our drinks in companionable silence for a few moments.

"You asked me about the guilt," I said after a while.

"And you should probably tell me to mind my own business. Grief is a personal thing and I shouldn't have intruded on that."

"I wasn't there when Joe died." I took a breath. It still hurt so much to think about it. I felt Xander shift on the sofa next to me. "I promised him I wouldn't leave him alone, that I'd stay with him as long as he needed me and I broke that promise." I heard the catch in my voice and I closed my eyes to stop myself crying. I felt Xander's hand, warm and comforting, on my back.

"I only went to get a coffee." I took another deep breath and opened my eyes, turning to look at him. "I don't think I'll ever be able to forgive myself. Some days I feel as though I'm finding myself again, that I'm starting to live again and then I remember what I did and everything spirals backwards and I feel so stuck."

"Is that how you felt just now?" he asked. "Just before Gus interrupted us?"

I nodded.

"And why you've found it so hard to move on?"

"Is it that obvious?" I tried to smile.

"Perhaps only to people who understand what you've been through."

"Everyone seems to think I should just be getting on with my life. Mum and my friends are always trying to encourage me to go out more, to start dating. Even Joe's parents think I need to stop living like a nun. But how can I, when remembering that day can stop me in my tracks still?" I hadn't meant to tell Xander any of this, but there was something about him that made me want to open up, to say the words out loud, to admit how far I'd come but also, no matter how hard I tried, how I sometimes felt as though I was being pulled back down.

"I think," he began slowly. "That when the time is right and when you meet the right person you'll be able to talk it through with them and then you'll be able to start letting it go. I don't believe that life is ever the same again after loss, but I do believe that life can be good again. Eventually."

"What if..." I asked quietly. "What if I meet the right person before I'm ready?" The words hung in the air between us and Xander's hand moved on my back.

"If that person is even remotely worthy of you, Megan," Xander replied, his voice almost a whisper, "then they'll wait until you're ready."

My stomach flipped over. Did he know I was talking about him? Was he talking about himself? Did he feel this spark of electricity between us or was I imagining it? But why else would he be taking me for lunch and dancing quadrilles?

I'd have thought that was obvious.

I turned to look at him and he was so close to me I could smell the woody scent of his aftershave; I could hear his breath. He leaned towards me as he tucked a strand of hair behind my ear.

"Megan, I..." he began.

"Can I get you anything else?" said a loud jovial voice from somewhere behind my shoulder. I turned, moving away from Xander to look at one of the waiters who had come to clear away our empty glasses. I realised we were the only people left in the bar.

"No, I think we're done, aren't we?"

Xander nodded, not meeting my eye, and I started to stand up. Gus woke up and started barking again.

"I'd better take him out for a pee," Xander said. "We'll take our time to give you a chance to get ready." He handed me a key card. "I got us one each so you don't have to worry about letting us back in."

By the time he and Gus returned from their night-time perambulations I was already in bed with the duvet pulled up to my chin, reading a copy of *Persuasion* that I'd found among the pile of Penguin classics by the side of the sofa in our room. The hotel had been as good as its word and sent up toiletries, and a fluffy robe, which I'd decided, in the absence of pyjamas, to sleep in. The thought of sleeping in only my underwear was more than I could handle, especially after whatever it was that had just almost happened in the bar.

"What are you reading?" Xander asked as he started to settle Gus down on some blankets the hotel had lent us.

"I found a copy of *Persuasion*," I replied.

"Your favourite romance," Xander said. "What's so special about it? No spoilers though – I haven't finished it yet."

I closed the book and sat up in bed. "There are a lot of problematic heroes in romantic fiction," I began. "Heathcliff for starters…"

"I'm afraid I never made it through *Wuthering Heights*."

"I don't blame you – but don't tell Bella I said that; she'd never forgive me. There's also Rochester in *Jane Eyre*."

Xander shook his head. "Borderline psychopathic," he said.

"Exactly! And you already know I'm not Darcy's biggest fan. But Frederick Wentworth in *Persuasion* is a genuinely good man. OK, so he's pretty crap at verbal communication but he loves Anne and…"

Xander held up his hand. "Stop," he said. "Spoilers! Let's have this conversation when I've finished the book."

He went into the bathroom then and shut the door and I realised that I was inordinately happy at the thought there would be further conversations about books with Xander on another day.

I stopped reading when he came back into the room and turned off the lamp by my bed so the only light was the lamp on his side – or the side I'd allocated to him when I'd got into bed and balanced precariously on the edge so as to be as far away from him as possible. I'd found some spare pillows in the wardrobe that I'd almost put down the middle of the bed but decided it was a step too far. He had promised to keep his body parts to himself after all.

"You sure you don't want me to sleep on the sofa?" Xander asked as he pulled his jumper over his head. As he did so, the T-shirt he was wearing underneath rode up, exposing a flat muscular abdomen and a line of dark hair that ran from his navel to his belt buckle. The wave of desire that hit me was so unfamiliar that it made me feel almost nauseous and I had to turn on to my side, rolling up into a tight ball with my back to him.

"No," I replied, my voice sounding tight and strangled. "It's fine."

I tried not to think about him getting undressed just a

few metres from me, but the harder I tried not to think about semi-naked Xander the more I thought about semi-naked Xander. It wasn't until I felt the mattress dip as he got into bed and heard the click of his light turning out that I found myself able to relax a little.

"Megan," he said quietly into the darkness. "You said that you knew you couldn't go back to work after your husband died, but do you see yourself working in the bookshop forever?"

"No," I replied immediately.

"What do you want to do?" he asked.

I thought for a moment – I hadn't got around to planning this far ahead.

"I have no idea," I replied.

Just before I fell asleep I remembered Philomena Bloom's card, which I'd kept in my purse.

13

When I came down to breakfast the next morning Xander was already there, drinking a cup of black tea and reading the morning papers. He looked more dishevelled than he had been the previous day – stubble shadowed his jaw and without whatever product he usually put in his hair, it was curlier and more tousled than usual and looked as though he had been standing in front of a wind machine. He was also wearing a pair of dark-framed glasses and the overall effect seemed to be making him even more devastatingly attractive than usual.

I remembered the way he'd touched my hair the night before, the way he'd said my name. Had he been going to kiss me? I knew that if he had, I would have kissed him back. I felt stuck again, this time on a see-saw rather than a carousel, stuck between wanting to kiss Xander and being lost in the guilt of not being with Joe when he died. Would this cycle never end?

"Morning," he said, looking up as I approached. "How did you sleep?"

"Really well, surprisingly," I replied. Xander hadn't spoken again after I'd told him I had no idea what I wanted to do, and I thought I'd be lying awake half the night worrying about our almost-maybe-kiss and whether I'd told him too much, but instead I'd fallen into a deep and peaceful sleep, tired from the long walk in the snow and sleepy from the brandy. When I'd woken, Xander was already up and showered. "You end up being an early riser when you have a dog," he'd said as he and Gus left me to get ready. I'd done the best I could to make myself look presentable in yesterday's clothes with the powder compact, mascara and lip gloss I'd had in my bag. Without my straighteners, however, my hair was beyond hope.

"How about you?" I asked, even though I could tell from the shadows under his eyes he probably hadn't slept as well as me.

"Not bad," he said. "Bit of a contact lens emergency though – unplanned nights away and contact lenses aren't very conducive. Luckily I had my glasses in the car or I might have had to get you to drive us home." He smiled at me but I thought it was very unlikely he let anyone else drive the Porsche and he'd have driven half-blind if he'd needed to.

A waitress took my order for coffee.

"Is that Lapsang?" I asked, pointing at Xander's teapot.

"No sadly, just Earl Grey," he replied. "But at least it's not a teabag."

"I really wouldn't have had you down as a tea snob."

"What did I tell you about pigeonholes." He smiled lazily. "Besides, it goes right alongside being a book snob." He paused and folded up his paper. "You were telling me about your friend's café last night."

"Yes, I think you'd really like it. They sell all kinds of loose-leaf artisan teas. I'll take you there when we get back, but for now I'm going to get some eggs and toast."

When I came back from the breakfast buffet he told me he had some good news.

"Any bad news?" I checked.

"No, not this morning. Apparently the roads have been cleared already and if we eat our breakfast slowly they'll have cleared the car park too, so it shouldn't be long before we can head back."

"That's a relief," I said.

"Had enough of me already?" Xander asked and I felt my cheeks burn. I'd never blushed so much in my life as I had since I met Xander Stone.

"Best to quit while we're ahead," I replied. "Before I find out what else you're unbearably snobby about. Still, at least we know we have similar tastes in theatre entertainment."

"God, that pantomime was…"

I held up my hand. "It's probably best to never speak of it again."

"While we're on the subject of not speaking of things," he went on. "I asked you a lot of questions last night that I probably shouldn't have done and I just wanted to assure you that everything you told me will remain between us."

"Thank you." I looked down at my eggs. "It was quite cathartic, so thank you for listening."

"Any time," he said and the silence between us suddenly felt awkward. I tried to eat my eggs but I wasn't hungry anymore. We'd shared more last night than the confessions we both poured out on our snowy walk back to the hotel. I was sure we'd shared what Missy always referred to as 'a moment'. Before I had too much time to overanalyse this further or to start wondering what he meant when he said 'any time', the assistant manager came over to our table to tell us that Xander should be able to get his car out now. I pushed my eggs to the side of my plate, finished my coffee and followed them out into the car park to see.

It was a glorious morning, the sky clear and blue, the sun shining, the air bitingly cold. The snow lay in big drifts at the side of the car park but the gravel itself looked safe enough to drive on.

"And the roads are clear?" Xander checked again.

"If you follow the York road back towards the dual carriageway then you're all set."

"Well, we should probably get going then," Xander said, turning to me. "Unless you want another coffee?"

"No, I'm good to go."

We went back up to the room together to collect our coats, Gus trotting at Xander's heels. I double-checked the bathroom and the table by the bed to make sure that I hadn't left anything, not that I'd had much with me to leave, and picked up the borrowed boots to take down and return.

When we got back to the reception area and the huge Christmas tree that stood there, Xander took the pink and yellow boots from me in exchange for his car key and Hunter wellies.

"Could you pop those in the car for me?" he said. "Just press this button – the storage area is in the front and it'll open automatically."

"In the front?" I queried. "With the engine?"

"Engine's in the back," he said, and I nodded as though I knew what he was talking about. "I'll take these back for you—" he waved the brightly coloured boots in the air "—and pay the bill."

"No," I said, catching his wrist. "We should go halves on the bill. Hold on and I'll get my credit card…"

"I asked you to lunch," he interrupted. "So I'll pay."

"It turned out to be a lot more than lunch."

"Please, Megan," he said. "Let me pay for this, just take the stuff back to the car. I won't be a minute."

I decided to let it go and do as he said. After all, I had the whole journey back to York to convince him to let me transfer some money into his bank account.

I pressed the button just as he'd said and the front part of the car opened up. For someone as immaculately turned out as Xander, the storage space in his car was an absolute mess and I started to move a few things aside to fit the boots back in. I picked up a brown leather satchel, thinking I could put the boots underneath, but I picked it up upside down and it wasn't done up properly. A sheaf of typed pages fell out.

I stared at them for a moment. Was this Xander's new novel? His current work in progress? I knew I shouldn't look but I couldn't resist a little peek. Just the working title, I told myself.

I picked up the pages and turned them over, but the manuscript wasn't Xander's latest work in progress. It was something quite different. I read the cover page again.

Naked Temptation

-a novel by-

RUBY BELL

★

"What the hell do you think you're doing?" Xander's voice was cold and clipped. It was the voice he'd used in the supermarket the first time we'd met. I hadn't meant to start reading the manuscript and now I'd been caught.

"I moved this bag and the pages fell out," I began. "I thought it was your latest manuscript. I only…"

"Don't," he said icily, snatching the papers from me and stuffing them back into the leather satchel.

"I shouldn't…" I tried again.

"No, you shouldn't." He snatched the car keys out of my hand and closed the storage space at the front of his car. He took Gus and settled him onto the back seat.

"Well, get in then," he snapped at me. "I really haven't got all day."

I knew I shouldn't have looked at the manuscript. I'd worked with authors for years and I knew how precious and personal those first drafts can be. The first draft, as I always told my authors when I worked at Rogers & Hudson, is for them and only them. The first draft is their version of the story, where they get to know their characters and the adventures they are to go on. Even if that had been a first draft of Xander's next book, it shouldn't have crossed my mind to look at it. I should have stuffed the papers back in the satchel and ignored them.

But it hadn't been Xander's next manuscript. It had been a new unpublished Ruby Bell manuscript – perhaps the one that hadn't been published this winter, for whatever reason. What was Xander doing with it? Did he know who she was? I had so many questions but the look on Xander's face when I got in the car stopped me from asking any of them. Gus had buried his head under his paws in an attempt to keep out of it.

"Do you make a habit of going through other people's private papers?" Xander asked as we drove out of the gates of Graydon Hall.

"I wasn't going through them on purpose," I said, but my excuse sounded whiny and pathetic even to me. I took a breath. "I'm sorry," I said. "I shouldn't have even thought about looking."

He didn't respond and I glanced at him out of the corner of my eye. He seemed even more tired than he had at breakfast and his knuckles were white from gripping the steering wheel so hard.

"I realise that you are probably full of all kinds of questions about why I have a manuscript by your beloved Ruby Bell in my car," he said after a while. "But I'm not at liberty to tell you."

He had changed back to the man I'd first met, as though everything we'd shared last night hadn't happened, as though... and then the penny dropped. I couldn't believe I hadn't thought of it straight away.

"There's only one reason why you'd have a Ruby Bell manuscript, though, isn't there?" I asked with more confidence than I felt. "So there aren't really that many questions."

He didn't say anything.

"Dot is a huge Ruby Bell fan," I went on. "Does she—"

"No," Xander interrupted. "She doesn't. And you're not going to tell her, are you?"

"Of course I'm not going to tell her if you don't want

me to – although, as she's been such an inspiration to your writing career, I'm surprised you haven't told her yourself."

"Told her what exactly?" he snapped back at me, his eyes not leaving the road ahead.

"That you're Ruby Bell, of course. What other—"

He reached out and flicked a switch on the driver's panel and loud classical music blared out of the car speakers.

"You may as well just admit it," I said loudly over the music, making it clear this conversation wasn't over. "I know I shouldn't have looked at the manuscript and I am sorry, but I've seen it now; we can't just pretend it hasn't happened."

"Oh I think you'll find we can," he said coldly.

Was he simply embarrassed? If Xander Stone did, in fact, moonlight as Ruby Bell – and honestly what other explanation was there – why was he so scornful of romance novels? After all, he must have made quite a lot of money out of those Ruby Bell books, almost as much as he'd made writing as Xander Stone – all of them had been best-sellers. I could understand why he would want it to remain a secret but I knew now, so why wouldn't he just admit it? Unless I'd jumped to the wrong conclusion? But if that was the case, you'd think he'd want to distance himself from Ruby Bell's writing as quickly as possible.

"I don't know why you're so embarrassed," I shouted over the loud music.

He sighed and turned the volume down, perhaps realising that I wasn't simply going to let this go. As if I could. This was huge.

"Why on earth do you think I'm embarrassed?" he asked.

"Well you've been totally disparaging of romance fiction

pretty much since the moment I first met you, and now it turns out that you're actually one of the best-selling contemporary romance authors in the country."

"At no point have I told you that. You really should stop jumping to wild assumptions about people."

"Right," I said, folding my arms across my chest. "Because there are so many other rational explanations as to why you have that manuscript in your car."

"For all you know, I could be one of the few people who know who Ruby Bell is. I could be sworn to secrecy." The corner of his mouth twitched slightly and I knew then that I was right. Xander Stone was Ruby Bell and now I was itching to get back to the bookshop and read a Ruby Bell book side by side with a Xander Stone one to see if I could find any similarities in sentence structure, or timbre, or narrative voice.

"Just because you're too embarrassed to admit it, doesn't mean it isn't true."

Xander made a grumbling noise in the back of his throat but didn't say anything else. I tried as many different tacks as I could to get him to admit it, until I saw that little twitch in the muscles of his jaw that I'd seen during the green tea incident at the pantomime and decided not to push it any further. It felt as though all the warmth and connection from the previous evening had vanished and I couldn't understand why, after everything I'd told him, he couldn't tell me this. Was I asking too much? Was he contractually obliged to keep silent in the face of inquisition? I guess I'd never know.

There was no sign of snow in York of course, which was a shame because now all the shops in our little street had their decorations up it would have looked so festive. Xander stopped his Porsche at the top of the road and I didn't invite him to pull into the parking space behind the shop.

As I reached for the car door handle I felt his hand on my arm and that familiar tingle of electricity. I wondered if he felt it too.

"I would really appreciate it if you didn't tell anyone about…" He trailed off, his eyes flicking away.

"I'm not going to tell anyone," I replied. "Everything we've talked about in the last twenty-four hours remains between us, OK?"

"OK." He nodded.

I didn't know whether to ask him if he was coming to book club on Thursday, if he was staying in York until Christmas or anything else. My mouth felt dry and I managed a feeble 'goodbye' as I got out of the car. It wasn't until he'd driven off that I realised I hadn't brought up the topic of paying for my half of the hotel room.

I walked up the street to the bookshop, trying to remember if I'd ever noticed any similarities between Ruby Bell's writing and the writing in *Boxed*. Of course I hadn't. Xander was too good a writer to make that mistake, but there had to be something – some quirk or nuance that he wouldn't have even noticed. My hands itched to start comparing the two authors' works properly.

But as I pushed open the door of the bookshop all my thoughts disappeared because it seemed we had a visitor. Somebody I hadn't seen since Joe's funeral.

14

"Look who's crawled out of the cheese," my mother crowed as I walked across the shop floor. Several customers turned around to see what was going on and, seeing nothing particularly unusual, went back to their book browsing. From their point of view all they could see was the owner of the bookshop and a tall, tanned man of about the same age.

But I saw my father, as large as life and standing behind the counter of the bookshop, somewhere I hadn't seen him stand in well over a decade.

The last time I'd seen him had been at Joe's wake. He'd written a poem for the funeral, which had made me cry when he read it because it had been so full of Joe's spirit and made me remember how well they'd got on, how they'd had the same sense of humour, the same camaraderie with the world around them and how Joe had helped me and Dad heal our relationship. It had been the first time I'd cried since the hospital.

Dad had spent the wake filling up glasses and talking to everyone – always the life and soul, even at a funeral. Afterwards we'd talked quietly in the kitchen at Joe's parents' house – he'd needed to get back to France and I'd just wanted to go home and be alone, but I'd promised to see him, promised to visit him in Paris.

The last I saw of him had been through the kitchen window as he'd kissed Mum goodbye and I'd felt a pang of jealousy that at least they still had each other even if they lived in different countries, even if their relationship was beyond my comprehension.

Three and a half years had passed since then and I'd never kept that promise. Now Dad was here and he looked older, slightly more stooped than he had when I'd last seen him, and I felt an overwhelming sense of regret. How had I let so much time pass me by in this strange bookshop limbo? Why had I shut myself away for so long, avoiding life and the people who loved me? Grief was awful, life-changing, but as Xander had said last night, life can be good again.

I shouldn't have left it so long to work that out.

"Dad," I said, walking over to him. "What are you doing here?"

"I came to see my daughter," he replied. "But it turns out I timed it all wrong and I got here on the night you finally left the bookshop."

He enveloped me in a huge bear hug. For a few moments it felt like being a little girl again, until Missy interrupted us by poking her head around the office door.

"You're back, you dirty little stop-out," she called across the shop and all the customers looked up again to see what the fuss was now. "I want to hear all about your night with Xander..."

"Shhh," I said, pulling away from Dad and walking over to Missy, pushing her back in the office. "Do not say his name. There are customers in the shop and they'll know who he is and they know who I am and anyway it wasn't even like that. We got snowed in."

"Yeah, yeah." Missy laughed.

"Don't," I said quietly. "It was actually quite awkward. I'm never going to be able to read another 'only one bed' romance again."

"If I make you a cup of coffee, will you tell me everything?" Missy asked. "Please?"

"I am supposed to be working and it's practically lunchtime and I need to get changed out of yesterday's clothes and find out why Dad is here. I'm assuming it's to do with the bookshop figures you emailed to him. Did Mum say anything?"

Missy shook her head. "He turned up late last night apparently. When I got here this morning your mum and dad were deep in discussion but they stopped talking as soon as I got near."

"I can't believe he's here," I said, turning to look at him again. He turned at the same time and caught my eye, smiling at me. "It's so good to see him. I can't believe I left it so long."

"Look, I know you want to talk to him but I'm desperate to hear about your night with Xander." She looked pleadingly at me and I sighed. There was so much I wanted to tell her but couldn't. "I'll make coffee and you get changed and meet me back here, OK?"

"OK." Hopefully the shop would be too busy to sit about chatting by then.

When I came down Colin was behind the till and Mum and Dad were nowhere to be seen.

"Morning," I said to him, wondering if he knew anything

about my accidental night away. Even if he did, he probably didn't care as he never showed any interest in bookshop gossip.

He raised an eyebrow at me in reply but didn't say anything. I thought he was probably still sulking about me making him join in the quadrille at book club on Thursday.

"Have you seen my parents?" I asked.

"Your parents?" Colin had never met my father and, other than the fact that he was the poet Walter Taylor, knew nothing about him. "I saw your mother with a tall, bald man leaving the shop a couple of minutes ago. Leaving me alone again," he pointed out.

"Yeah, that tall, bald man is my dad," I said.

He goggled at me. "That was the infamous Walter Taylor?"

I nodded.

"Damn, why does nobody ever introduce me to these people?" I opened my mouth to try to placate him but he continued. "I didn't recognise him. He looks much older than his author photo," he said.

"Doesn't everyone look older than their author photo?" I mused. Except Xander, of course, who looked exactly like his author photo, cheekbones and all. Xander was also probably one of those men who got better-looking with age as well so could update his author photo at will. I felt my stomach flip. *Damn Xander Stone and his stupid secrets*, I thought to myself before realising Colin was talking to me.

"Pardon?"

Colin sighed. "I said Missy wants you in the office."

I looked around the shop but it didn't seem too busy, which was more than a little disappointing less than three weeks before Christmas, but it was only a Monday morning and I had to keep hoping that things would improve.

"Will you be OK on your own for a few minutes?" I asked Colin.

"Aren't I always?"

I didn't reply to that. I was getting a bit tired of Colin's attitude, as though he were doing us a favour by gracing us with his presence. But I also knew that we unintentionally left him out of bookshop stuff a little bit and made a mental note to invite him to book club again on Thursday. He probably wouldn't come though.

As soon as I walked into the office, Missy pushed me into the wing-backed chair and thrust a cup of coffee into my hands. "Tell me everything," she said.

I told her almost everything – about the delicious roast lunch and our easy conversation, about the blizzard and the realisation that we'd have to stay the night, about the awful pantomime and there only being one bed.

"I couldn't believe it when your mum told me," she squealed, clasping her hands together in front of her. "Bella is delighted, of course – firstly that you've finally met someone and secondly that you are living out her favourite romance trope…"

"Can you all stop gossiping about me behind my back?"

"Blame your mum, not me," Missy retorted. "She's practically got you and Xander married off already."

"Desperate to get rid of me," I said with a smile.

"You know we all just want to see you happy," Missy said softly. "Now what is it that you're not telling me?"

"How do you know I'm not telling you something?"

"I always know."

There was a lot I hadn't told her and the thing I wanted to tell her more than anything was the one thing I couldn't talk to anyone about – Ruby Bell's new manuscript.

I would really appreciate it if you didn't tell anyone.

"And I'm right, aren't I?" Missy said, peering at my face. "There is something you're not telling me. You didn't sleep with him, did you?"

"No I did not," I snapped, even though I knew she was teasing. "The whole one-bed thing is a lot less romantic than you'd think. We both slept right on the edge of the bed so as not to touch each other." I didn't tell her that I had a feeling Xander might not have slept at all.

"Disappointing," she sighed. "But there's always next time. But tell me what's on your mind."

"There was a lot of time for talking," I said. "And honestly I haven't really talked to anyone like that in ages. I told him about Joe."

"About his illness?" Missy asked.

I nodded, feeling a bit guilty because I'd never really spoken to Missy or Bella about Joe's long illness or how I felt after he died. "And about afterwards," I said. "When Mum had to come and get me and I moved up here. About what a mess I was in."

"Wow," Missy said quietly. "You must really trust him."

"His mum died of leukaemia too," I said. "Although I'm sure he'd prefer it if that didn't become public knowledge. But it meant he understood. He talked to me about his mum and I talked to him about Joe, but..." I trailed off as I thought about that moment on the sofa in the bar as we sipped our brandies. I could still feel the sensation of his fingers in my hair.

"But…?" Missy prompted.

"We sort of… well… we had a moment."

"Of course you had a moment!" Missy's eyes were wide. "It's obvious to everyone that he's mad about you. Tell me, tell me!" She was practically bouncing in her seat.

"We'd just got back from the pantomime and I was feeling warm and sleepy from the double brandy he bought for me, and we were talking about dating again and how on earth I'd know when I was ready and… I thought just for second that he was going to kiss me."

"But he didn't?"

"No, we were interrupted by the barman – who I think just wanted to shut the bar for the night. Then Xander took his dog out for a quick walk and I got ready for bed and everything became awkward again."

"Did he mention if he was dating?" Missy asked.

"Hasn't done since his divorce apparently," I said, realising as soon as the words were out that Xander probably didn't want that to be public knowledge either.

"Divorce? I never knew he was married! It doesn't say anything about that on his much-read Wikipedia page."

"No, apparently Philomena manages that and he only likes the bare minimum to be made public – so I've probably told you way too much. Please don't tell anyone."

She mimed zipping up her mouth and throwing away the key, but a second later her mouth was open again. "How did you leave things?" she asked.

"Oh you know." I tried to sound breezy. "He dropped me off, he was in a hurry to get back to Dot's. I'm sure I'll hear from him later in the week." I hoped that was true and I hadn't pushed him too far trying to get him to admit he was

Ruby Bell. I should probably give him a ring. "Did Mum and Dad say where they were going?" I asked, changing the subject to stop any more Xander-related questioning.

"No. They didn't say anything."

"Colin said they'd left the shop together. He was annoyed nobody had told him that was Walter Taylor."

Missy rolled her eyes. "Colin is permanently annoyed about something."

I spent the rest of the day helping Colin on the shop floor as we got much busier after lunch, thankfully. While I knew I didn't want to work in the bookshop forever, I loved helping customers choose the right books either for themselves or as a present for a loved one – I adored matching people with the right books – so the afternoon flew by and I barely had time to think about Xander, Ruby Bell or my father.

My parents returned to the shop just after closing time, with Bella in tow, so I didn't get a chance to ask them where they'd been.

"Missy and I are going out for cocktails and you're coming too," Bella said. "I want to hear all the gory details about your one-bed romp and…"

"I'll be going," Colin said grumpily, putting on his coat. I felt myself cringe at the idea that he had heard what Bella said.

"Colin, would you like to come to book group again on Thursday?" I asked, swallowing my mortification.

"Will I have to dance?"

"Only if you want to."

"Will Xander be there?"

"I'm not sure," I admitted. "But everyone else will be, and we'd love to see you."

"I'll think about it," he said as he slunk out of the shop.

"What did you do that for?" Bella asked.

"I feel a bit sorry for him. I feel like we forget he's a part of this bookshop too."

Bella huffed. "Anyway, I haven't got time to think about Colin. Go and get your glad rags on so we can go out."

"I was hoping you and your mum would have dinner with me tonight," my father said.

"Have you met my dad?" I asked Bella.

"Oh yes," she replied, waving at him dismissively. "Your mum introduced us." She seemed wildly uninterested in my previously absent father.

"Well, you and Missy will have to go out without me tonight," I said.

"But…"

"Don't worry," I interrupted. "Missy already knows everything, so she'll fill you in."

Almost everything, anyway.

15

When I woke up the next morning, the first thing I thought about was Xander. The second thing I thought about was that this was the first morning in over three years that Joe hadn't been the first thing on my mind.

I hadn't had a chance to call Xander the previous day, so I had no idea how he was feeling about my working out his secret – if I had worked it out and wasn't letting my imagination run away with me. I had jumped to the right conclusion though, hadn't I? Xander might not have admitted to being Ruby Bell but he hadn't denied it either. Lots of authors wrote in multiple genres under different pseudonyms, so it wasn't that unusual. But I was never going to get to the bottom of it if I didn't give him a ring.

I had found out why my father was back in York though – to 'save the bookshop' as he kept telling us throughout dinner, when he wasn't telling me how much he'd missed me, which just made me feel terrible all over again for how thoroughly I'd cut my life off from everyone around me for so long. He'd told us about Paris and about how he was thinking of moving to Spain in the new year.

"I fancy some time by the sea," he'd said as he and Mum had exchanged a look that I couldn't quite work out.

Mum had already filled him in on everything Xander-related, including my unplanned night away.

"About time," my father had said. "Welcome back to the real world." He didn't mean it unkindly; he could just be very blunt sometimes.

"Megan is organising a Regency Christmas Eve party in the bookshop," Mum had said then, which had distracted my father from asking any embarrassing questions about my night at Graydon Hall and instead had allowed him to spend some time snobbishly criticising our love of romance novels (he and Xander would have a lot in common) and then invite himself to the next book group because he wanted to dance the quadrille too.

It wasn't until we got back to the bookshop that Dad had taken me to one side and told me the news I'd been dreading.

"You know I can't really save the bookshop, don't you, love?" he'd said. "You know we're going to have to sell it."

I'd nodded sadly, because I did know. Deep down I'd known for a while that there was no other way out of this and so had Mum; we just hadn't wanted to talk about it. Missy had mentioned the possibility of selling once to both of us, but Mum had just waved the idea away, saying we couldn't do anything without Walter and walking out of the office. I'd known then that it was only a matter of time.

"It'll take a while to sell though," Dad had gone on. "Which will give you plenty of time to work out what you're going to do next. Maybe this thing with Xander Stone will work out and if not you could come and stay with your old man in Spain for a while."

"That would be great," I'd said. "And I'm so sorry I never

came to Paris. I hadn't realised how much I'd cut everyone and everything out of my life since Joe died. I wish I could…"

"Shhh," Dad had said gently, his hands on my shoulders. "It's OK, I understand. We all do."

When I came down to the bookshop on Tuesday morning Dad was nowhere to be found again, typically. I'd been wanting to talk to him about a pre-Christmas sale we could have in the shop. If selling the bookshop was the only way forward, we had a lot of stock to get rid of.

"He's gone out," Mum said, without telling me where he'd gone. "And you've got a visitor."

"At eight-thirty in the morning? Who?"

"Who do you think?" Mum replied. "He's in the cookery section." Why on earth did everyone end up in the cookery section?

I turned into the section of shelves that housed recipe books and food memoirs. "Hi," I said quietly to Xander's back. He turned around, still holding the copy of *Medium Raw* that he had been flicking through.

"Hi," he replied and smiled at me. My heart skipped in relief.

"Can we talk?" he asked. "Somewhere quiet."

"Um… sure. Colin will be in soon to help Mum, so do you want to come upstairs?"

He nodded but didn't really look at me.

"Where's Gus?" I asked.

He looked around him as though he was trying to remember where Gus was. "Oh, um, he's at Dot's," he said.

He seemed miles away and was still clutching the copy of *Medium Raw*, which I gently took from him and put back on the shelf and then I led him upstairs to the flat.

He started talking as soon as we stepped into the living room.

"I'm so sorry about yesterday," he said. "The way I shouted at you and then was so rude and obstinate again. I know you didn't go looking for the manuscript; I know it was an accident." His hands were deep in his coat pockets and he looked almost as dishevelled as he had done at the breakfast table at Graydon Hall. "I have a tendency to be rather reactionary. And then regret my behaviour. You might have already noticed that after the supermarket incident."

I had noticed of course, and I wondered why. Had he always behaved like that or was it something that had happened in the aftermath of his mother's death? I knew I was a lot more hesitant since Joe died, unable to make decisions, anxious and shy – even more so than I had been before. Despite feeling more like the old me than I had in years I still wasn't quite the same. I wondered if I ever would be.

"I probably shouldn't have started to read the manuscript though," I replied. "When it fell out of the bag I should have just put it back and forgotten about it."

"You're a reader," he said, looking at me for the first time. "It's natural that you'd want to read it." He stood hesitantly in the middle of the room.

"Would you like to sit down?" I asked. "Can I get you a cup of tea? We've only got teabags though, I'm afraid."

He smiled. "Then no, I'm OK." He took off his coat and sat on the sofa.

"Well we can talk about your unbearable snobbery later," I teased, sitting next to him. "Is there anything else you're like this about or is it just romance novels and tea?"

"Well," he replied quietly, "I have a snobbish inability to admit, as you've already worked out, that I write romance novels under the pen name Ruby Bell." He slumped against the back of the sofa miserably.

"If I was a best-selling romance author and a Booker Prize nominee I think I might be quite happy about my achievements," I said. "What's wrong?"

"Do you like Ruby Bell?" he asked.

"You know I do. It's you who sneers whenever I mention her name. Dot's the big Ruby Bell fan though." I paused. "As you know."

"She doesn't know. I've never told her."

"Who does know?"

"Philomena, of course, my brother and sisters and my ex-wife… and my mother knew." He paused. "And now you."

"I won't tell anyone," I said.

"I know. I trust you."

"You do?" I asked. I didn't feel as though he'd known me long enough to trust me, and then I remembered all the things that we'd talked about when we'd been stranded in the blizzard. Perhaps some people were easier to trust than others.

"I do," he said. He turned to me and took my hand in his. I felt the familiar electricity at his touch. "I reacted very badly to you finding that manuscript. I'm struggling to finish it, to be honest, and I'd just read an awful review of *Mists of Our Waters* in *The Sunday Times*. When I saw you with the manuscript it just made me feel…" He paused. "Vulnerable, I guess." I could tell by the way he said it that it was almost killing him to admit this to me. "I don't do vulnerable very well, I prefer to try to be in control of things."

"I'm beginning to realise that," I said. "I'm sorry about the bad review though."

"Oh don't be," he said, looking down at our hands. "It's part of the job and Philomena had warned me about it. I should know better by now than to read these things."

"I'm sorry you're struggling with the new Ruby Bell book," I said, not moving, not wanting him to take his hand away from mine. "Is that why there wasn't one this Christmas?"

He nodded. "I'm under contract for one more and I just… I don't know. Romance is bloody hard to write." He smiled.

"Thank you! Most of my authors at Rogers & Hudson were romance writers and I got so sick of hearing about how easy romance must be to write, as though there was a magic formula or an assembly line. There are still the same character arcs and motivations to work out, the same plot holes, the same struggles to get the pace right. Writing books is hard, whatever the genre. I'm not sure I could do it." I looked up at him. "Although when you first arrived in the bookshop you were extremely scornful of romance novels yourself."

"Yeah I know." He pulled a face. "When I first met you in the supermarket I was doing some Christmas shopping as a favour for Dot and I had no idea who you were and then when I arrived here and realised who you were, I was so angry with myself for being rude to you the first time that I ended up being rude all over again. I was pouring scorn on everything, not just romance novels."

"You were particularly scornful of romance novels though," I reminded him. "You told me we had an awful lot of them and from your tone I didn't take it as a compliment!"

"Perhaps so," he admitted. "I've struggled with the whole romance writing side of my persona for a while. It's been really hard and…"

"Are you embarrassed about being Ruby Bell?"

"Sort of, but there's more to it than that." He looked away from me and shifted in his seat, but he didn't let go of my hand.

"I mean, there's a big difference between *Boxed* and *A Night to Remember*," I said, referencing the two debut novels of his writing alter egos. "But you should be really proud of them both. They're great books in their own way… although the sex scenes in *A Night to Remember* are definitely racier."

"Yes well, let's not think about those too much," he interrupted. "This story of how I came to write as Ruby Bell gets particularly weird if you think too much about the sex scenes. Do you think you can handle it?" I swallowed, trying and failing not to think about Xander having written those sex scenes.

"I think so," I said.

"Believe it or not, I read a lot of romance novels when I was growing up. I mean, I read a lot of novels but my mum loved romance novels so our house was full of them. Whenever I ran out of library books I just picked one of those up. I was probably too young to be reading them, certainly at first, but they taught me a lot."

I felt myself blushing again at the thought of what he learned from his mother's bookshelves. For heaven's sake, I had to get my face under control.

"What sort of romances did your mum like?" I asked.

"Anything and everything from Georgette Heyer to

Jackie Collins. She really loved medical romances though; she used to get a subscription box of those. She read medical romances the whole way through her chemotherapy and beyond, even when she was in palliative care. You'd think she'd have been sick of anything to do with hospitals by then but she could never get enough." He smiled sadly at the memory.

"So you read a lot of romance as a teenager, but what made you start writing it?"

"That was Mum again," he said. "While I was doing my degree I started writing – short stories, poems, anything really, but it wasn't going anywhere so Mum challenged me to write a romance novel."

"And the rest is history?"

He laughed. "Well my first draft was terrible, even Mum couldn't put a good spin on it, but she suggested some changes and between us we wrote the book that became *A Night to Remember*."

"But that didn't come out until after your mum died," I said.

He rubbed a hand over his face. "I suggested trying to get it published but she always said no, even after Philomena signed me and I got my book deal for *Boxed*. She always said it was just for fun and some days I wish I'd listened to her."

"What happened? How did you come to publish them?"

"I wrote all five of the published Ruby Bell novels with Mum. We started years ago, before she got ill, and we just carried on right through her treatment until she was too sick to concentrate on much. It was our thing. My siblings thought it was hilarious and mortifying in equal measure

– I guess finding out your mother and brother are writing sex scenes like that is the epitome of awkwardness, and to be honest I loved embarrassing them all." He smiled. "But from their point of view it was another reason to take the piss out of me – especially after I became Xander Stone and *Boxed* was being reviewed in every newspaper – and it helped to distract us all from what was happening with Mum."

He stopped talking for a moment and took a breath.

"Sorry," he said. "It's hard to talk about this sometimes, you know. I miss her so much."

"I know," I said. "Trust me, I know."

"After Mum died, during my darkest days when I was under contract to write a third Xander Stone book and wasn't writing anything at all, I told Philomena about the books I'd written with Mum. I don't know why I told her – I think I just wanted to talk about Mum, to keep her alive – and she jumped on it and talked me into sending her the manuscripts. Before I knew it she had a book deal all sorted for this character she'd invented called Ruby Bell. It happened so quickly I barely realised. My first book deal had taken so long to get I didn't even know that you could get a deal that fast but romance and digital-first publishers are a whole different world."

"And she's never told anyone," I said quietly, thinking about loud, outrageous Philomena and the secret she'd kept for so long.

He laughed softly. "You wouldn't think she'd be able to keep a secret for so long, would you?"

"No I…" I paused, not really sure what to say. "Thank you for telling me. I know this must be really hard for you."

"It actually feels like a huge relief to tell you. I should have done it yesterday."

"Would you have told me if I hadn't found the manuscript?" I asked.

"I'd like to think so, yes." He paused. "Eventually anyway."

"Fair enough." We were still sitting facing each other; he was still holding my hand. "And Dot really doesn't know?"

"She has no idea," he replied. "I know she was disappointed there wasn't a new Ruby Bell this Christmas but I'm not sure I can do it anymore, not without Mum."

"But you've started," I said. "And that's the hardest part. There's a first draft sitting in the back of your car."

He sighed. "It's absolute crap though. Utter nonsense, and I'm saying that because it's rubbish, not because I'm being derogatory about romance novels."

"Hmmm," I murmured, the kernel of an idea coming to me. "Maybe I can help you out."

"Really? How?"

"Well, I used to edit a lot of romance novels you know. So if you liked I could take a look at it, give you some pointers."

He beamed at me, looking like his normal self for the first time that morning. "You'd do that?"

That flicker of who I used to be burst into a flame just for a moment. Yes, I would do it; I wanted to do it. For the first time since the day of Joe's diagnosis I wanted to get my teeth into an author's manuscript again, if the author wanted me to, of course.

"I'll do it," I said. "Besides, you might be doing me a favour."

"How do you figure that out?"

"Well, remember on Sunday night when I admitted that I didn't want to work in a bookshop forever?"

He nodded, his eyes on mine.

"Things have escalated."

"In what way?"

"The bookshop is doing really badly," I admitted. "We're barely breaking even and I've known that for a while."

"It's a really hard time for bookshops at the moment."

"Particularly this one."

"It's a wonderful place you've got here, Megan," he said. "I see a lot of bookshops and this one is really special. There are loads of amazing books coming out in January. Philomena will know exactly which authors will fit in with your aesthetic here. I know she'll be able to help."

"Thank you," I said, "but…"

"You don't want to work in a bookshop forever," he said.

"No, and I don't think Mum does either. This bookshop was Dad's passion – well his parents' really. Dad just took it over from them when they got too old to run it. I think we might all be holding on to it in a sentimental way. Dad owns the building and he thinks it's time we sold it."

"God, I hate it when bookshops go out of business. It's heart-breaking."

"I know," I said. "I haven't even begun to sift through all the mixed feelings selling this place is going to bring. Dad told me last night that it will take a while to sell so I should have plenty of time to work out what to do, but I've always needed more than this bookshop – it's why I went to London in the first place. I've known for a while that I can't stay here forever, but now Dad wants to sell up, I need to start thinking about what to do next."

"And you think my shitty manuscript can help you?"

"Perhaps putting my editing hat on again while I read your manuscript will help me work things out."

He didn't say anything, he just sat there looking at me, his thumb gently massaging my knuckles.

"What?" I asked. "Do I have something on my face?"

"You look happy and excited," he said.

Whenever I thought about editing again, that spark of life flared up inside me. "I guess I'm ready to get my teeth into something new," I said.

"Well, if my terrible attempt at a sixth Ruby Bell novel can make you smile like that and might even help you work out what to do next, then I'm happy to let you read it."

"Thank you," I said. I felt a bit overwhelmed, but in a good way, as though a cloud had lifted.

Xander was still looking at me.

"Megan," he said. "On Sunday night when we were talking in the bar... I told you that any man who was worthy of you would wait..."

"Don't," I interrupted. "I know what you're going to say."

"Do you?" His voice was low and soft and I felt all of my nerve endings fire up. I suddenly couldn't take my eyes off him either.

I'd known on Sunday night that he'd been talking about himself. I'd felt the chemistry between us. I wasn't so switched off from the world that I didn't recognise chemistry. I felt Xander's fingers brush my hair again, just as they had on Sunday. There was nobody to interrupt us this morning and a part of me, the part that was still scared of the huge changes that were looming up ahead in my life, wanted to stand up, make some excuse, put some distance between us. But I couldn't do it. I didn't want to do it. I wanted him to kiss me.

His fingers moved to the back of my neck, massaging the muscles in small, sensual circles. I felt my breath catch in my throat…

And then I heard the creak of the floorboard in the hall outside and footsteps on the stairs. I'd been wrong about there being nobody to interrupt us.

I sprung up, ignoring the look of disappointment that flashed over Xander's face, but when I looked out into the hall there was no one there.

"Sorry," I said. "I'm really sorry." He had no idea how sorry I was. "I thought I heard someone on the stairs and my dad arrived on Sunday and he's been asking all sorts of awkward questions about you and I just…"

"Walter Taylor is here?" Xander asked.

"Sorry, I didn't tell you that bit, did I?" My voice sounded flustered. "He turned up while I was with you on Sunday. He's here to sell the bookshop, like I said and…" I paused because I was babbling. "Do you know Dad?" I asked.

"I've met him at a couple of events over the years but I don't know him." He picked up his coat. "I should go," he said. "Check that Gus isn't destroying Dot's house."

"Xander," I began.

"It's OK, you don't need to explain."

"I do," I said. I didn't really know why, when I'd wanted Xander to kiss me, I'd jumped up at the faintest sound. Was I really bothered if Dad walked in? I was a grown woman, after all. I felt as though I was stuck on that carousel again, unable to get off no matter how much I wanted to.

And for the first time in three years I really, really wanted to.

"Look, I really like you, Megan – I think that's fairly obvious – but I'm not going to rush you." Xander walked up to me and gently placed his hands on my shoulders. "We take things at your pace."

But I didn't want him to go, not without knowing when I would see him again. I wasn't sure I was ready but I was sure I wanted to see what happened.

"Are you free this evening?" I asked. "I can take you to the Two Teas, the tearoom I was telling you about. You can talk Lapsang Souchong with Ben."

He nodded slowly. "I could meet you there," he said. I watched him take a breath. "Maybe we could have dinner afterwards?"

"I'd love to," I managed, my voice not really sounding like my own.

"Seven-ish?" he asked, and I nodded like an idiotic nodding dog, not really knowing what else to do.

"I can see myself out and I'll see you tonight." As he left he pressed a kiss on the top of my head and I collapsed on to the sofa, suddenly completely exhausted.

16

"He almost kissed you!" Missy squealed, her eyebrows higher than I'd ever seen them. "Why did he not completely kiss you?"

"There's a family in Aberdeen who didn't hear you," I said.

"I repeat, why did he not completely kiss you?"

"I thought I heard someone on the stairs and…"

Missy sighed and rolled her eyes heavenward. "So you backed out?" she asked. "Again?"

"No, I… well… I guess. Sort of. The first time wasn't backing out – we were in a public bar."

"Do you actually want him to kiss you?"

"Yes, of course I do," I replied, almost too enthusiastically. I could feel myself blushing again. "How's Bryn?" I asked, trying to change the subject. "Is he coming to book club again this week?" I thought about Bella and Missy and the two Vikings, and how out of place they'd looked dancing a quadrille.

"Bryn isn't really my type, but he's fun for now," Missy replied. "Let's get back to talking about Xander. You definitely want him to kiss you."

"Yes," I said, more quietly this time but with no less enthusiasm. "I want him to kiss me."

"Hallelujah," Missy shouted, throwing her hands in the air, and for the second time that morning I was glad I'd shut the office door behind me. "Progress."

"He did kiss the top of my head as he left," I said, smiling at the memory. "Although it was mostly awkward."

She shook her head. "You're both as bad as each other."

"Once bitten twice shy, I guess," I replied. "You must get that too?"

She nodded and looked away. "And he's taking you out tonight?" she asked, pretending to do something on her laptop like she always did whenever I mentioned her first love. "Where are you going?"

"I'm not sure, but we're meeting in the tearoom at seven and I have no idea what to wear…"

"The black dress with white spots," she interrupted.

"Thanks." I should have left then, the shop was busy and I knew Colin would be seething if I didn't get out there soon, but I hovered near the door. Missy must have noticed my hesitation as she looked up.

"Are you OK?" she asked.

"I am… it's just a lot has happened over the last few days. It's a bit…"

"I think we both know you're ready to get on with your life," she interrupted. "Or at least to work out what your next steps are – and I personally think Xander Stone is a good person to do a bit of moving on with, if you get my drift." She winked at me, just to make sure I knew what she was talking about, even though we all always knew what Missy was talking about. "Now get out of here and sell some books so these spreadsheets don't look so depressing."

The bookshop was busy for the rest of the afternoon. The Christmas shoppers had finally decided to descend upon us, and I had to drag Mum down from her writing cave to help for a few hours. Xander's new book was selling fast, which might have had something to do with the brilliant window display Colin had done for the book launch. The shop had two big bay windows either side of the main door, perfect for bookish window displays, and in the other window I'd made a Christmas tree out of festive romance novels, but the romance novels weren't selling anywhere near as well as Xander's book. For a moment I thought about how much Xander would gloat when he found out but then I remembered the shocking truth – that Xander was Ruby Bell and that perhaps he'd quite like it if some of Ruby's books sold as well. I made a mental note to do a table display of Ruby Bell books when I got a chance.

I was glad the shop was busy, and not just because it stopped me from spending the afternoon overanalysing my dinner with Xander tonight. Thinking about the fact that this was probably the last Christmas that Taylor's Bookshop would be trading was almost too much to bear. I knew Dad was right; I knew there really wasn't any option now other than to sell up, but as Xander had said, it was heart-breaking when bookshops closed – especially one that you'd grown up in. I knew that behind his bravado, Dad would be feeling the same too. By being busy at least we had some hope of going out with a bang rather than a whimper.

Halfway through the afternoon, my father reappeared with Fred Bishop in tow. I hadn't seen Fred for years – he'd retired from his former career as a bookseller at Taylor's just after Joe's leukaemia came back and I hadn't been able to come to his leaving party. I had no idea that he and Dad kept in touch, or indeed that Fred still lived in York. I wondered why he hadn't been in to see Mum and me over the last three years.

It was good to see him, but we didn't have much time to stand and chat as the shop continued to be busy and every time Colin was left behind the till on his own he started growling and grumbling and rolling his eyes – goodness knows how he'd react when I told him Dad was selling up. In the end Fred himself decided to help out. "Things can't have changed that much," he said as he went to help a Christmas shopper choose some books for her teenage grandchildren. Not long after that, I noticed Mum and Dad disappear upstairs and I pondered what was going on there.

But I didn't have much time to overanalyse that either, and before I knew it we were ushering our last customer out of the door and I had less than an hour to get ready and get myself to the tearoom to meet Xander.

I had time to change my clothes, perform one of those 'day-to-night' miracles on my makeup and defrizz my hair, which was the best I could manage with it at the moment – it didn't seem to have recovered from getting caught in the snow on Sunday. I set off quietly for the tearoom without shouting goodbye to my parents – I couldn't face the fuss they'd make.

The Two Teas Café was a very welcome addition, even if I wasn't as into tea as most of the people who frequented it. It was heaving with Christmas shoppers when I arrived and Xander was already there, chatting to Ben and purchasing his beloved Lapsang Souchong.

"You should try the Russian Caravan too," Ben said. "I love that one."

As Ben was ringing the purchases through the till, I walked up to Xander and lightly touched his arm.

"Hi," he said softly, turning to me. "This place is fantastic; I can't believe I hadn't noticed it before."

I grinned. I knew he would love it.

"I was going to suggest staying for a cuppa," Xander went on. "But it's so busy – shall we just go and get food instead?"

"Sure, what did you have in mind?"

"Pizza?"

Of all the foods.

Pizza had been what Joe and I ate on our first date and suddenly everything about that first night out with him came back to me in flashes – his leg against mine under the table, the way his eyes crinkled when he laughed, the anticipation…

I made myself look at Xander, to ground myself in this moment. His suggestion of pizza didn't mean anything. I had a whole life in front of me and only I could choose what to do with it. I took a breath.

"Pizza would be great," I said.

The pizza place that Joe and I had gone to had long since gone out of business. It had been a greasy, hole-in-the-wall sort of place that should probably have been condemned.

It served the sort of pizzas that were overly doughy and covered in oily yellow cheese. The only reason I'd ever had fond memories of it was because of what it represented. I usually ended up with stomach-ache every time we ate there.

Xander took me to a trendy Italian restaurant on the other side of the city and as we sat down I knew there were no similarities between that night thirteen years ago and tonight. Then Joe and I were two kids excitedly taking our first steps into adulthood. Tonight Xander and I were two slightly jaded, slightly broken adults getting to know each other after our previous faltering first steps had been rather disastrous.

Once we'd ordered our food we started talking about the Ruby Bell manuscript. We'd agreed beforehand to not mention the name Ruby Bell in public, but to just refer to it as 'the manuscript'.

"I'm ashamed to even let you read it," Xander said. "But I've emailed you a copy. I can get a hard copy to you if you prefer."

I shook my head. "No, it's fine, I'll do a first edit on screen." I hesitated. "I did see your email but I haven't opened it yet. I'm happy to just delete it if you prefer."

"Part of me wants to say yes, delete it and we'll forget this whole sorry affair. Philomena can invent a tragic story that explains the disappearance of our dear, beloved Ruby and we can pretend none of it ever happened..."

"I sense a but," I said.

"But I'm contracted to write one more so I'm going to swallow my pride, ask you not to judge me and be very grateful for your help."

"How soon do you want me to get to this?" I asked. "If I get my head down I can probably get through it in a day or two."

"It might not even take you that long. It's not even a full manuscript – only about 50,000 words. I sort of... ran out of steam."

He looked sad and dejected and I was about to change the subject when our pizzas arrived.

"These pizzas are so good," Xander said, cutting into his. "Almost as good as the Sunday lunches at Graydon Hall. There's a reason I come up to York as often as I do."

"How often do you come up?" I asked.

"I've visited a few times since Dot moved here the year before last, and I'd come up more often if I could – I originally only came to see her but I sort of fell in love with the city." He paused. "It gave me some distance from London, from Mum's death." I understood that well enough.

"And you always stay with Dot?"

He smiled. "She won't hear of me staying in a hotel and of course it means I can usually bring Gus with me."

"And it's the food you come up for?" I asked. "Because there aren't any restaurants in London?" Although admittedly these pizzas were excellent, with just the right balance of tangy tomato and stringy, melt-in-the-mouth mozzarella. I wondered how long this restaurant had been open and why I'd never noticed it before. I really had been living inside my own bubble for far too long.

Xander laughed. "Between you and me," he said, "sometimes I grow tired of London." He looked up from his pizza. "And don't you dare quote Samuel Johnson at me – being tired of London has nothing to do with being tired of life and everything to do with wanting a smaller, quieter life. God," he went on. "I sound like an old man, but there it is."

"I didn't just leave London because of all the memories," I said. "When I was rational enough to think about life after Joe's death, I didn't think I could navigate London on my own and, perhaps more importantly, I didn't want to. We didn't even live in central London but it all felt a bit too much."

"Where did you live?" he asked.

"Kingston," I replied. "By the river, but I wanted to live in a smaller city, somewhere where I could walk from one side to the other without navigating buses and trains and the underground." I paused. "Coming back to York was just coming home for me though. You grew up in London."

"If you'd told me ten years ago that I'd grow tired of it, that I'd want something quieter, I'd have laughed in your face. But the more time I spend in York the more I realise that it makes me happy. Plus, if I sold my flat I could probably find something bigger up here – maybe even with a garden for Gus."

"You really love that dog, don't you?" I asked, noticing his almost misty-eyed expression.

"He changed my life for the better." Xander shrugged. "The least he deserves is a garden to dig holes in rather than my expensive rugs!"

I thought about my father then, about his desire for a bigger life – the opposite of what Xander wanted. I had to admit that I'd been surprised that he'd come rushing back as soon as Mum had told him about the shop – after all, if he'd wanted to sell he could easily have done that from overseas through a lawyer. I wondered if there was more to his sudden reappearance than just the dire state of the bookshop finances, and if perhaps he'd already known the shop hadn't been doing well – he hadn't seemed very surprised, after all. And why did he and Mum keep disappearing together?

"When you offered to look at the manuscript, was it a tentative step back into editing?" Xander asked.

"I honestly don't know. When I left Rogers & Hudson I genuinely never thought I'd want to return, but now I'm having second thoughts. I'm not sure I want to do the same thing though."

"Not editing again?"

I shrugged. "You know, it's funny," I said. "But at the end of your book launch Philomena gave me her card and told me to call her. She seemed to be having some sort of premonition that I'd want to change career imminently."

"I told you she was good." Xander smiled. "Too good, most of the time." He looked at me, his final piece of pizza halfway to his mouth. "Perhaps you should call her though."

"You think so?"

He nodded. "She knows literally everyone in publishing and beyond. At the very least she might be able to help you with your next steps."

"She seemed quite pushy," I said. "And a bit rude."

"You thought I was rude when you first met me and yet here you are, having dinner with me."

"You wore me down," I acknowledged. "But she seemed to know so much about me, it was a bit creepy."

"Like I said, she knows everybody and their business. But she's one of the hardest-working people I've ever met. She gets a bit over the top at my book launches – I think it's to compensate for the fact that I hate doing them so much – but I'd say it would definitely be worth getting some advice from her at the very least."

I felt a bubble of excitement erupt inside me as though something great was on the horizon, if I just let go a little and allowed it to happen. It had always been Joe who had pushed me forward in my career – insisting I apply for the internship in the first place and then encouraging me to go for each promotion. There had to be something out there for me, and maybe Xander was right, maybe Philomena Bloom was the person to guide me in the right direction.

I felt Xander's leg against mine under the table and the bubble of excitement turned into something else, something that made my breath catch in my throat. I remembered how he'd almost kissed me in the living room this morning, how I'd wanted him to kiss me.

"Would you like dessert or coffee?" he asked.

We ordered dessert and coffee and brandy, neither of us eager to leave or for the evening to end.

"I finished *Persuasion*," he said.

"And?" I felt genuinely apprehensive that he wouldn't love one of my favourite books.

"My favourite of your recommendations so far," he replied.

"Phew."

He put his hand on his chest. "That letter," he said, pretending to swoon.

"I know, right! That's exactly what makes Fred Wentworth the greatest romantic hero – so much better than Darcy. Darcy would never write a letter like that."

"So you like a man who can write," he replied with a wink.

After we'd dragged dinner out for so long that we were the last people in the restaurant, Xander walked me back to the bookshop. My hand automatically found the crook of his elbow, as though it belonged there. As we walked through the cold, frosty streets of York – signs of Christmas all around us – I felt a contentment that had eluded me for years, even before Joe's death. I'd been living for him for so long I'd forgotten how to live for myself. This contentment might be temporary but right now I felt I was exactly where I wanted to be.

When we got to the bookshop there were no signs of life and we stood outside for a moment, murmuring our goodbyes quietly. The last thing I wanted was to alert my parents to our presence and for them to invite Xander inside. I wanted to come home as quietly as I'd left.

"I've been wondering for days what it would be like to kiss you," Xander said softly as he leaned in towards me, stroking my hair again. My stomach flipped. Tonight felt like a night of new beginnings and steps forward.

A night to kiss someone new.

I moved closer and tilted my head up towards him. In the porchway of the shop that doubled as my childhood home, Xander Stone finally kissed me – tentatively at first, as though asking for my permission and then harder, more persistently, his tongue stroking against mine. The flicker in my belly turned into a fire as I pressed myself against him.

His kiss was different to Joe's – quieter, more serious, just like Xander himself, and I wondered if everyone kissed in accordance with their personalities and if so, what were my kisses like?

It surprised me that he was the one who pulled away first. I had thought it would be me – filled with nerves or shame or guilt, especially as we stood in the same doorway in which Joe had kissed me for the first time. But I felt none of those things. Just a vague disappointment that Xander wasn't kissing me anymore.

"Stop overthinking it," he said gently.

"I'm sorry," I replied. "It's just this is the first time I've kissed anyone new…"

"I know," he whispered as he stroked my hair. "Me too. But I've been wanting to do that since I first met you."

"Really? When you met me in the supermarket?"

"Well I did mean the first time that we stood on this doorstep," he said, his lips curving into a smile at the memory. "But you certainly left an impression in the supermarket too!"

"But you were so rude to me on both those occasions!"

He shrugged. "Like little boys pulling the pigtails of the girls they fancy at school."

I laughed, leaning my head against him until he tilted my chin up with his fingers to kiss me all over again.

"I'd better leave you to get your beauty sleep," he said eventually, reluctantly. "Can I see you tomorrow?"

"I'll be here all day," I replied.

"We can practise our quadrille before Thursday."

"You're coming to book club again?" I asked.

He tilted his head on one side. "Is it a book club anymore when all we do is dance quadrilles and talk about mock-turtle soup?"

17

"We need to discuss Christmas carols and food," Trixie announced, once all the Die-Hards plus honorary members – Stan, John, Norm, Bryn, Xander and the newest member, my father – had all arrived for book group on Thursday night. "But first may I just say what a joy it is to have not one, but *two* published authors with us tonight." She smiled at Xander and Dad.

"Because I'm just chopped liver, I suppose?" Mum muttered beside me. Trixie definitely heard her but didn't say anything. She'd always been a little derogatory about Mum's writing and I had no real idea why – perhaps because it was published in weekly magazines rather than between the pages of a book. But weekly magazines had been good enough for Dickens. I suppose we're all snobbish in our own ways when it comes to reading.

I felt Xander's hand on my thigh under the table and I let myself lean against him. I'd felt self-conscious when he and Gus had first arrived and he'd gently kissed me on the cheek in front of everyone, but it felt right, comfortable. The whole book group seemed quite cosy and coupled up – Bella and Norm with their arms around each other, Dot and John sitting closer together than was necessary, Missy and Bryn making eyes at each other over the top of Trixie's head. Even my parents seemed to be getting on better than usual. It must be the spirit of Christmas. Either that or the sheer volume of Christmas decorations that had appeared in the shop over the last twenty-four hours, which I assumed my father was responsible for, meant that there wasn't much space and we all had to squeeze in close.

Xander had cooked for me the night before, while Dot had been at a college dinner (to which, apparently, she'd taken John as her guest). He'd picked me up from the bookshop and had been press-ganged into having tea with my parents.

"Come upstairs, Xander, won't you?" my father had said as though the two of them were old friends.

Instead of questioning Xander on his intentions with their daughter, my parents had questioned him on his writing and I'd had to look into my cup of tea for the whole excruciating hour, convinced that if I'd looked at either one of my parents I would just blurt out the secret to Ruby Bell's identity.

Eventually they'd let us go, mostly thanks to Gus barking his head off, and we'd gone back to Dot's and eaten lasagne and apple pie before curling up on the sofa to ostensibly watch television – although there had been substantially more kissing than watching.

Xander and Gus had walked me back to the bookshop once Dot had arrived home again.

"We can take this as slowly as you need to," he'd said as we'd walked. "I know this must be hard for you and I'll take your lead."

But kissing Xander hadn't been as difficult as I'd made

it out to be in my head. I wanted to be with him; I liked having him around. I leaned my head against his arm. "It's not as hard as I thought it would be," I'd said quietly. He hadn't replied but I'd felt him pull me a little closer.

"How long will you be in York?" I'd asked as we stood outside the bookshop.

"I'm staying for the Regency shindig, if that's what you're asking?"

"That's not the only reason I'm asking," I'd replied.

He'd smiled his devastating smile and my knees had felt weak. I hadn't known that was possible outside of the pages of a romance novel. What on earth was happening to me?

"I'm going back to London early on Christmas Day to spend Christmas with my family, but I'll come back in the new year if you want me to."

"That would be nice."

"Nice?" he'd replied, raising an eyebrow. "High praise indeed." He'd paused for a moment, locking his gaze on mine. "You could always come to London."

I felt a lump in my throat. Was I ready to go back? I thought about what came next, where I wanted my life to go. Could I do any of it without going back to London? Avoiding London meant I could avoid memories of Joe, avoid seeing his parents, but I didn't want to avoid the hard parts of my life anymore, and if I did want to get back into publishing in some way, London was where the jobs were.

He must have sensed my hesitation and the tiny step I took away from him. "You don't have..."

"I haven't been back since..." It was time I went back. "I could come to London," I'd said. It didn't sound as terrifying as I thought it might have done. Maybe if I said it out loud enough times I'd feel comfortable doing it.

And now he was here at book club with Gus asleep at his feet, listening to a long lecture about Regency Christmas carols while gently massaging my thigh in a way that made me wonder exactly how many nerve endings a person had in their thighs. I relaxed into him, into the sensation, trying to stay in the moment and not think about the man who couldn't be here tonight.

After making a list of carols that were suitable to sing at a Regency Christmas party – including, I was surprised to learn, 'Deck the Halls' and 'We Wish you a Merry Christmas' – and ones that were not – anything by Noddy Holder (which my mother pointed out weren't carols anyway) – Trixie started bemoaning the new Christmas decorations that had appeared all over the shop.

"They are just not suitable for our Regency theme, Megan," she said sternly. "I said we could keep the Christmas tree but those flashing Santas are just too much."

I was inclined to agree with her. I'd tried very hard not to let the shop look tacky, but then Dad came along. "The Santas are nothing to do with me, I'm afraid," I said. I looked over at Dad, who shrugged.

"Oh come on, let them stay," he said. "It's Christmas."

One smile from Dad and Trixie was putty in his hands. After agreeing that the Santas would be taken down on Christmas Eve in time for the party, we moved on to food.

"We agreed on finger food version of Regency delicacies, I think," Trixie said, peering at her copious notes.

"We thought we could all try to make one dish and bring it," I replied.

"Do you think perhaps we should get Ellie at the tearoom to do some back-up dishes?" Xander said quietly to me. He'd become rather enamoured of The Two Teas since I'd met him there. "Just in case?"

"Already sorted."

"I've written up some recipes," Trixie went on. "And you can all choose something to make and bring. I'm going for mini Yorkshire puddings." Typically she'd chosen the easiest dish to make. "There's also potato pudding, pasties, savoury pies, bubble and squeak, colcannon, mince pies and fruit cake, so I suggest you all get practising."

Because we all had time to be cooking up a disgusting-sounding storm as well as everything else. This party felt as though it was getting out of hand, and I wished I'd never suggested it. I was just going to get Ellie to make some extra mince pies and hope Trixie didn't notice.

"Now before we start dancing, I need all the men's measurements," Trixie announced. "If you don't know them I can measure you." She unrolled a tape measure ceremoniously.

"God help me," Xander whispered under his breath.

"What do you need our measurements for?" Bryn asked.

"Your Regency costume, of course."

"What? Nobody told me..." Bryn began but Trixie silenced him with a look.

"Us ladies already have our gowns, and we expect our dance partners to be appropriately attired," Trixie went on, as I wondered if they made breeches to fit Bryn and Norm. "I need to get everything ordered from the costume rental this week. It's very last minute—" she gave me another of her knowing looks "—so it is imperative this is done tonight. If you don't know your measurements, please come and have them taken."

My father was first in line, flirting outrageously with Trixie.

"Will you take my inside leg measurement please," Xander growled quietly into my ear and I felt as though my whole body had caught on fire. "I've never known anyone blush as much as you." He laughed as he got up. "And don't worry, I know my measurements so I don't need to be manhandled by Trixie – these inside legs are for you alone."

I shook my head at him but I couldn't stop smiling. How was this the same man who'd rammed his trolley into my legs just a few weeks ago?

"And now we dance," Trixie said, when all the measuring was sorted out.

"Have you been practising?" Xander asked.

"When have I had time to practise?" I asked. "And I think I've forgotten everything that we learned last week. You did mention practising together but…" I paused, narrowing my eyes at him. "You've been practising, haven't you?"

He nodded sheepishly. "Yes, with Dot and John," he admitted.

"Humph." I looked over at Dot. "So she's been seeing a lot of John outside of book group then?" I asked.

"Well, you know she went to that college do last night with him."

"Is he suitable, do we think?" I joked.

Xander laughed. "I think Dot is capable of looking after herself. If anyone is going to be taken advantage of then it's John."

Mum was sitting out the quadrille as Colin hadn't turned

up. I'd asked him several times but he was clearly more annoyed with us for leaving him to work alone during the Christmas rush than I'd thought. I had to make it up to him somehow – we'd all been taking him for granted for far too long – but I didn't know what I was going to do, especially once he found out he wasn't going to have a job at all soon enough.

"Dance with me," Dad said.

"No, it's fine…" Mum began but Dad was insistent. Always the life and soul of any party and never one to be left out, Dad was ready to dance a quadrille, even though he had no idea how to or even what a quadrille was.

"Really, Walter," Trixie said, pretending to be cross with him, but I could tell already that he was going to get away with it. He always did. "We can't be starting from scratch. We'll never catch up and we don't have long to go now."

"You just carry on from wherever you're at," Dad said. "I'll follow along."

We gathered in the middle of the shop floor where we'd cleared space once again. I took the opportunity to speak to Missy for a moment while everyone was still finding their places.

"Has Dad talked to you about the bookshop?" I asked.

She glanced over towards where Dad was being shown the opening steps of the quadrille by Dot and then looked back at me.

"He's selling up, isn't he?" she whispered.

I nodded.

"I think it might be the only way, Meg. It would have to happen eventually," Missy replied as Trixie called us to order once again.

My father had two left feet at the best of times, but he wasn't going to let the quadrille defeat him. What he lacked in skill he made up for in effort and if nothing else he had us all roaring with laughter – even Trixie. This was typical of my father – everyone loved him.

"You're all hopeless," Trixie announced. "But we are getting there. I'll see you all next week." She packed up her lists and dance demonstration designs in her handbag and slung it over her arm. "Come along, Stan," she ordered. "Dot, John, are you coming with us?"

"I'll help Megan clear up and see you back at the house," Xander said to Dot.

"I'm sure you will," she replied, squeezing his arm and giving me a little wink. "Would you like me to take Gus?"

"That would be great, actually," Xander said, clipping Gus's lead to his harness and handing him over. Gus looked a little disgruntled at first but then Dot mentioned treats and his ears pricked up as he trotted next to her.

When everyone had left and my parents had disappeared upstairs, clearly thinking I was too smitten with Xander to notice their constant whisperings in corners, Xander and I were alone.

"What's the matter?" he asked.

"Nothing. Can you help me move this bookcase?"

He took my wrist gently and pulled me towards him. "Something's the matter. Talk to me."

"I'm being ridiculously sentimental about the bookshop. I know I want to move on, I know I haven't got what it takes to save the business – I'm not even sure if it can be saved – but the thought of it not being here next Christmas is just…" I shook my head gently, looking at the bookshelves around me.

The bookshop had been my home for so long that I couldn't imagine it not being here. It had also been my solace and my shelter since Joe's death, a place I could return to and lick my wounds. I hadn't minded paying for the refurbishment; I'd enjoyed rejigging all the bookshelves and making the space more welcoming, but I'd never felt I'd had the energy for much else. It had only been over the course of the last few months that I'd felt like throwing myself into a new project again, and that's when Missy, Bella and I had decided to broaden our horizons when it came to book launches, to try to get big-name authors in rather than local authors. It had been a great idea and there was no denying that Xander's launch had boosted sales, but I couldn't see that even the unlimited energies of Philomena Bloom would get us out of the woods. Dad and Missy were right: eventually we'd have to sell. It was sensible to do it before we ploughed any more money into the business.

And I'd known, when we were all making the initial plans for Xander's launch, that this wasn't what I wanted to do – that marketing and budgets and double-entry spreadsheets were not where either my heart or my skill set lay – but I hadn't wanted to face that fact or think about the future. Until Xander rammed his trolley into the back of my legs and everything changed.

My heart lay in the actual words that surrounded me every day. The words on the pages that sat upon the sage green bookshelves all around me. I was passionate about stories, about those stories being told in the best possible way and read by as many people as possible. I was good at selling books, at convincing people that this particular story was the one that would speak to their heart. I knew I could match people up to the right book, just as I'd always known the books that would light people up when I'd been an editor. But I had no idea how to get people through the door of Taylor's in the first place so they could buy the books.

"I'm worried about Mum as well," I said. "It's been just the two of us for so long now and I couldn't have got through the last few years without her. What will she do when I go off to pastures new and Dad has sold the only home she's had for the last thirty years?"

"Your mum will understand," Xander said, stepping closer to me and gently brushing my hair back from my face. "She wants you to be happy. After all, she was the one who encouraged you to have coffee with me in the first place."

"Against my better judgement."

He smiled slowly. "Maybe it was, but do you regret it?"

"No, I..." I hesitated again, my mouth dry at the proximity of him, the warmth of his body next to mine. I never thought I would feel like this again. "I don't regret it at all."

"Good," he said. "And we can work the rest out together..."

"We?"

"If you want me to help, I will," he whispered, ducking his head so his lips were close to mine and I could feel the warmth of his breath. "But before we do that, I want to do this."

And then he kissed me, his lips hard against mine and his hands on my hips as he backed me against the nearest bookcase. As I kissed him back I felt, in that moment, that there was nowhere else I'd rather be and nobody else I wanted to be with.

"It's late," Xander whispered into my hair as we sat wrapped around each other in the reading nook of the shop. "I should go."

"I don't want you to go," I murmured.

"I don't want to go either," he said softly, folding his fingers around mine. He looked down at our hands as though he couldn't quite meet my eyes and I was suddenly very aware of the beating of my own heart.

When he looked at me again the air between us grew thick. I watched as he leaned back against the chair and closed his eyes for a moment.

"I want you to be comfortable," he said. "I don't want to rush you."

"I never expected this," I said quietly. "I never expected the man who hit me with his trolley to be..."

"It wasn't on purpose, you know," he said quietly.

"Wasn't it?"

He looked at me, catching my eye as though challenging me to guess the truth. "I never expected this either," he said. I felt him shift, his thumb gently stroking my temple.

"Stay," I said. Just one little word, but it felt like so much more. It had only been a few days since Xander had kissed me for the first time in the bookshop doorway, since I'd wondered if it was possible that I could have another relationship again, but already I knew that I wanted to try. I had to know where this was going.

"Are you sure?" he asked.

My head was telling me to change my mind, to say 'no I'm not sure', to give one of a thousand excuses as to why it would be a terrible idea... but they were nothing but excuses. My heart wanted him here with me. I wanted to get on with my life and I wanted to do that with Xander.

"I'm sure." I paused. "Are you?"

"I'm sure," he whispered, his lips brushing my forehead.

18

Xander woke me gently, very early the next morning. "I need to get back to take Gus out," he said, blinking sleepily. "And I really shouldn't have slept in contact lenses."

"I'm sorry," I said, remembering how he'd told me at Graydon Hall that contact lenses weren't conducive to unplanned nights away.

"It was worth it." He smiled.

We crept downstairs together so I could let him out the back way. It was still dark as we stood in the doorway and he turned towards me to kiss me goodbye, pressing me against the doorframe.

"Thank you," he whispered. "Thank you for trusting me."

I went back to bed after he'd gone, falling into a fitful doze, and it came as no surprise to me that when I woke up I felt suddenly sad and guilt-ridden, my head full of thoughts of Joe and how I wasn't with him when he died. I could still hear the 'drip, drip, drip' of the coffee machine as it deposited its almost undrinkable contents into the white plastic cup, just as I could still hear the 'beep, beep, beep' of the machines that helped to keep Joe alive, the palpable silence in his room when those machines weren't needed anymore and the sound of my cup of coffee hitting the floor when I realised what had happened.

Healing is never linear. I learned that when I first moved back to York. Some days I would wake up and feel almost normal, as though I could get on and face the world, and then the next day I would wake up floored with grief again, unable to move, unable to get out of bed. The five stages of grief aren't linear either – they all seem to exist together in one fiery hell ball of emotion that feels as though it will last forever. People will tell you that time heals but, in my experience, time just takes away the intensity. The grief and the anger and the rage are still there, but less so with each passing month until it becomes something you simply carry with you, like the memory of the person you've lost.

Usually when I woke up feeling like this I would panic, desperate not to spiral back into that place I had been in the immediate aftermath of Joe's death. But today I lay there with my feelings, the duvet pulled up to my chin, the scent of Xander's aftershave still on the pillow, and allowed all the sensations and the memories to wash over me. Things were different now, change was happening – it had started happening the day that Xander Stone and his eccentric agent walked through the door of Taylor's Bookshop. As the feelings and the memories started to fade again, I allowed myself to remember the night before without guilt. I knew Xander would understand how I was feeling because he understood grief. He understood that it changes you, that it never fully leaves. I had no way of predicting the future, no way of knowing whether whatever was happening between Xander and me would last. But it felt right, and I felt a clarity that I hadn't felt since before Joe's diagnosis.

I pushed myself out of bed and into the shower, and vowed that today I would phone Philomena Bloom. I knew it would take a while to sell the bookshop and that Mum and Dad would probably need my help over the next few months, but it wouldn't hurt to start putting feelers out into the publishing world again. I never thought I'd get to this place again, where I wanted to go back to working in publishing.

But I also wanted to enjoy the remainder of my life as a bookseller, especially these busy days before Christmas, and I promised myself that I wouldn't abandon Colin in the shop on his own quite so much.

Of course, like all best laid plans, the day did not work out like that at all.

The bookshop had been open about half an hour when it happened. We were surprisingly busy for nine-thirty on a Friday morning and I felt a little spark, like the fairy lights on the Christmas tree, light up inside me, washing away the last vestiges of the memories and dark feelings I'd woken up with.

"You're in a surprisingly good mood," Colin said as he went off to restack the shelves in the cookery section. (Why was the cookery section so popular?)

"It's Christmas," I replied to his retreating back.

I manned the till while Colin was on the shop floor and gentle Christmas music played in the background – a playlist I'd been recommended by Ben at the tearoom when I'd complained about the quality of Christmas music that my father insisted on. I was feeling full of seasonal contentment.

Mum was upstairs pretending to write but I'd heard her and Dad talking in loud whispers about something up in the attic earlier.

"Happy Christmas." I smiled to the woman who had just paid for a stack of children's books for her grandchildren.

My smile turned into a grin then as I saw Xander walk through the bookshop door. I hadn't expected to see him until closing time and I was about to step out from behind the counter to talk to him when I saw that this wasn't the Xander from last night, the one who'd shared my bed and kissed me until my lips stung, or the Xander whose smile could light up a whole room. This was the Xander who I'd first met in the supermarket back in November – his face white, his mouth set in a hard line.

He stood in front of me, tapping a rolled-up newspaper against his leg.

"We need to talk," he said.

I felt an immediate sense of dread. It had only been a few hours since he'd kissed me against the back door of the shop. I wanted to tell him that we were too busy for me to talk, that Colin shouldn't be left on his own again. I felt torn between my responsibility to the shop and Xander's mercurial moods. What could possibly have happened since this morning to change everything so much?

"Not here," I replied quietly. "Go into the office while I get Colin to cover the till."

Colin complained, of course. "He's here every five minutes," he moaned about Xander. "What does he want now?"

"Please, Colin, I'll be as quick as I can."

Xander was standing with his back to me as I walked

into the office, but he turned around as soon as he heard me shut the door.

"What the hell have you done?"

I looked at him blankly. What had I done?

He unrolled the newspaper and held it in front of him.

LITERARY WONDERKID IS SECRET BONKBUSTER NOVELIST: EXCLUSIVE

I stared at the headline and the air seemed to still around me. At first I couldn't work out what on earth the article was talking about, and then my eyes moved down from the words to the headshot of Xander that sat beneath. Somehow his secret was out, and a national newspaper had got hold of the story that Xander Stone was Ruby Bell. But how had they found out? I hadn't told a soul, even though I'd desperately wanted to. I'd promised Xander that I wouldn't breathe a word and I hadn't. I thought of the manuscript he'd emailed me that was sitting on my laptop still unread, mostly because I'd been so distracted by the manuscript's author. But my laptop was locked and password-protected. Nobody would have looked at it... would they?

"I trusted you," he said, his voice cold and hard.

"You seriously think that I would do this?" I asked him, incredulous.

"Who the hell else was it, then?" His voice was louder now and I hoped Colin wasn't listening at the door. "Who else would have gone running to the press? You are the only person I've told recently."

"Oh, there's lots of people who could have done this..." I began.

"Don't make it worse, Megan," he said, folding the paper up again as though he couldn't bear to see the headline any longer. "I told you in confidence, and you broke that confidence." I thought about the night before, his body wrapped around mine. How could he possibly think I could betray his secrets after all we'd shared? "I thought we had something… something…" he went on. "I thought we were… My God, Megan." He stared at me, his anger palpable. "How could you?"

I stared back at him for a moment and I felt a ball of rage rise up in my throat, its taste so bitter I couldn't bring myself to speak. I was furious that he could think I would do this to him and furious with myself for trusting him, for letting him in, for spending the night with him.

"How dare you," I said eventually into the silence. "After everything we've talked about, after last night…" I paused for a moment, taking a breath. "How dare you come into my shop, my home and accuse me of this."

"Who else could it be?" he repeated.

"Anyone," I snapped at him. "And you know it. You think this is some big secret that only you and the chosen few know about; but come on, Xander, you know what publishing is like. Lots of people will know. Creating a book isn't a solo act you know – it's not all about you. There are huge numbers of unsung heroes behind every single paperback and it would only take one of them to be fired or disgruntled, and bingo – the secret's out."

He stared at me as though this hadn't even crossed his mind. Had he really thought that I could do this to him?

Something about him changed then and he suddenly looked exhausted. "I can't trust you," he said, putting the

folded newspaper down on the desk. "I can't trust anyone."
He turned away from me, towards the door.

"We're still talking," I snapped. "Do not walk away."

He turned back towards me, his hand still on the door
handle.

"What else is there to say?" he asked.

"This isn't about me, is it?" I said, trying to keep my voice
calm even though I didn't feel calm at all. "You don't really
think I could do that, do you?" I pointed at the newspaper.

Xander shrugged, not meeting my eye. He looked as
though he'd completely run out of steam.

"This is the part of the romance novel that you hate," I
went on, remembering what he'd said to me on that first
night when he'd arrived unexpectedly at the bookshop.
"This is the bit where the couple have a ridiculous
misunderstanding and an enormous row that isn't really
about what they think it's about."

"All I want to know is why you told the papers?" he
persisted.

"I can't answer that because it wasn't me and you know
that – you must do. This isn't about your secret being spilled,
this is about us, about last night." I paused, feeling frustrated
and angry. "For some reason you're scared and I need you
to tell me why." I thought it would be me who got scared,
me who pulled away. I'd assumed Xander was the stronger
one of us, but why should he be? He'd been through so
much over the last few years too, he'd hidden himself away
and refused to acknowledge it just as I had, so it made sense
that he'd find our burgeoning relationship difficult as well.
Admittedly I wouldn't storm into someone's place of work
and accuse them of things they hadn't done but I already

knew he was reactionary; he'd already admitted that. When he wasn't caught up in his own emotions he could be quite self-aware.

"I'm not scared," he said firmly and unconvincingly. "I'm bloody furious. How could this have happened?"

I remembered then how he'd told me he liked to control things, that he didn't do vulnerable very well. After last night he must be feeling vulnerable. I knew I was. It was natural after spending so long alone. I just wanted him to admit it.

"Xander…" I began, stepping towards him.

He shook his head. "I can't do this," he said.

When he turned back towards the door again I let him go.

"And you didn't tell anyone?" my mother asked for what felt like the fifteenth time.

"No, Mum, I haven't told a soul; stop asking me. Don't you think if I was going to tell anyone you'd have been the first to know? I don't know how it got in the paper. Does it really sound like something I would do?"

"Nobody's accusing you of telling the paper," Dad said from the armchair opposite.

"Xander is," I reminded him. Had he even been listening?

"Oh yes, well, apart from him nobody is accusing you."

We were sitting in the living room in the flat above the shop – Mum had taken me up there when she'd come down and Colin had told her what was going on. Dad had joined us after tea in mismatched mugs – the Great British solution to any crisis, even if in this house we tended to use teabags.

And this must have been one hell of a crisis as Missy was helping on the shop floor, something she always refused to do. She hadn't asked any questions – just stared at the newspaper headline in disbelief.

"We're just checking you didn't inadvertently tell anyone who may have spoken to the paper," Dad went on.

"No," I said again. "I did not tell anyone else. How many times?"

"Xander Stone is Ruby Bell, though," Mum said. "That is a surprise, especially when he's so disparaging of romance novels." She turned to me. "Was that a cover?"

"Sort of," I replied. Despite Xander's accusations, I still wasn't going to betray any of his secrets and tell my parents about him writing the books with his mother and that he avoided romance novels to stop himself thinking about her too much. Not that avoidance ever worked – I'd avoided all kinds of things in an attempt to stop myself thinking about Joe over the years but I'd still thought about him every day. And as I thought about him again now, sat in the living room with Mum and Dad – the newspaper headline spread between us – I got that familiar sinking feeling. Joe was never coming back; he'd never hold my hand or kiss me again. He'd never be there to help me. I was on my own now.

"I finally allow myself to have feelings for someone who isn't Joe," I said, "and then this happens."

"I know, love." Mum pulled me into a cuddle. "But this is just a silly misunderstanding that you and Xander need to sort out. You just need to give him time to calm down. Seeing this newspaper headline will have been a huge shock to him."

"Who would have told the press though?" I asked. "I tried to placate him by telling him it could be anyone in the publishing industry, that loads of people would have known, but he wasn't buying it." I wasn't sure if I bought it myself.

And then I remembered the footstep in the hallway that I thought I'd heard on the morning that Xander told me his secret. I'd convinced myself I'd just imagined it, on edge at the thought of Xander kissing me for the first time. But now I was sure it must have been someone.

"Was it you?" Mum said, looking scornfully at my father.

"Of course it wasn't me," he replied, sitting up and looking affronted. "Why on earth would it be me?"

"Well, you're in those publishing circles," Mum said.

"Trust me, I had no idea that Xander Stone was Ruby Bell."

Mum was about to say something else when Missy came rushing in. "I'm so sorry," she said. "But the shop is really busy and Colin has disappeared and I really have no idea what I'm doing. Can someone help?"

"We'll both go down," Mum said. "Come on, Walter." She patted Missy's shoulder. "Thanks for your help. Why don't you stay up here with Megan for a while?"

"How are you feeling?" Missy asked as Mum and Dad headed downstairs.

"Awful," I replied.

"More tea?" she asked, clearing up the empty mugs.

I shook my head. "I slept with him last night."

"What?" she said, almost dropping the mugs in her surprise.

"You heard," I said as she put the mugs back on the table and sat down next to me.

"You slept with Xander?"

I nodded.

"Here? After book group?"

I nodded again. How many more inane questions was she going to ask?

"Wow," she said. "Well... That's a good thing though, right?"

"I thought it was, until he accused me of selling his secrets to the press."

Missy had clearly run out of questions.

"How dare he speak to me like that. How dare he think I'd go to the papers. I can't even..." I could feel myself starting to cry again. Xander Stone was not worth this.

"I hadn't really realised you were this serious about him," Missy said.

"He's the first person I've liked, the first person I've even trusted since Joe. He seemed to get me; he'd been through similar stuff. I thought..." I shook my head. "Urgh, I should have known better than to think anything."

"This whole argument," she said slowly. "It wasn't really about the newspaper headline, was it?"

"No, I don't think so. If he feels anything like I do then he'll be feeling tired and a bit vulnerable after last night. It's not that I didn't want it to happen, it's just a big step. For both of us."

Missy squeezed my shoulder. "And neither of you are used to having to deal with stuff like this."

"It kind of makes me not want to bother. It feels easier to just go back into hibernation."

"Totally understandable. This is the first time you've opened yourself up and allowed yourself to trust someone since Joe died. It's scary and raw and when something goes wrong it's tempting to just disappear back into your foxhole."

"What else is there to do?"

"Not disappear into your foxhole."

I thought about that for a moment. It had felt good to be doing something new, getting to know someone new. And those good feelings weren't all to do with Xander's cheekbones or his kisses or how good his hard, muscular body had felt in my bed. I'd started to feel more like me again – the me I'd been before Joe first got sick. I'd even kickstarted my career – although I'd have to work that out on my own now. I would hardly be flavour of the month with Philomena Bloom after this.

"The fact is," Missy went on, "you didn't tell anyone about Xander being Ruby Bell – although I have to say I'm wounded you didn't confide in me…"

"Trust me, I was soooo tempted!"

"But you didn't – you didn't tell anyone. You kept your side of the bargain and if Xander can't see that when he calms down then… well… he doesn't deserve you."

I thought about Graydon Hall, about sitting in the bar with Xander after our long snowy walk home when I'd asked him what would happen if I met the right person before I was ready.

If that person is even remotely worthy of you, Megan, then they'll wait until you're ready.

But what if that person wasn't ready either? What if we'd both rushed into this too quickly? This wasn't the first time Xander had reacted like this and I wondered again if this was something that he'd started doing after his mum died. I'd learned over the last three years that I can't control anything but my own reactions to things, but God knows I'd tried, in an attempt to never feel pain again. Was that what Xander was doing? Did he hold himself so tightly that sometimes he snapped?

Was he the one who wasn't ready for what was happening between us?

"Somebody went to the papers," I said to Missy. "I wonder who it was?"

"Who else knew?" Missy asked.

"His agent, of course, but contrary to appearances he says that she is able to keep a secret. His family know and his ex-wife. I imagine a lot more people at his publishers know than he realises though. It was almost impossible to keep secrets when I was at Rogers & Hudson."

I was about to tell her about the footsteps I'd heard in the hallway on the morning Xander told me about Ruby Bell, when I heard footsteps in the hallway again. This time they were my mother's. She sounded angry.

"Martha, for God's sake, come back," my father called after her as he followed her towards the kitchen.

"It's very clear you don't need me," Mum replied. "You've made all these decisions without me."

"I haven't—"

"You're about to sell my home from under me without any warning," Mum shouted.

Missy stared at me. "Has he found a buyer?" she asked in a whisper.

I stared back at her. "Not to my knowledge."

"I'm not selling your home from under you," Dad said, trying to keep his voice quiet. "I've come back for you, like I promised I would."

"And what about Megan?" Mum asked.

I stood up then and walked out of the living room and towards the kitchen.

"Yes," I said. "What about Megan?"

19

"Tell us about the sex," Bella pleaded, gin in hand. "Was it like his Ruby Bell books?"

My face was on fire.

"She's blushing," Missy teased. "Which means it was good."

"Did he throw you down on the bed and ravish you?" Bella asked. "Like Nico Skyvros in *A Night to Remember*. God I loved that book, it was just so…"

"Stop it!" I begged them both. I couldn't stand it anymore. "Please stop! The sex was nothing like a Ruby Bell book, but that doesn't mean it wasn't good and that's all I'm going to tell you. Besides, I have more important things to think about right now."

"Come on, Megan, things really aren't that bad," Bella said.

"I feel as though I've lost everything."

"You haven't lost everything. Don't be so dramatic," Bella replied as she replenished my gin glass and passed me another tissue. "You have Missy and me for a start, and you can stay here with us for as long as you need."

"Don't make it too long, though," Missy interrupted. "The delightful Norm is moving in next month."

"What?" I said, finally distracted from the tragedy of my own life. "That's great news. When did…?"

Bella held up her hand. "We'll come to that in a minute," she said. "As I was saying, you have us and somewhere to stay. Xander will cool down and realise he's being ridiculous and come begging your forgiveness like the deeply flawed romantic hero that he is…"

Missy tutted. "You don't have to forgive him though," she said. "That was a total dick move, blaming you for selling his secret to the press the morning after he slept with you."

Even Bella looked deflated at that. "It was a dick move," she said. "But so far he hasn't kidnapped anyone like Sebastian St Vincent – so he's not beyond redemption, right?" She looked at me. "Those are the rules, aren't they?" She grinned at me hopefully. She was absolutely right of course; I hadn't lost everything.

I was about to lose my home a lot more quickly than I'd thought, as Missy and I had found out earlier when my parents had finally confessed to us what was going on.

"Your father has found a buyer," Mum had said bitterly. "Who wants us all out by the end of January."

"What?" I'd replied. That was so soon, just six weeks away. I knew we'd have to sell the shop but I hadn't expected this. I thought it would take months, maybe even years to sell. Who would want a failing bookshop, after all?

"You knew we'd have to sell it, love," Dad had said. "We'd talked about it."

"You said it would take ages. You said I had plenty of time."

"Yes, well, the speed of the sale has been a surprise but the developers…"

"Developers?" I'd asked. But of course it was being sold to developers. The answer to the question 'who would want a failing bookshop?' was 'nobody'.

"I'm sorry, love, we'll work something out."

"I expect he's got your whole life planned out for you," Mum had said. "Just like he has mine."

"Where are Mum and I going to live?" I'd asked.

"Apparently we're all going to Spain," Mum had snapped.

"What?" None of this had made any sense, especially on top of Xander's earlier accusations.

"It might be the new start you need," Dad had said. "We can have a chat about it and—"

"No." I was sick to death of being told what I'd done and what I should do and what would be best for me. "I can't do this. Not right now." I'd walked away from their protests, grabbing my coat from the hook in the hallway as I'd passed. I'd run down the stairs and through the shop, pushing past Colin.

"Megan," he'd called after me. "I need to talk to you."

"Not now, Colin," I'd replied, already breaking my vow to be less dismissive of him as I'd marched out into the street.

I'd started walking, with no idea of where to go, when Missy, who must have only stopped to collect her laptop from the office, had caught up with me.

"Where are you going?" she'd asked.

"I have no idea," I'd replied.

She'd taken me back to her flat and Bella had been

summoned. As soon as she'd been able to get out of work she'd appeared with a bottle of gin and sensible words.

"Do you think you'll move to Spain?" she asked now.

I shook my head. "No," I said. "I have absolutely no desire to move to Spain."

"Is your mum going to go?" Bella asked. "With your dad?"

"I've no idea. Dad said something about coming back for her, as though they'd been planning this for years, but Mum seemed really pissed off. I don't think she'd been expecting the shop to sell so quickly." I paused. "That's all I know though. I didn't give them much of a chance to explain."

"But you're staying in York?" Bella confirmed.

"I think so. I mean, I'd really like to. I love it here, but the publishing jobs are all in London. Xander did mention briefly that I should go to London but…" I shrugged. Who knew what was happening anymore?

"You should make that call to Philomena Bloom," Missy suggested. "See what she thinks."

"I don't think Philomena Bloom will want to talk to me now, will she? Not after what Xander will have told her about me."

"Don't be ridiculous," Missy said. "Nobody really believes you're the one who leaked the story, not even Xander. Philomena probably knows who did it. This has inside job written all over it."

"You don't know that," I said.

"I'm fairly sure of it, though. What could you possibly gain from blabbing to the papers? He'll be at home right now regretting he ever accused you and working out how to win you back, just like Bella said."

I doubted it. This wasn't a romance novel after all, despite what I'd said to Xander in the office this morning and all the romance tropes we'd inadvertently encountered.

And it wasn't the first time he'd reacted like this.

"I never told you why Xander told me about Ruby Bell," I said.

"I thought he just told you," Bella replied.

"He did, but only because of what I found in his car." I told them about coming across the manuscript and about how Xander had reacted, how angry he'd been and how he'd refused to admit to the obvious explanation at first. "I couldn't tell you because I couldn't tell anyone," I said. "But the next day, when he came to see me at the shop to apologise and admit the truth he also told me that he can be reactionary and then regret his behaviour afterwards."

"Which is exactly what he's done again now," Missy said.

"It's not a very healthy way of living, though, is it?" I replied.

"Nor is locking yourself up in a bookshop for three years or only dating men who look like your first love," Bella snapped.

Missy and I stared at her as she clapped a hand over her mouth.

"I'm sorry," she said. "I didn't mean it to come out like that."

"What did you mean then?" I asked warily.

"Look, you told us about Xander's mum and his ex-wife and how the two of you talked about grief and how hard it is to go on after you've lost someone important. I just wonder if his behaviour is something to do with how he's handling his mum's death. He's human, after all – although it's hard to believe with those cheekbones – and maybe his way of trying to control his life when it spiralled out of control was to keep people at arm's length, which he does wonderfully by being rude and arrogant – something I think we discussed when you first met him."

She gave me a knowing look and I had to agree with her. We all find our ways of coping after trauma and those behaviours can quickly become a habit – an unhealthy habit most of the time.

"Xander told you he'd take the relationship at your pace," Bella went on. "But maybe he needs to hear that from you as well."

"Go on," I said. It was something that had already crossed my mind after all.

"From what you told us he lost both his parents and got divorced before he turned thirty," Bella said. "Perhaps he's not as ready for a new relationship as he thinks he is. Perhaps he's scared too. And perhaps last night was as big a step for him as it was for you."

"You think he regrets last night?" I asked.

"I didn't say that," Bella replied. "I said that it would have been a big step for him after everything that's happened." She looked at Missy and me and rolled her eyes. "You'd think you two would be able to see that."

"Megan and I don't go around accusing people of things they haven't done," Missy said indignantly.

"No, but like I said, until recently Megan had barely left the bookshop and you only date guys who remind you of your first boyfriend – even though it always ends in disaster and even though good men like Bryn are besotted with you." Bella folded her arms across her chest decisively.

I turned to Missy. "She has got a point," I said.

"Humph," Missy replied.

"What can I do about it, though?" I asked. "Xander must know I didn't sell that story to the papers. I understand that he was shocked and probably a bit scared and this week has been a total rollercoaster for both of us, but it's up to him to apologise now and so far I haven't heard from him."

"Give him time," Bella said.

"But he was the one who asked me out for coffee," I replied. "He was the one who took me to Graydon Hall."

"And look how that turned out. That whole one-bed thing can't have been particularly easy for him either. Especially if he had feelings for you and had no idea if they were reciprocated."

"Wouldn't it have been easier for him to just talk to me about how he felt?" I asked. "Rather than shout mad accusations at me?"

"From what you've told us, he's not much of a talker," Missy said. "Not when it comes to talking about how he feels, anyway."

"He probably wasn't expecting to fall in love with you," Bella went on. "This is all as much of a shock to him as it has been to you."

"In love? He's not…" Of course he wasn't in love with me. We hadn't known each other long enough.

"Isn't he?" Bella interrupted "Let's look at the facts."

"Must we?" I moaned.

"Firstly…" Bella began counting off her points on her fingers. "He never takes his eyes off you. Even before he took you to the Christmas Market, when he was still being an arrogant snob about romance novels, he was always looking at you with these big soppy eyes, just like his dog."

"No he wasn't…"

"Secondly, he is willing to come to a romance book club, be bossed around by Trixie, learn to dance the quadrille and, I'm presuming, put on a Regency outfit just so he can spend time with you."

"Well Norm is doing the same for you," I said.

"I bullied Norm into doing it. Xander turns up voluntarily."

That was true.

"Thirdly, there's all the kissing…"

I felt the hairs on the back of my neck stand up when she mentioned the kissing. I would miss the kissing.

"And now the sex, of course," she went on. "Which you are being disappointingly coy about."

"And she's blushing again." Missy laughed.

"Fourthly, and most importantly," Bella said, sounding triumphant, "he listens to you."

"Have you any idea how rare a man who listens is?" Missy muttered.

"What? How do you know he listens?"

"Because you told us," Bella said softly. "You told us how he listened and understood, how he'd been through a hard time himself and understood if you found it all a bit difficult."

I swallowed; it was true. He had listened quietly without opinion while I'd told him things that I'd never really talked about with anyone else.

"The woman has a point," Missy said. "It's fairly obvious he's pretty besotted."

"If he really likes me and had really listened to me then he would never have accused me of going to the papers."

"Look at it from his point of view though," Bella said. "His deepest darkest secret was all over the front of that tabloid just a few days after he told somebody new about it. He put two and two together and made fifty-four, but can you imagine the state he would have been in? It clearly wasn't something he wanted to be common knowledge, for whatever reason."

I had to admit that Bella's theory made sense, especially as I already knew the reason he kept it a secret, the reason he always wanted it to be a secret. Because it was something he'd shared with his mother, something he'd written for his mother and had published in her memory.

And something he couldn't do anymore without his mother. He'd probably been hoping to quietly kill off Ruby Bell until that newspaper headline appeared.

"You really like him too, don't you?" Missy asked.

"I do but..." I sighed. "I also wonder if I've just fallen for him because he's the first man since Joe to pay me any attention."

"Rubbish," Bella said. "Whenever we go out for a drink, men are interested in you. Xander isn't the first guy to pay you attention but he is the first guy you've responded to."

"That's not true..."

"It really is," Missy agreed, nodding vigorously. "I hate to say it but I think Bella is right."

"Yesssss!" Bella cheered, fist bumping the air.

"Right about what?" I asked.

"Everything," Bella said.

"About Xander needing to know that you'll give him

time if he needs it," Missy said, ignoring Bella. "Just as he's promised to take things at your pace, maybe he needs that reassurance as well. If he hasn't dated at all since his divorce, this has probably all come out of the blue for him as much as it has for you."

"Call him tomorrow," Bella said.

"I'll think about it," I said. "I promise, but…" I trailed off. There was something else I wanted to talk to Bella and Missy about, something I'd been thinking about all afternoon, something I'd been wondering about since Dad told me the bookshop would have to be sold, and it had nothing to do with Xander.

"What is it?" Missy asked. "There's something else on your mind, isn't there?"

"Do you think I should try to buy the bookshop?" I asked.

"What?" Bella said, staring at me.

"I know it sounds out of the blue. I did consider it when Dad said he was selling up but I thought it would be OK because in my imagination, when the shop was sold, it would become the thriving bookshop that Mum and I hadn't quite managed. But as soon as Dad mentioned developers I felt this overwhelming sadness – both my home and the shop are going to disappear forever. If I could put the money in to stop that from happening…"

"How?" Missy interrupted, her eyes wide. "What money?"

"I've still got some money left over from the sale of the London flat, plus…" I trailed off. I hated talking about this. I didn't even want to think about it, but I was going to need money for the future whether I bought the bookshop or not. I had to think about it sometime. "When Joe died I got a pretty hefty life insurance payment, as well as a death-in-service payment from his firm."

Bella leaned closer to me. "You never told us about that," she said softly.

"I've never wanted to think about it," I replied. "It's always felt like tainted money and I didn't want it. But needs must, and next month I'm going to be losing my job and my home if I don't do something drastic."

There was a silence, interrupted only by the sound of more gin being poured.

"I don't think you should buy the bookshop," Missy said thoughtfully.

"You don't?"

"I agree," Bella said. "It would be a step backwards, I think."

"Exactly." Missy sat up and shifted across the sofa towards me. "You said you were ready to move on, to maybe go back into publishing. You even mentioned London."

"Yes, I guess," I said hesitantly.

"And if you buy the bookshop you'll stay exactly where you are. Yes, you'll still have a roof over your head and a job, but for how long? I know those bookshop accounts like the back of my hand and I'm fully aware that you haven't taken a wage from the shop for months. If you use Joe's life insurance money to buy the shop, what will you live on?"

"Whereas if you start again, the money will give you a buffer," Bella said. "Something to live on while you work out your next steps, which is probably exactly why Joe took the insurance out in the first place."

They were both right of course, but it felt like too much,

as though two gin-sozzled bulldozers were coming at me with the truth all at once when all I wanted was for things to carry on as normal. I put my head in my hands and groaned.

"I know you weren't expecting your dad to sell this quickly – and neither was I, to be honest. It's a lot to take on, especially when Xander had already ruined your day," Missy said, rubbing circles on my back. "But I think this might be exactly what you need."

I thought about the bookshop, my childhood home and refuge. I'd been unable to save it, unable to do anything. The bookshop had needed more effort than my broken heart had been able to cope with, and as my heart had started to mend I'd known I needed something else, something more. Yes I'd given everything a new lick of paint, I'd had a new sign commissioned, I'd made the bookshop look welcoming with its reading corner, monthly book recommendations and the children's read-along. I'd listened to Bella and Missy about marketing and finance. I'd even managed to get Xander Stone to launch his book from our shop. But it wasn't enough and I'd always known it wouldn't be enough because, as I'd finally admitted, my heart wasn't in it and never had been. I loved books and I was desperate for stories to be told and sold, but I needed to move away from what was, essentially, my grandparents' dream – just as my father had had to move away from it years before.

When Joe and I had first started talking I knew I'd wanted to go, but even when we getting ready to move away, I couldn't imagine not having the bookshop as part of my life.

"Just because you were brought up in a bookshop doesn't mean you have to sell books forever," Joe had said. "The circumstances of your birth don't dictate your destiny, Megan."

But what was my destiny?

"Where will I live?" I asked.

"I've already told you that you can move in here for a while until you find something else," Bella said.

"What? And sleep on the sofa?" I laughed. "That's really lovely of you but I don't think you want me living here on top of you, Norm and Missy."

"You don't have to sleep on the sofa," Missy said. "You can have my room."

"Why? Where are you going?" I asked. "Is Norm that bad that you need to move out or are you running off with Bryn after all?"

"Neither. I'm going back home."

I stared at her. "What? To America?"

She nodded, looking into her almost-empty gin glass. "Not forever, just for a while."

My stomach sank. "Is this something else I haven't realised because I've been so wrapped up in myself for so long, like Norm moving in?" I asked.

"No," Missy said. "Both our decisions have been rather spur-of-the-moment, haven't they, Bella?"

"Norm and I only decided to move in together on Monday. He got a letter asking if he wanted to renew the lease on his flat and we thought it was daft paying rent on two places when we're always here."

"And I phoned my parents on Wednesday," Missy said. "I

think they thought it was their annual Christmas phone call come early. I don't think they were expecting to hear me say that I wanted to come back for a few weeks."

"What made you decide to do that?" I asked. "Don't get me wrong, if you're happy I'm happy, but you always said you'd never go back. Not after what happened."

"I listened to my own advice," Missy replied. "I'd been nagging you about moving on and starting again. I pushed you into seeing Xander and into thinking about what else you wanted, to find a life outside of the bookshop, and then I realised that I was no better…" She paused. "Bella was right about that too."

"Wow, this is huge, Missy."

"I've had itchy feet for a while," she went on. "I've been thinking about doing some travelling for months, but I just never got around to it. I felt sort of overcome by this sense of inertia."

"I know that feeling," I said.

"And then I saw you on Wednesday morning after your date with Xander, after you finally kissed him, and you were glowing."

"I was?"

She nodded, smiling at me. "You really were. I was so happy for you – your dad was back, you'd met a guy you wanted to spend time with. I was a little bit jealous, truth be told. I wanted to feel like I was glowing again. And so I phoned my parents."

"Just like that?" I asked. "After all this time?"

"Not at all." Bella smiled. "She spent an entire evening stomping around the flat debating whether she should or not first. It was quite disconcerting."

"I thought that if I was going to go travelling then visiting my parents might be a good starting point. We'll have a lot to talk about, a lot to work out, but it's something I know I need to do and I can't do it over the phone." Missy shrugged as though it was no big deal, but I knew exactly how big a deal this was for her. She would have had no idea how her parents would react and she would have been opening up the box she'd stored her heart in for the first time in years, just as I'd done when I let Xander kiss me for the first time.

As I sat there with my two friends I realised I had no regrets. Opening up to Xander had allowed me to be honest about so many things in my life and allowed me to admit that I was ready for whatever happened next. I knew, no matter what happened when she arrived at her parents' house, Missy wouldn't regret doing this either.

"You're doing the right thing," I said, taking my turn to rub her back.

"I'm scared shitless," she admitted.

I shrugged. "Me too. I think that's normal though."

"And you'll take Missy's room?" Bella asked. "She's booked a flight for mid-January so it all works out perfectly."

"You've booked a flight?"

Missy nodded. "I had to do it straight away," she said. "Otherwise I'd never do it."

"OK, I'll move in," I said, although I was reluctant to live with the happy couple. "But just temporarily until I find somewhere else. I don't want to cramp Norm's style."

"So that's your home sorted," Bella said. "And tomorrow you'll phone Philomena and that will be your job sorted."

"I'll think about phoning her," I corrected.

"And then all you have to do is phone Xander."

"No," I said. "That's not all. There's something I have to do that's more important than any of that."

"What?" Bella asked.

"I need to talk to Mum."

20

Mum was in the kitchen attacking some potatoes when I got home the next morning. She was making a loud banging noise and it ricocheted off my head, which was sore from too many gins the night before.

"What on earth are you doing?" I asked.

"Practising," she replied breathlessly.

"Practising what?"

"Potato pudding. It was the recipe I got in Trixie's ridiculous Regency food lottery." There was potato all over the kitchen surface and little bits of it were stuck in Mum's hair.

"I never meant it to go this far – it was meant to be fun."

Mum stopped mashing and looked at me. "What did you get?"

"Mince pies. I've asked Ellie at the tearoom to make them for me."

"Cheat," Mum said, continuing to attack the potatoes.

"I'll leave you to it," I said. "I need to get changed, get coffee and go and help Colin." I felt terrible, both from too much gin and from the fact that I'd stormed out of the bookshop like a bratty teenager the day before rather than sit down and talk to my parents.

"Wait," Mum said, blowing hair out of her face. "Your dad's helping Colin and they'll be fine until lunchtime. Can we talk?"

I hesitated.

"I'll make a pot of coffee," she said.

I nodded and sat down at the table, brushing potato crumbs off the seat before I did, and watched Mum make the coffee.

"Are you really going to Spain?" I asked.

Mum placed a mug of coffee carefully in front of me and sat down. "That depends," she said.

"On what?"

"On you."

"I don't think I want to go to Spain," I said. "I'll come and visit of course; I won't let things get bad again like I have with Dad over the last three years. I know I should have been to see him and I've been so selfish but I just…"

"Megan, it's OK," Mum interrupted gently. "We don't expect you to come to Spain to live with us. You've no idea how happy it makes both me and your dad to see you wanting to get on with your life. We've been so worried."

"I never meant to worry anyone."

"We know you didn't, love, but there were times when I thought you'd never move on. You seemed so stuck, but this year it's felt as though you've started to wake up a little bit and since Xander appeared you've been like your old self again."

I smiled weakly. "Tell me about you and Dad," I said, not wanting to talk about Xander. "Tell me about Spain."

"You know your father and I have stayed in touch over the years?"

"Yes, but I've never really understood it," I admitted. "You were so upset when he first left."

"I was. I was devastated. But you see, Megan, it was my fault as much as your father's."

"How? It wasn't you who left."

"No, but he asked me to go to London with him. He wanted both of us to go, but I told him I didn't want you to be uprooted – you were in the middle of your A levels and…"

"I wouldn't have minded being uprooted though," I protested. "I'd have loved to live in London."

She reached across the table to take my hand. "I know, love," she said. "It was an excuse. I was the one who was scared. I've lived in York my whole life and I used your schooling as a reason not to go to London, because I was scared. When it came to the crunch I couldn't do it; I couldn't leave. But I couldn't stop your dad from going and after he left I was so angry with myself for letting my fear hold me back, so angry that I refused to talk to him."

"Until my wedding," I said, starting to put the pieces together.

"Yes, Walter and I talked a lot at your wedding."

"You knew by then that I'd be moving to London too. Did you still not want to join him then?"

"It felt as though we'd have to get to know each other again and your dad wasn't ready to sell the bookshop. I said I'd look after it for him."

"So he's been thinking of selling it for a long time then?"

"Your father has been thinking of selling the bookshop for almost as long as I've known him." Mum laughed. "It was his parents' dream, not his, but it was also his home and he's found it hard to let go." She paused and looked at me. "I think you probably understand that?"

I nodded. "But the bookshop isn't your dream either," I said. "Why did you stay so long?"

"It's a beautiful place to live in the middle of a beautiful city," she replied. "It's easy to get lost in it, to lose track of time, to hide away among the bookshelves and, for me at least, in my writing room in the eaves. I think you probably understand that too, don't you?"

"More than you could ever know," I replied. "Moving back to York was meant to be a new start, but it ended up being a good excuse to disappear from my life."

"I probably exacerbated that, didn't I? I've been overprotective of you since Joe died. I should have started to encourage you to spread your wings much sooner."

"I might not have listened, though." I paused, there was a missing part of Mum's story that I needed to get to the bottom of. "Mum, it's been nearly ten years since my wedding," I said. "Since you and Dad started talking again. Why has it taken you so long to agree to try again?"

"The timing has never been right," she said and I noticed her eyes flick away.

"What aren't you telling me?" I asked.

"I was going to go to Paris with him," she said quietly. "When he first moved there for that 'writer in residence' job. We'd only just started talking about it when Joe was first diagnosed and we wanted to support you, support both of you. We loved Joe like he was our own son, you know."

"I know," I managed, my throat burning.

"In the end I persuaded your father to go without me. It was too good an opportunity for him to turn down. Joe's prognosis had been good at the beginning and I thought I could join your dad in Paris when you were over the worst."

She passed me a tissue from the box on the kitchen table as I cried at the memory. She was right – we'd been told that a high percentage of people made a full recovery from the type of leukaemia Joe had. When he first went into remission, we all thought it was over. We never expected it to come back.

"I'm sorry, my darling," Mum said, taking my hand. "I'm sorry to bring this all back up again for you."

"I need to know," I replied. Mum had been amazing the whole time Joe was sick, both times he was sick. She'd come down to London whenever she could, filled our freezer with casseroles and lasagnes, and had been a tower of strength to both of us and to Joe's family. I never knew how she did it. And I never knew she'd given up Paris to do it. "Why didn't you tell me all this before? I can't believe you gave up Paris."

"Perhaps we should have told you. I don't know. We were both trying to do what was best, and at first I just thought I was delaying Paris. After Joe died, both your dad and I were devastated. None of us were thinking straight, and you needed me. I couldn't go to Paris then; you needed the stability of home, of the bookshop."

"I'm so sorry," I said. "I'm so sorry I haven't been able to be there for anyone else."

"You have nothing to be sorry about," Mum said. "Your dad and I just had to wait for you to find your feet in your own time. You came first."

"And now we've come full circle," I said. "And we're selling the bookshop."

"So it would seem."

"This is what you want, isn't it, Mum?" I asked. "You seemed so angry with Dad yesterday." I thought of Joe's money sitting in my account. I could still buy the bookshop if Mum didn't want to leave. She'd looked after me for so long...

"Of course it's what I want," she replied, interrupting my thoughts. "I know I was angry yesterday but that was because Walter had agreed this sale without running it past either of us. Six weeks doesn't give us much time to get our heads around everything, and I was worried about you as well. This is your home."

"You don't need to protect me anymore, Mum. I know we need to sell the bookshop; I've known it for a while. Admittedly, I didn't think it would happen so fast, but I need to learn how to live life again on my own. Like you, I've been almost too comfortable here and I haven't found any reason to leave. I even thought I might use Joe's insurance money to buy it because..." I shrugged. "I don't know. I don't really want to buy it, but some days it's hard to imagine not being here."

"I don't think you should put that money into the bookshop," Mum said, looking a little horrified. "It's for your security, not to plough into a sinking ship."

"Don't worry, I'm not going to."

I told her about the conversation I'd had over too much gin the night before, about Bella and Norm and about Missy's upcoming trip to America, about moving in with Bella and working out what I wanted to do once the bookshop was sold.

"Who is this mystery buyer, anyway?" I asked.

"Fred Bishop," she replied. "Who used to work here."

"So that's what he and Dad were talking about the other day. Dad said it was going to a developer. Since when was Fred Bishop a developer?"

"Apparently he found retirement boring and got into property development. It seems to have made him rather ruthless. He's transforming the building into two flats and a retail unit – open to the highest bidder."

"Fred Bishop is a ruthless property developer?" I was rather astounded. He'd always seemed so kind and gentle, such a lover of books.

"Well, maybe he can help you find somewhere to live. It's the least he can do in the circumstances."

"And what about a job?" I asked with a smile. "I'm probably going to need one of those too."

"I thought you were going to talk to Philomena Bloom about that."

I pulled a face. "That's what Bella and Missy said. I'm convinced she won't speak to me after all this Xander and Ruby Bell stuff but…"

"You won't know until you ask her," Mum interrupted.

"I guess not." I didn't really have any excuse not to phone Philomena. I had to do something.

"I still can't believe that Xander wrote those raunchy Ruby Bell books," Mum said. "Did you ask him what made him do it?"

"Money, I think." I knew it was a lie and so did Mum – the massive six-figure advance he had got for *Boxed* had been all over the trade press – but I wasn't going to betray any of Xander's secrets, no matter what he might think of me.

"Do you think Dot knew?" Mum asked.

"Xander says not," I replied. "I keep thinking I should call Dot and ask her how Xander is, but…"

"You haven't heard from him then?"

I shook my head.

"Give it time," she said, echoing Bella.

The week that followed was one of the longest of my life. The days seemed to drag interminably, even though the bookshop was almost constantly busy with customers needing advice and attention. My father helped as much as he could when he wasn't disappearing to have meetings with the bank or Fred Bishop, but mostly it was just Colin and me on the shop floor every day – and Colin was acting more mysteriously than ever since Dad had spoken to him about the bookshop being sold. He barely seemed able to look at me, and whenever I tried to talk to him about it or to ask him what it was he had wanted to talk to me about on the afternoon I'd found out that my father had found a buyer, he just waved me away dismissively.

On top of everything else, Trixie phoned every five minutes about the Christmas Eve party. If I ignored my mobile phone she just called the shop landline instead, which she knew I had to answer.

"I think we should have a proper dress rehearsal on Thursday," she said.

"A dress rehearsal?" I queried. "It's a party, Trixie, not a play."

"We all need to check that our gowns still fit," she went on. "And the men's outfits have arrived now so we need to check them too. If we need to do any alterations I don't want to be doing them at the last minute on Christmas Eve."

I thought of Xander's Regency outfit, his jokes about his inside leg measurement, his hand on my thigh. He still hadn't phoned and I guessed I'd never know what he looked like in breeches now.

"I suppose that makes sense," I reluctantly agreed.

"And we should set the bookshop up as we will be doing for the party," Trixie said. "With the dance floor and card tables and buffet area – just to make sure everything fits."

"Fine," I said, without enthusiasm. "A dress rehearsal on Thursday. I'll let everyone know." The last thing I felt like was a dress rehearsal for something that was meant to have been a casual party and I wished I'd never come up with the Regency Christmas idea. I knew Mum agreed. When she wasn't shut up in her writing room trying to meet a Christmas Eve deadline, she was making inedible attempt after inedible attempt at potato pudding. Plus, without Xander we were one man down for the quadrille and I wondered if I should attempt to invite Colin again. He was much shorter than Xander but perhaps we could make some alterations to the Regency costume for him to join in.

"Or you could just phone Xander and make sure he comes," Missy reminded me.

I don't know how much time I wasted looking at Xander's number on the screen of my phone and not ringing him that week, but it was a lot. So much so that it had Colin sighing and moaning that he was once again running the bookshop single-handedly.

"I'll phone him if you like," Missy said.

"Maybe I could phone Dot instead," I suggested. But I

didn't do that either. I couldn't bear it if she thought I'd been the one who'd told Xander's secret to the press. Dot would come to book club on Thursday surely, although she hadn't replied to my email about the dress rehearsal. Maybe she'd bring Xander with her.

If he was still in York.

One thing I did manage to do, in between pretending to be festive for our customers and staring at Xander's number on the screen of my phone, was call Philomena Bloom.

"Megan," she boomed when she answered. "I'd have expected to hear from you before now."

"There's been quite a lot going on," I began, intending to assure her that it wasn't me who had told Xander's secrets to the press, that I was completely discreet and fit for work in the publishing industry. But of course I never got a chance.

"So Xander's been telling me," she said and I felt myself blush as I wondered exactly what he had been telling her. "He's being quite ridiculous over all of this Ruby Bell stuff, in my opinion. I've been telling him for years the truth will out in the end. You can't keep a secret like that, especially not in this industry where everybody knows each other."

"You think it was somebody in the industry?" I asked.

"Megan, I know full well you're not the whistle-blower. I'm fairly sure it was an inside job, as it were, and I've told Xander that several times. Have you heard from him?"

"Um... no," I replied. "I haven't seen him since he..." I hesitated.

"Since he accused you of blabbing his private business to the national press? Oh he is such a hot-headed boy, almost incapable of dealing with his own emotions, especially since his mother died." Exactly as Bella and I had thought.

"His mother's death hit him hard, you know," Philomena went on. "He's never really been the same since. He'll have told you all about that, of course – she died from leukaemia like your dear husband."

"Yes, yes – he said." I was being spectacularly inarticulate, but Philomena seemed to have that effect on me. How did she know so much? I was still finding it very hard to equate this loud, blabbermouth with a woman who'd kept Xander's secret for so long. "Anyway," I went on, pulling myself together. "I didn't phone about that."

"No," she said. "You phoned to talk about your future."

"Yes, although I'm not really sure what I want to do with my future."

"You enjoyed your job as an editor?"

"I loved it, I loved working with authors and helping them create their best work. I loved shouting about books and being around people who were excited about new stories all the time, but I'm not sure if I want to go back to doing exactly what I used to do. I feel the need for something new. I'm just not sure what."

"I have a proposition for you," she said mysteriously.

"You do?"

"I'd like you to become Cuthbert."

21

"Ow, you're hurting me," I complained, as my mother was a little bit too enthusiastic with the hairbrush while putting my hair up into something that resembled a Regency style. My mother's hair was too short to do anything with, so she was wearing a bonnet. Trixie was going to tell her that women wouldn't have worn bonnets at dances but we were all mostly wearing day dresses anyway so our authenticity could only go so far.

"This is far too tight," Missy moaned, pulling at the bodice of her pale blue gown.

"We could let it out," Mum said as she stabbed at me with a few final hairpins.

"We let it out last time," Missy said. "There's nothing left to let out."

"It does look rather ravishing though," I said. With her tattoos, 1950s style makeup and green diamante glasses, Missy made the whole outfit look amazing. But again, it wasn't exactly authentic.

"You look rather good yourself," Missy said to me.

"I really don't." I was wearing a rose-pink gown, which I thought made me look washed out. I looked pale and exhausted and, standing next to Missy, I felt small and dowdy.

"You do," she insisted. "You look dainty and demure. You'll have Xander on his knees."

"We both know Xander isn't coming," I said.

"Dot will bring him," she replied. "You'll see." Dot had, at least, confirmed that she'd be here tonight in full costume, which I supposed was something. If Xander didn't come maybe I could talk to her. I wasn't sure what I wanted to ask her, though. Since my conversation with Philomena Bloom I'd moved from upset to angry when it came to my emotions around Xander. He knew, according to her, that it couldn't possibly be me who was the whistle-blower and yet he still hadn't got in touch to apologise. Did the night we'd spent together, the things we'd shared, not mean anything to him?

Perhaps it was better if he had gone back to London and we both moved on. As my father liked to remind me, there were plenty more fish in the sea. At least his choice of words was slightly more appropriate now than they'd been after Joe had died. He means well but for a poet, my father was terrible at subtlety.

"So tell me more about Philomena's proposition," Missy asked as we went downstairs to the bookshop to start getting the space ready and wait for everyone else to turn up while Mum got her latest batch of potato puddings out of the oven.

"It was quite cryptic really," I replied. "Which is fairly typical of her. She started off by saying she wanted me to be Cuthbert."

"Cuthbert?"

"As in 'Bloom & Cuthbert Literary Agents'."

"But I thought Cuthbert didn't exist," Missy said, her brow furrowed in confusion.

I laughed. "He doesn't, but he will as of January. He will be me."

"She asked you to go into partnership with her?"

"Not exactly, I mean I have no experience of being a literary agent, after all. But she wants me to work for her. She says she wants to take on someone who can go through the editing process with her newer authors. Apparently she doesn't like that bit very much and she knows how good I am at it. In return, she's going to train me up to start taking on my own authors in due course."

"Wow, that's amazing," Missy said. "Don't take this the wrong way, but why you?"

I laughed again. "Who knows? She says she liked me from the first time we spoke and that she's done lots of research into me, which is a bit scary, and I'm exactly what she needs."

"Will you have to move to London?"

"That's the best bit," I replied. "She works from home so sees no reason why I can't too. I'll have to go to London for events and some meetings but, as she pointed out, not all authors live in the south so it might be nice for my, so far mythical, clients to live nearer their agent too. So basically I get the best of both worlds – I get to go to London and stay here."

"This is amazing Megan. I'm so happy for you."

"To be honest it feels a bit too good to be true and I probably won't fully believe it's happening until I've got the contract in my hand." I paused, looking around the bookshop sadly. It was strange to think that in a few weeks' time I wouldn't be living here anymore. "Anyway, come and help me move these bookcases."

Just as we started to move the furniture, Bella, Norm and Bryn arrived, which helped matters a lot. The three of us stood around in our gowns bossing the Viking duo about until the bookshop looked exactly how I hoped Trixie would be expecting it. We'd just finished when Mum came down with her potato puddings.

"I think these are worse than the last lot," she said. "They are hard as bullets. I give up."

Admittedly they looked horrible but Norm and Bryn valiantly tried one each without complaint.

"Let's see what Trixie thinks," I said. I was quite looking forward to seeing Trixie try to defend Mum's potato puddings. "It might be that they are supposed to taste disgusting."

Trixie arrived not long after that, carrying a huge pile of what looked like suit bags and with Stan, John and Dot in tow – and my dad appeared from wherever he'd been all afternoon as well. Trixie looked around the bookshop and nodded before counting us all.

"No Xander," she said.

"No, he couldn't come tonight," Dot said quietly, and my stomach dropped. It turned out I had been hoping that he'd come after all, no matter how angry I was.

"Well that makes us one short for dancing," Trixie huffed in annoyance.

"I can sit out the quadrille," I said.

"Could Colin not come?" Trixie asked.

I shook my head. I had been going to ask him, but he'd been avoiding me all day again so I hadn't bothered.

"Well, we'll just have to manage," she sighed. She sorted through the pile of suit bags and threw one aside. I noticed the label on it simply read "X.S." and I felt another wave of anger. Trixie had gone to all this trouble and Xander couldn't even be bothered to turn up.

Trixie started to organise the men, giving them their outfits and telling them to find somewhere to change. Mum opened the office area for them to go into.

While all that was going on, Dot came up to me.

"I tried to get him to come," she said quietly. "But he wouldn't. He's..."

"Rude and arrogant," I said.

"More mortified and embarrassed, I think," she replied. "He knows it wasn't you, but..."

"Would it hurt him to pick up the phone and tell me that?"

"He wrote you this," Dot said, handing me a white envelope with my name written in dark blue ink on the front. "He's usually better at writing things down than trying to say them. He asked me not to give you this until later but I think you should read it now. If you want to, once you've read what he has to say, you should still be able to catch him at my house."

"Did you know?" I asked. "That he was Ruby Bell?"

Dot shook her head. "I had no idea. That newspaper headline was as much of a shock to me as it was to anyone. I'd never have guessed."

"Did he tell you..." I began.

"About his mother?"

I nodded.

"Yes," she said simply. Then she smiled and stepped

away, leaving me to read the note on my own. I stepped
behind one of the taller bookcases, hiding from the chaos
that the trying on of costumes seemed to have created, and
slit open the envelope with my index finger.

Megan

*For a man who can write 800 pages of drivel and
call it a book, it appears I am hopeless when it comes to
writing letters. If you could see the discarded drafts that
surround me...*

*I am no Captain Wentworth then, but I am half
agony and half hope. I am a lot of other things as well
– arrogant, rude, heartbroken, confused, embarrassed,
foolish... but most of all I am sorry. I am sorry for
so many things – for every time I've been rude or
demanding, every time I've pushed you, but most of
all I am so sorry for storming into your shop without
thinking and for accusing you of something I know you
didn't do. Once again I reacted badly to something I
couldn't control, and treated you appallingly – just as I
did at Graydon Hall.*

*Most of all I am sorry that I haven't called and that
it has taken nearly a week to write this letter. That is
unforgiveable and I have no excuse other than my own
cowardice.*

*Everything that has happened between us over the
last couple of weeks has taken me by surprise. For nearly
four years I have closed myself off from the world and
hidden myself behind a brick wall of my own making.
And then you came along and smashed the wall down.
I fell head over heels for you the night I pushed my way*

*into your bookshop and realised you were the woman
from the supermarket.*

*I told you that anyone who was worthy of you would
wait until you were ready to move on, but I don't think
either of us was prepared for what happened between
us. I have loved watching you talk about the future, I
have loved seeing you opening yourself up to start again
and I hope you still want to take those big steps into
your new life – because you deserve to shine, Megan.
You deserve to know a life full of your biggest dreams.*

*But I don't deserve you, not after what I've done. The
fact that I can't bring myself to say these things to your
face, that I can't bring myself to pick up the phone, is
enough to know that I am not worthy of you. I hate that
I have hurt you and I wish I could turn back the clock
but without that ability I just wanted to say goodbye, to
tell you that I'll be thinking of you as you step into the
beautiful life I know you're going to have, and to wish
you nothing but happiness.*

*Love, Always,
Xander*

I stared at the letter, my eyes scanning the words a
second time. His writing was big and loopy, exactly like the
signature I'd seen him write in Sharpie on the front pages
of all those copies of his book on the night of his launch.
I remembered his smile that night, the way his hair kept
falling into his eyes.

He was right when he said what had happened between
us had been unexpected. I'd spent the last few years building

a very similar wall around myself as well, but Xander hadn't smashed that wall down in the way he claimed I had. Instead, he had quietly dismantled it brick by brick, until I'd been able to talk to him, to open my heart to him. I hadn't realised it at the time but as each brick was pulled away, I had slowly begun to allow myself to fall in love with him a little bit more. I suddenly missed him so much it felt like physical pain.

As I read the words again, I felt anger as well. His letter was self-pitying, claiming he had failed me somehow, failed me so badly he couldn't show his face again. If he had really fallen 'head over heels' as he claimed and as Bella had suspected, why wasn't he here? He was right when he said that was cowardice. This letter wasn't written by the Xander whose smile lit up a room, who had sat opposite me and listened to every word I said, who had spent the night with me and made me feel confident again. This was the Xander who gave in to self-doubt, who listened to his own inner demons, who cared too much about what the world thought of him.

That Xander wasn't going to fight for us, that Xander wasn't going to sit down with me and talk this through.

And if he wouldn't, maybe I had to fight instead. Because all of those different parts of Xander made up the man I was falling in love with. A man I wanted in my life, whatever he may think I 'deserved'. I had to see him; I had to let him know how I felt.

"Megan, where are you?" Trixie was calling me from across the shop floor.

I popped my head out from behind the bookcase. "Here," I said.

"Ah yes, now come over here and tell me what you think."

I walked out a little way towards her so I could see the men in their outfits. I thought they all looked amazing, and from the way Bella and Missy were fawning over Norm and Bryn it seemed they agreed. I hadn't been able to imagine what the two Vikings would look like in breeches, stockings and tailcoats but the overall result really worked in the same way that Missy's tattoos worked with her gown. Even my father looked good, despite Mum's relentless teasing.

I looked at the couples around me – Bella and Norm, Missy and Bryn, Trixie and Stan, Dot and John, even Mum and Dad were back together. Usually in circumstances like this I ached for Joe, for him to be here with one arm slung around my shoulder, but this evening it was Xander who I missed, Xander who I wanted next to me – his hand on my thigh, his sarcastic whispers in my ear.

"Shall we start with dancing or cards?" Trixie asked me. I looked down at Xander's letter, which I was still holding, and then back up at Trixie. "Perhaps if we do the quadrille first you can watch us and tell us what it looks like. You could even record it on your phone so we can watch it back and…"

I tuned out, thinking about Xander again. I wanted to tell him he was a coward, to ask him who he thought he was, making decisions for me, that I would be the one to decide who I wanted in my life and who was worthy of me. I wanted to tell him that I wanted him in my life, that the days I'd spent with him were days when I'd felt more like myself than I had in years, that I wanted to finish whatever it was that we'd started.

"Megan, are you listening to me?" Trixie asked, poking me quite hard in the arm.

I looked at her and then down at the letter once more, and remembered that Dot had said he was still at her house, that I should still be able to catch him. Out of the corner of my eye I saw the suit bag with his initials on and got angry all over again at how Trixie had gone to all this trouble and he hadn't even bothered to turn up. I picked up the bag.

"Megan," Trixie said again.

"I'm sorry, Trixie," I replied. "I have to go."

I turned on my heel, the letter in one hand and the suit bag in the other, and ran out of the shop.

"Go where?" Trixie's voice followed me out of the bookshop. "You don't even have your coat."

Regency skirts are not conducive to running through the streets in, however much period dramas might try to tell us otherwise. I had to hold the suit bag and letter in one hand, because of course there were no pockets, and hitch up my skirts with my other hand to enable me to run. Dot's house was about a fifteen-minute walk away from the bookshop but somehow, despite the skirts, I made it in just under ten. I dropped the skirts and held on to the wall as I took some wheezy breaths. I was totally unused to such exertion and was probably beetroot red so I gave myself a minute to calm down.

The house was in almost complete darkness, which didn't bode well. Had he left already? Had he and Gus gone back to London? I felt sick and I wasn't sure if it was the running or the thought of not seeing either Xander or his dog again. I pressed my forehead against the cool brick and took a deep breath before walking up the steps to Dot's front door.

I'd only been here twice before – once to drop off some books to her when she'd had the flu and then again, just over a week ago, when Xander had cooked for me and we'd kissed on the sofa until Dot had come home from her college dinner. I took a shaky breath and knocked on the door knocker.

I was expecting to hear Gus bark but all I heard was silence. I tried again, pressing my ear to the door to see if I could hear anything. After the third knock I knew it was pointless. He wasn't here. He'd already left.

I was too late.

22

I got up early the next morning, sneaking out of the back door of the bookshop before either of my parents had emerged, to sit on my bench outside York Minster. I bundled up in as many layers as I could find as it was one of those beautifully clear, frosty mornings – blue skies and sunshine but bitterly cold.

I'd known it was going to be a morning like this as I'd walked back to the bookshop from Dot's house the night before, shivering in my gown. By the time I'd arrived back – it had taken a lot longer on the return journey – my mother and Trixie were in the middle of what appeared to be a stand-up fight about what time the shop should shut on Christmas Eve.

"Christmas Eve is our busiest day of the shopping year," Mum had said. "We're staying open as long as possible."

"What's the point?" Trixie had fired back. "You're selling the shop to a developer in January anyway."

While Mum had looked as though she was going to punch Trixie in the face for that, everybody else was ignoring what was going on and pretending to eat the potato puddings.

I'd felt exhausted and wanted everyone out of the

bookshop so I could go to bed. I'd walked up to them, standing in between them so they didn't come to fisticuffs.

"We'll close at 5.30 p.m.," I'd said.

"Megan, where on earth have you been?" Mum had interrupted. "You look terrible and you're freezing. Let me get you a jumper."

"Leave it," I'd replied. I'd wondered if they'd ever gotten around to any dancing or card playing. "We'll close the bookshop at 5.30 p.m. on Christmas Eve, so if you could all be here about 6 p.m. to help me set up that would be great. Please don't forget to bring greenery to decorate the bookshelves and whatever item of Regency food you've been allocated. I'll see you all then."

I'd turned away and walked towards the back of the bookshop, to the stairs that led up to the flat. I'd heard Bella, Missy and my parents calling my name as I went but it had been Dot who'd caught up with me and touched my arm.

"Did you talk to him?" she'd asked.

I'd shaken my head. "He wasn't there. He must have left already."

"Leave Xander to me," she'd said. "And I'll make sure he gets this too." She'd prised the suit bag out of my hands. "Now go and get some sleep."

I hadn't slept well, of course, but instead of tossing and turning and worrying about what had happened with Xander and feeling guilty over my memories of Joe, I'd got out of bed, turned on my laptop and started to edit the new Ruby Bell manuscript. I hadn't really known if I was doing it to distract myself from my overly anxious mind or to prove to either myself or Xander that I knew what I was doing, but as soon as I'd started I was engrossed. The flicker of who I used to be had burst into flame once again, just as it had done when I'd first suggested doing this. I'd found myself full of ideas and inspiration on how to improve the manuscript, which really wasn't as bad as Xander had made out. By the time I'd finally fallen asleep I'd been ready to send him an email with my initial thoughts. If that was the way I would need to reach out to him, then so be it. I wasn't going to let him make all my decisions for me.

I'd woken early though, my brain a mess of anxiety, worry and guilt. So I'd taken myself to my bench, armed with a copy of *Persuasion* so I could read Fred Wentworth's letter to Anne Elliot, with Xander's letter tucked into the pages.

"Hello," a voice interrupted me after a few minutes. A pair of expensively clad feet appeared in front of me, alongside a sausage dog in a bright blue polo neck jumper. I let my gaze drift upwards, following the line of his beautifully cut wool coat until my eyes locked on his. My stomach flipped over. He hadn't gone after all.

"Hi," I said. "I thought you'd left."

"We got as far as the M62 junction before I realised what a coward I was being and turned back. When I arrived at Dot's she was waiting for me, ready to give me a piece of her mind and a Regency outfit." He rubbed his fingers over his forehead. "I was hoping I'd find you here."

We'd talked about the bench on the night he'd cooked dinner for me. I'd told him why I sat there, how it was the place I'd first met Joe, what it meant to me.

"I know it sounds ridiculous," I'd said.

He'd looked at me in that disarming way he had. "It's

not ridiculous," he'd said. "Joe will always be part of your life and there'll always be places you want to go to be alone and remember him. I'm just sorry I interrupted you that morning and was so rude about your book."

He was looking at me again now in that same disarming way. "How could I walk away from you, Megan?" he said. "I should never have left it so long."

"Do you want to sit down?" I asked.

He sat next to me, not quite touching, and picked Gus up to sit in his lap.

"Dot said you came looking for me last night," he said.

"I read your letter. I…" I hesitated. "It's probably just as well you weren't there. I was so angry with you I'd probably have said something I'd regret."

"There's nothing you could have said that I don't deserve," he said, sounding dangerously close to self-pitying again.

"This isn't about what you do and don't deserve. You made so many assumptions in that letter, telling me what was best for me, that I didn't deserve you. But it's up to me to decide who I have in my life."

He didn't say anything; he just sat and scratched the spot between Gus's ears.

"I trusted you," I went on. "I told you things I'd never talked about with anyone else. I slept with you; the only person other than my husband I've…" I stopped, took a breath, lowered my voice. "I rather stupidly thought that meant something, but you couldn't even come and talk to me when things got tough, you just accused me of something I didn't do and walked away from me because you thought that was easier than fighting for us. How could you do that? Why couldn't you talk to me like we talked at Graydon Hall?"

He looked up then, those deep dark eyes locking on mine again. "It did mean something," he said quietly. "It meant so much to me, but I find it really hard to articulate things sometimes; it's easier to write them down."

"But this is me, Xander. We've talked about everything over the last couple of weeks."

"I know," he said and he closed his eyes for a moment as though he was summoning up the courage to say something or do something. "Walking away from you in the bookshop was one of the stupidest things I've ever done. And you were right, it wasn't about Ruby Bell at all, not really. I was scared by how fast things were moving, by how much I cared about you. I've kept people at a distance for so long in an attempt to stop them from getting to know me, but you... I couldn't keep away from you."

"Why?" I asked.

"Because you're beautiful and funny and clever and—"

"No," I interrupted, even though it was nice to hear. "I meant why do you keep people at a distance?" I already thought I knew the answer though.

"When Mum died everything felt as though it was spiralling out of control," he said quietly. "I needed a way of getting some control back in my life, a way of making sure I never had to feel that kind of pain again."

I could imagine Bella hearing this and doing some sort of triumphant dance about how she was right all the time, while fist bumping the air.

"But you don't need to push me away, do you?" I asked.

"It becomes a kind of habit," he said. "Sometimes I don't realise I'm doing it."

I thought about how I'd tried to hide myself away after Joe died, how I'd allowed the bookshop to become my entire world, how I hadn't even left York until Xander came along and how I still felt guilty about the day Joe died, the promise I'd made to him to never leave him alone, the promise I'd broken. I understood the need to protect yourself and how it could quickly become habit, until you didn't even realise you were doing it.

"I get that," I said softly. "I really do. But I've come to the conclusion that trying to protect yourself like that doesn't really work."

"I know," he replied. "And for the record, I also know it wasn't you who went to the papers about the Ruby Bell thing."

"Who was it?" I asked.

He shrugged. "No idea. Philomena thinks it was a publishing insider but I'm not sure. She says it was bound to get out in the end so maybe it's just inevitable. Maybe you were right and it's a disgruntled employee from my publishers. I tried to control who knew, but it was bound to have got out. I'd never really thought about it like that."

It was when he said the words 'disgruntled employee' that I realised. I couldn't believe I hadn't worked it out before. There had been someone else in the shop that morning when Xander and I had talked about him being Ruby Bell, someone else whose footsteps I could have heard in the hallway. But now wasn't the right time to bring that up.

"I would never betray my friends' confidences," I said quietly.

"Are we still friends?" he asked.

"I thought we were more than that."

I watched him take a slow, shaky breath. "I have absolutely no idea what I'm doing, Megan," he said. "I've never dated anyone in my life. I married my childhood sweetheart and when she left I just shut myself off from the world. The night I spent with you was the first time for me as well…"

A bubble of laughter welled up inside me out of nowhere and exploded into the cold morning air.

"I know it's a sad and tragic story," he said. "But there's no need to laugh." He sounded annoyed but I watched the corner of his mouth twitch as though underneath the hurt and the pain he was amused at himself, at this ridiculous situation.

"Xander, do you think I have any idea what I'm doing either? I met Joe in my first term of university, and we got married the summer after we graduated. There has never been anyone else until now."

I shifted along the bench a little bit, closing the gap between us, and stroked Gus's head. Xander placed his hand on top of mine, squeezing my fingers.

"You were the one who asked me for coffee," I said softly. "The one who asked me to lunch…"

"I know," he replied, his voice barely more than a whisper and his eyes on our intertwined hands. "I never expected…" He paused, still not looking up. "I never expected to fall for you so hard after so many years of being alone and I was so scared of hurting you. And then I did hurt you."

He had hurt me, it was true. But I understood the unexpectedness of what was happening between us. I understood how overwhelming that was, how uncertain. In a world that we both knew was full of endless uncertainties.

"Xander, the fact that you came back and you're sitting here on this bench in the freezing cold next to me has to mean something, as does the fact that I'm still here despite being so angry with you. You've told me how you feel and honestly, while it's taken me completely by surprise as well, I feel the same. I don't want either of us to walk away from this."

He turned around on the bench to face me. He lifted his hand, the one that wasn't wrapped up in mine, and ran his thumb over my cheekbone. Gus shifted position in his lap as my breath hitched in my throat.

"I'm bloody terrified of screwing this up," he said.

"You won't…"

"You don't know that. Some days it feels like I screw everything up and I couldn't bear the thought of hurting you again – not after everything you've been through."

"I'm not some delicate little flower," I said, trying to keep the irritation from my voice. Why was everyone so invested in protecting me from unknown evils? "I know that this might not work out." I paused, my eyes dropping to his lips and my mouth going dry. "But I also know that moving on with my life means opening myself up to the bad as well as the good."

He moved his head then, just a little closer to me, and I thought for a moment that he was going to kiss me, before he pulled away.

"Megan, I don't want—"

"It's OK," I interrupted, my voice unnaturally bright. "I get it…"

"No," he said. "Let me finish. I don't want to walk away from this either. I realised that as soon as I got to the motorway last night. It's the reason I'm here. But it doesn't make it any easier."

Neither of us said anything for a moment. We seemed to have reached an impasse, a place where we both knew how we felt but had no idea what to do with those feelings.

And then I remembered the other thing Bella had said to me.

"You told me that we could take this at my pace," I said. "That you would take my lead. But I think that perhaps you need the same thing and that what we actually need to do is take each other's lead, to give each other the space we need, to work this out together."

He exhaled and slowly closed his eyes. I waited, my hand still wrapped up in his.

And then he smiled at me. "That's exactly what I need," he said and I could sense the relief in his words.

"Then that's what we'll do," I said, leaning my head on his shoulder. It felt like a breakthrough. And it felt like enough. For now at least.

"Philomena told me your father has sold the bookshop," he said. "That was quick."

"Yeah and don't ask me how I feel about it because I honestly don't know. I knew it was going to happen but I hadn't thought it would be so fast! Part of me feels as though everything I've ever known is being taken away from me and another part of me feels that it's a push in the right direction." I paused. "I thought about trying to buy it myself but…"

"You heart wasn't in it," he interrupted, squeezing my hand again.

"Missy and Bella talked me out of it, not that I needed much persuading." I knew it was the right decision. I knew I had to walk away from the bookshop to be able to start again. "How did Philomena know about it anyway?"

"I assumed you'd told her."

"No, she already knew when I called her."

He laughed. "She knows everything," he said. "I bet she knows who went to the press about Ruby Bell too, but she'll never let on."

I bet she doesn't know, I thought to myself.

"She offered me a job," I said.

"Will you take it, do you think?"

"We've got a lot to talk through and I won't believe it until I've got the contract in my hand," I replied. "But in theory, yes, absolutely."

"Will you move back to London?" he asked.

"I don't know. She's given me the option to stay in York and for now that's what I'll do, except when I'm needed in London of course. I know that means we'll be living in different cities but…"

He smiled. "York and London aren't that far apart," he said. "And I like it up here – you know that. I like the food and the architecture…" He paused. "And there are other attractions that keep me coming back."

And then he did kiss me, gently and carefully, and it was all I needed. We could work the rest out.

Gus barked and Xander pulled away from me.

"I started editing your manuscript last night," I said, changing the subject.

He looked surprised by that. "You did? Even when you were so angry with me?"

"I couldn't sleep," I said. "You know it's really not as bad as you told me it was. You need to pad out the subplot a bit more and move the big reveal a bit later. Anyway, if you want me to email you my thoughts I can."

"I..." He shook his head. "I can't believe you did that for me after everything."

"I enjoyed it actually. I told you that you'd be doing me a favour by letting me get my hands on it."

He took my hand again, raising it to his lips, pressing a kiss to it.

"I've got some bad news, I'm afraid," he said.

"What?" I didn't want bad news, not now. I felt as though we'd come so far this morning.

He looked away from me. "I do have to go back to London today," he said.

"You're leaving?" I felt anger rising up inside me again, just as it had done the night before when I'd read his letter, and I tried to pull my hand away from his but he held on, refusing to let me go. I didn't want him to go anywhere.

"I'm not walking away," he said.

"It sure as hell feels like it."

"I need to see my brother tomorrow," he said. "I made the stupid mistake of telling my nephews that I was coming to London this weekend and they're expecting me and..." He trailed off.

"What?"

"Philomena has arranged this interview for Monday with the *Observer*. They want it to be face-to-face and I hate face-to-face interviews."

I felt myself soften a little, my features relaxing into a smile. "Is there anything you don't hate about being a famous author?"

"I don't hate the writing part," he said quietly. "But I'm not famous, Megan, I'm just ordinary. And I want to be ordinary with you."

He let go of my hand and I felt his fingers under my chin as he tilted my head towards him.

"I'm not walking away," he repeated, his eyes locked on mine.

I don't know how long we sat there staring at each other but eventually he stretched and placed Gus gently on the floor. Standing up, he turned to me, offering me his hand. I took it and stood next to him.

"Thank you," he said.

"What for?"

"For listening, for understanding."

It was my turn to look away from him then. I couldn't hold his gaze anymore; it was too intense.

"I'll be back for the Christmas Eve party," he said. I'd almost forgotten about Christmas Eve. I stepped a little closer to him.

"You will?"

"I will, I promise."

I felt Xander's hand on my waist, drawing me close. He bent to kiss me gently on my temple. "I'll call you," he whispered into my hair.

I knew this wasn't going to be easy. Easy would be him walking away. Easy would be me buying the bookshop from Dad and staying in the same routine until I went bankrupt.

To live a life that is full of all the things we want, we

sometimes have to take risks. We have to step out of our comfort zones. We have to do the hard things.

After he'd left I took his letter out of my copy of *Persuasion* and read it one last time before tearing it in half and putting it in the bin. I knew how he felt now and I knew how I felt. I didn't need to read it again.

I had no idea how this would work out, but it was time for that leap of faith everyone else was taking.

23

"Colin, can you come into the office?" I asked later that morning.

He looked up at me. "Don't you need me to stay on the shop floor?" he asked.

"Dad will be OK for a few minutes on his own," I replied. My father had been working on the shop floor almost full-time all week. He said it was his last chance to relive his youth. I didn't remind him that it was a life he'd once claimed was too small for him. I was a bit exhausted from trying to work out the motivations of the men in my life, and Colin was no exception.

The office was already almost bare. Missy had collected most of her things and was going to do the winding-up procedures for us from home. I'd started packing up paperwork into boxes, which I moved out of the way so Colin could sit on the wing-back chair.

"Take a seat," I said, gesturing to the space I'd cleared.

He didn't say anything as he sat, and I rubbed a hand across my face. I didn't even know how to begin this conversation. I had no evidence, only a feeling, and if he denied it he could probably take me to a tribunal or something.

"Colin," I began.

"Is this about Xander Stone?" he asked.

"Sort of."

"And Ruby Bell?"

A wave of relief washed over me. Was he actually going to make this easy for me? It could only have been Colin, and he must have overheard Xander and me talking that day.

"I think you'd better tell me everything," I said.

He sighed and sank back in the chair. He looked very young all of a sudden. I think we all forgot sometimes that he was only twenty-two – because of the way he dressed he seemed so much older.

"I'd overheard your mum and dad talking about selling the shop," he began. "I know what you're going to say but I don't think any of you realise how much I overhear in this place. None of you notice me. Sometimes it feels like I don't exist."

He was right of course – we had always excluded him. We always said that he didn't try to be included, but that wasn't an excuse for us not to try.

"Anyway, I was furious that you hadn't said anything to me," he went on. "It was just another thing everybody knew about except me and I'd had enough, so I came upstairs to talk to you about it."

"But you knew I was with Xander."

"You're always with someone, Megan," he said. "You're either with someone or too busy to talk or your mum tells us not to bother you."

"Mum does that?"

"Yeah, she's kind of overprotective of you, isn't she?"

I nodded. After our conversation last week I'd begun to realise that both my parents had been a little overprotective for a while.

"You've been through a lot. It's no surprise she's worried about you."

"She's still worried about me?" I asked.

"Perhaps she always will be," Colin said, with wisdom beyond his years. He was right about everything he'd said.

"Anyway," I said. "You came upstairs to talk to me and I'm guessing you overheard Xander and me talking about him writing as Ruby Bell."

"It took me a while to work out what you were saying, but when I realised it was a bit of a shock and I didn't really know what to do. I could hardly come in then because you'd have known I heard, so I just sort of froze and then it went silent and I thought that maybe he was kissing you so I went back downstairs."

I nodded. That must have been when I heard him, just as Xander was going to kiss me.

"What made you go to the papers though, Colin?" I asked.

"I was just so angry with you both," he said.

"I can understand you being angry with me. I've been very self-absorbed over the last few years and that's not been fair on anyone. I guess I've been really hard to work for, but I don't understand why you were angry with Xander."

Colin looked away. "It's stupid really, but I felt as though he'd let me down. He's one of the greatest writers I've ever read – *Boxed* totally changed my life and made me realise that ordinary people could do extraordinary things, but then he was this romance writer as well and he went to your book group and danced your Regency dances."

"But you just said yourself that Xander is ordinary. He was just having fun."

"It didn't feel like that to me though. It felt like another slap in the face on top of you all ignoring me and not telling me what was going on." He paused. "They always say you shouldn't meet your heroes."

We had all treated him badly, every single one of us – me, Mum, Missy, even Dad to an extent. We'd taken him for granted, assumed he'd run the bookshop and cover shifts at the last minute, never invited him to book group or on outings. It was no wonder he'd had enough of us all. It was no wonder he was so angry. He never spoke about his life outside of the bookshop and as far as I knew none of us had ever asked. I wondered if he was lonely.

"I tried to talk to you again later that day," Colin continued. "After Xander had gone, but you didn't have time and I was so furious that I..." He broke off, clearly embarrassed by what he'd done. "I know someone who's a journalist so I phoned her up. I wasn't expecting it to make the front page." He put his head in his hands. "I'm so sorry, Megan, I've been a complete idiot. I did try to talk to you after Xander brought the paper in but..."

"I ignored you again, didn't I?" I sighed. "We're both at fault here, Colin. I'm sorry that I've ignored you when everything in the bookshop is so turbulent. You probably knew things weren't going very well financially too, didn't you?"

He nodded. "I'm surprised you kept me on this long," he

said. "And I don't mean that in a 'poor me' sense at all. I'm just surprised you could afford to pay me. But I'll go now – that's probably best."

"What do you mean?"

"Well, you won't want me working here after this."

"Colin, the shop is closing forever in a few weeks. I'd like you to stay until the end – if you'd like to."

"Really?" His eyes widened in surprise.

"And I'd like you to come to the Christmas Eve party too," I said.

He hesitated. "OK," he said. "But I really don't want to wear Regency costume or dance."

I held up my hands. "Fair enough," I said. "And if I were you, I'd avoid the potato pudding too."

He smiled a little at that.

"Colin," I said, as he started to leave. "You know I'm going to have to tell Xander, don't you?"

He nodded. "What do you think he'll do?"

"I honestly don't know, but I'll do my best to try to let the whole thing fizzle out, OK?"

Colin's smile widened. "Thanks, Megan," he said. "I do appreciate it."

"It's OK. I'm sorry you felt so left out of everything over the last few months."

He hesitated at the door of the office as though he'd just thought of something. "Is Xander coming on Christmas Eve?" he asked.

"He is, yes but I'll make sure he doesn't try to challenge you to a fight or whatever ex-boxers do."

"I can't really imagine Xander as a boxer, can you?"

I laughed. "He was welterweight apparently."

Colin's brow crinkled. "I don't know what that means."

"No, neither do I."

After Colin had left, I texted Xander.

I know who your whistle-blower is, I typed. And then, before I lost my nerve, I scrolled through my contacts list and dialled a number I should have dialled a lot more often.

"Hi, Christine," I said when Joe's mum answered. "How are you?"

"Megan, how lovely to hear from you!"

"I'm so sorry that I haven't called in such a long time."

"Oh that's all right, love," Christine replied. "We know you're busy in the shop this time of year. I was just saying that to Neil the other day. He isn't here right now, I'm afraid."

"That's OK," I said. "But I do have some news."

"You've met someone, haven't you, love?"

I was taken aback a little. That hadn't been the main reason I'd been calling, although I had been intending to tell Christine about Xander.

"Um... well... yes. Sort of," I replied.

"Well it's about time," she said, and I could hear the genuine happiness in her voice. "Everybody needs a somebody."

"It's hard," I said. "And a bit complicated, and I just keep thinking about Joe."

"It's bound to be hard. It's a big step for you. But you know it's what Joe would have wanted – just for you to be happy."

"I know."

"As long as the man concerned understands."

"Oh, he does." And I knew it was true. I knew Xander understood that Joe would always be part of my life.

"So," Christine went on. "Who is he? Where did you meet him?"

"I met him here in the bookshop actually," I said. "Have you heard of the novelist Xander Stone?"

"Oh my goodness yes, of course," she exclaimed. "And it turns out he writes as Ruby Bell too. I love those Ruby Bell novels, although I read them on my e-reader so people can't see I'm reading dirty books!" She laughed at her own joke. I'd always loved Joe's mum's sense of humour and she'd always been on my side, even when his dad took offence that I didn't change my name after the wedding.

"Ah, you saw the story about Ruby Bell in the papers then?" I asked, and gave her an abridged version of everything that had happened.

"Well, you have been busy," she said. "Neil will never believe it when I tell him. I hope it all works out for the two of you. You deserve some happiness, Megan, you really do."

I squeezed my eyes together to stop myself from crying. I could have another relationship, meet another man, maybe even one day get married again. But Christine and Neil would never have another son. Joe had been their only child and I'd never been able to imagine how they lived with their sadness.

"Thank you, Christine," I said. Her blessing meant everything to me. "Although that wasn't actually the main reason I called."

"No? What else have you got going on, Megan?"

"My dad came home a couple of weeks ago. He's selling the bookshop, and he and Mum are going to live in Spain."

Even Christine was silent for a few moments after that.

"Oh, Megan," she said eventually. "But the bookshop is your home. What will you do?"

"I'm moving in with my friend until I find a place of my own. I think it's time I stood on my own two feet for a while, don't you?"

"Yes, yes I do," Christine replied. "But what made your dad suddenly decide to sell the shop?"

"It wasn't as sudden as it seems," I said. "The shop hasn't been doing very well for a long time and I think Dad wanted to release the capital he had in the building. It's the right thing to do but we all thought it would take months and months to sell so the short time-frame is a bit of a shock."

"And your mum's going to Spain with him? That's a turn-up."

"I know, it was a bit of a shock for me too." I paused. "They asked me to go with them, you know."

"But you prefer the weather in Yorkshire." Christine chuckled.

"This is my home," I said. I knew Joe's parents had always been a bit sad when I'd moved away from London, even though they understood why I needed to. "I know this is where I want to be and I might have a job that means I can stay here too." I told her about Xander's agent and the possibility of working with her. "But I'll definitely be in London a lot more than I used to, so hopefully we'll be able to see more of each other too."

"That would be lovely. And your young man is in London too, no doubt," she said.

"Yes," I said, unable to stop myself smiling. "He is."

Speaking to Christine had made me feel more settled,

surer of my recent decisions. I had always been so grateful to her and to Neil for understanding that I needed my own space after Joe died and I was equally grateful now for her reaction to what I'd told her. But talking to Christine had also made me think about Joe, about how much I still missed him and how much I probably always would. I spent the afternoon in the bookshop, busy with customers and helping choose Christmas presents and stocking fillers while listening to the awful Christmas music Dad insisted on playing, but Joe was there with me all afternoon, just out of reach, and when we closed the bookshop I knew I needed to end the day in the same place in which I'd begun it.

We had scattered Joe's ashes in the park behind his parents' house in south London, the park he'd loved as a child and played football in as a teenager. We didn't get permission to do it because we knew that permission would be denied, so Neil, Christine and I had gone out in the middle of the night to let Joe rest in one of his favourite places.

I knew that both of Joe's parents would sit in the park to be with him but I had never been able to feel close to him there, because it wasn't a place where I had memories of him. His park and football-playing days had been long over when I met him. The place where I felt closest to Joe was the bench near York Minster.

I sat down and curled my legs underneath me, snuggling deeper into my winter coat. I closed my eyes and remembered the first day we'd met, the sensation of the book in my hands, the way Joe's smile had made me feel. I remembered our wedding day, an almost unbearably hot August afternoon, the makeup melting off my face and the photographer who wanted every photograph to be perfect. And I remembered Xander sitting here on the morning I was reading *The Devil in Winter*, not knowing the importance of the bench, both of us already attracted to each other but too afraid to admit it.

The last three and a half years had been the hardest of my life, but I knew now that life wasn't meant to be easy. The hard things help us to change and to grow; they help us to move forward and to become better, stronger versions of ourselves. Eventually anyway. All things take time, and usually a lot more time than you expect.

Human beings have grown impatient, wanting instant gratification – social media likes and next-day delivery. But the really hard things in life take time to get over and the really good things require patience to achieve. I'd come so far in the last three years by being quiet, being patient, wrapping myself up in the bookshop and the friends I'd made through it.

But now it was time to spread my wings and I was excited.

"Be brave, Meg," Joe had told me on my first day as an intern at Rogers & Hudson. This evening as I sat on our bench and remembered everything we'd been through together and everything I'd been through without him, I could hear his voice as though he was by my side.

Be brave, Meg.

24

Xander called early the next morning as I was opening the shop. I didn't want to answer in front of Dad and Colin, so I let it ring out and shut myself in the office half an hour later to call him back.

"Colin?" he said when I told him who had gone to the press about Ruby Bell. "The student who works for you?"

"Yeah, he…" I paused, wondering how much to tell Xander. "It was him I heard on the landing. He'd come up to talk to me about something else and he overheard. He was trying to get back at *me* by going to the papers though, not you. He's a big fan of yours and is terrified you're going to hit him." Xander didn't need to know that Colin had been disappointed in his writing hero.

"I try not to hit anything except punchbags these days," Xander said. I could hear the smile in his voice and felt relieved. I had thought he'd be angry when he found out that Colin was his whistle-blower. "You can assure him I won't hit him on Christmas Eve."

My stomach flipped over at the thought of seeing him again. "How's your quadrille practice going?"

"I think I've forgotten everything I've learned," he said, but he probably hadn't. "Will you dance with me anyway?"

"Well I'll have to check my dance card." I smiled. "But I should think I could fit you in."

He didn't say anything for a moment and I heard him take a breath. "I don't just want to dance with you," he said. "I want to talk. I want to say the things I should have said last week and I don't want to say them in an email or over the phone."

"I want to see you too," I said.

"My brother tells me I've been a bloody fool over all this. He says I should have cancelled on my nephews and told the *Observer* I'd do the interview over the phone. He says I should have stayed with you."

"Your brother is quite wise, isn't he?"

"Don't tell him I said this, what with him being younger and everything, but yes. He really is. I should have stayed and I'm sorry."

"It's OK, Xander," I said. "We'll see each other in a couple of days."

"You know, the people I care about call me Alex."

I felt something come undone inside me then and I didn't know what to say.

"Dot doesn't call you Alex," I managed.

"She does sometimes."

"But you don't look like an Alex."

He laughed. "Well, it's up to you." he said. "As long as I get to see you soon, you can call me whatever you want."

It took me a few minutes to pull myself together after the call – talking to Xander (he really didn't look like an Alex) had made me feel like a teenager again. We both knew there were no certainties, but we both wanted to try to make this work and that was the leap of faith I'd been looking for.

★

We shut at 5.30 p.m. on Christmas Eve, just as I'd promised Trixie we would. Mum complained quite a lot about it all afternoon and it took some persuading to get the last customers to pay for their purchases and leave, but we managed it, and by 5.32 p.m. Missy was in the office cashing up and Dad was helping me move the bookcases to clear the space for the card tables and dance floor.

"This was a great idea of yours," Dad said. "I never saw myself as someone who dressed up and pretended they lived in the past, but now I've done it I can see the appeal."

"When Trixie first got us into this last summer, to go the Jane Austen festival in Bath, I wasn't sure about it either, but it's actually a lot of fun. I just hope other people will think so."

"Not everyone's dressing up though, are they?" Dad asked.

"No, I put on the invitations that Regency dress was optional so I don't expect many people will do. I'll have to make sure Trixie doesn't insult anyone who does and has the details wrong!"

"She's quite a force of nature, that one!"

"I know and she totally takes over everything but, to be fair, I'd never have got any of this off the ground without her. She's worked so hard to make this party happen. I'd never have been able to do it on my own."

"Shame about your mother's potato puddings," Dad said. Mum had kept at it but the recipe hadn't improved. The last batch had come out of the oven with a blackened crust. "None of us in this family are very good at cooking."

"I wouldn't hold on to much hope for any of the other Regency food either," I said. "Everyone's been having problems making it edible."

"Great," Dad said, without enthusiasm.

"Don't worry, I've asked the tearoom to do some back-up catering."

"Thank God for that."

As if on cue, Ben from the tearoom pushed the door open and came into the shop carrying several platters of sandwiches and cakes.

"Hi, Megan, Ellie sent me down with these," he said. "Where do you want them?"

I directed him to the buffet table that we'd set up. "Great," he said. "There's a few more loads to go."

"I'll give you a hand," Dad said. "You go and get ready, Megan love."

They disappeared out of the door together and I went upstairs to join Mum and Missy.

"Put your dress on and I'll do your hair," Mum said.

"Please try not to hurt me today," I replied as Missy poured me a glass of champagne.

"Have you heard from Xander?" Missy asked.

The people I care about call me Alex. I still couldn't imagine calling him Alex, but did that mean he cared about me? I hadn't heard from him since he'd phoned on Saturday morning.

"Not since Saturday, but he said he'd be here," I replied. I had no reason to think he wasn't on his way but the nerves were taking over and I wouldn't believe he was coming until I saw him in the bookshop. My stomach had been in knots all day and I'd hardly been able to eat a thing.

"Is he wearing Regency dress? He's going to look hot as hell in breeches."

"Missy." I laughed. "Can you just not?"

"Sorry." She giggled. "But you know it's true."

"All the boys look pretty good in their Regency outfits, I think," Mum said, doing up the tiny buttons at the back of my gown. "I thought it would all be a bit bizarre you know, especially your father, but I've been pleasantly surprised."

"I think we all have," Missy said. "Who knew Bryn and Norm would look good in tailcoats?"

"Who knew they made tailcoats in their size?" I replied.

When we went back downstairs the bookshop was in a state of transformation. The Die-Hards and their partners had arrived in full costume and they had all remembered to bring greenery with them, which they were laying out along the bookshelves and display cabinets. Most of them had brought various sorts of ivy but Dot had arrived wearing protective gloves and carrying a huge bunch of holly.

"It's from my garden," she said. "But it's very prickly, so please be careful."

I tried not to notice that Xander wasn't here yet and I still hadn't heard from him. "Everything looks wonderful," I said. "Thank you so much."

"Traditionally," Trixie said. "It was the mantelpieces that were decorated in each room, but I think bookshelves work just as well."

"They really do."

"And they kept the greenery inside until twelfth night,

but I suspect you'll need to take it down when you reopen on Boxing Day."

"Sadly yes," I replied. "I don't think Dot's holly will pass any sort of health and safety inspection."

"I've got mistletoe," Bella announced, waving a big bag of the stuff in my face. "For kissing under," she went on, as though we had no idea what mistletoe was for. "I'm going to get Norm to put it up everywhere."

"Do you have to?" I asked.

"Of course I have to," she squealed. "Norm and I don't need any help on the kissing front of course, but some people—" and at this point she poked me hard in the ribs "—need a little bit of a kickstart."

Missy walked over to see what Bella had in the bag. "Oooh mistletoe," she said.

"For kissing under," Bella replied and they both made kissing faces at me.

"For God's sake, stop it," I hissed.

Missy looked around. "Where is Xander anyway?"

"He's not here yet," I replied, trying to keep my face and voice as neutral as possible, but by this point I was a mess of anxiety. What if he didn't come? What if, after everything, this didn't work?

"He's on his way," Dot confirmed, squeezing my arm. Clearly my attempt at neutrality wasn't working. "And he's bringing someone."

My stomach sank. "What sort of someone?" I asked, all attempts at neutrality out of the window.

"You'll see," Dot said. "Brace yourself."

"Oooh, a secret wife." Missy giggled. How much

champagne had she had? "Oh sorry, Megan, I didn't mean... He's actually got one of those, hasn't he?"

"Ex-wife," I said. "Keep your voice down."

"Stop worrying, Megan," Dot said. "It's nothing like that. He'll be here soon; the traffic was bad – that's all."

I didn't have a lot of time to think about it because the guests started to arrive. Mum and Dad were in charge of food and drink and I heard Dad explaining that the Regency food was more of an experiment and the real party food was on the other buffet table and supplied by people who could actually cook. None of us had had any success with Trixie's recipes and the food sat on the table looking greasy and forlorn.

"I had to use lard to make these pasties," Bella said, picking one up and looking at it in disgust. "I didn't even know you could still buy lard."

The guests were a mix of suppliers, book reviewers and bloggers, local writers and regular customers – and a surprising number of them had done their best to wear Regency dress, although quite a lot of it looked more Victorian. Once everyone had arrived (everyone but Xander, who was still missing) Trixie took over.

"Good evening, ladies and gentlemen," she said. "And welcome to our Regency Christmas Eve." She went on to talk about various Regency traditions, which included pouring scorn on the Christmas tree and trying to force people to eat the disgusting lardy food. ("Avoid the potato puddings," Dad called out.) She showed everyone the card tables and encouraged them to all have a game of whist or pontoon. "And later on there will be a demonstration of

Regency dancing." I glanced at the door again at that point. I wouldn't be dancing at all if Xander didn't show up soon.

"He'll be here," Dot whispered in my ear.

Everyone started to settle into the party spirit. Quite a few people were playing cards – I ignored the fact they were clearly playing for money – and others were already on the dance floor pretending to be in a Jane Austen adaptation. Bella, Missy, Norm and Bryn were trying to organise an unofficial quadrille while Dad appeared to be showing how inedible the potato pudding was by bouncing it on the floor.

I looked around me at the bookshop I'd dedicated the last three years of my life to, and felt a wave of sadness. It didn't seem real to me that in just a few weeks the shop would be stripped bare, the sage green bookshelves empty and door locked for the last time. I'd known this place for my whole life – it had been the home I'd come to as a newborn baby straight from the hospital, the place where I'd laughed with friends and cried over scraped knees and teenage fallings-out, where I'd studied for my GCSEs and A levels. It was the place where I'd first met Missy and Bella, where we'd hosted countless Die-Hard Romantic Book Clubs and, while it might not be the place where I'd first set eyes on him, it was the place where I'd first got to know Xander, where we'd first tentatively admitted how we felt.

I was ready to step into the next phase of my life. But I was going to miss the bookshop with every ounce of my being.

I was snapped out of my memories by the bookshop door bursting open.

"Darlings we're here. So sorry we're late!" boomed a voice. Philomena Bloom had arrived, dressed in what can only be described as a peculiar steampunk outfit that included top hat, goggles and stripy tights. It was as far removed from Regency as it was possible to get while still wearing a corset. As far as I was aware she hadn't been invited. I presumed that she'd just invited herself.

"They're here," I heard Dot say next to me, but I wasn't looking at Philomena anymore because behind her, dressed in tailcoat and breeches and looking even more gorgeous than I thought possible, was Xander. His face was pale and grim-looking and he was laden down with three huge tote bags, which must be Philomena's.

But then he saw me, his eyes locked on mine, and he smiled that smile that lit up the whole room.

25

"Hello," he said with a little Regency-style bow. He was suddenly in front of me, tote bags gone, and it felt as though we were the only people in the room.

"Hi," I replied as he took my hand and pressed a kiss to my knuckles. "No Gus tonight."

"He had other plans, I'm afraid."

"I didn't think you were coming. I thought perhaps you'd changed your mind."

"I wouldn't miss the chance to dance with you, Ms Taylor."

"You don't have to act Regency all night you know," I said with a smile. "Although can I just say you look magnificent dressed like that."

"Hmmm," he replied doubtfully. "It's not the most comfortable outfit I've ever worn. But this gown..." He looked at me and smiled again, his eyes dropping momentarily to my chest.

"Also not that comfortable," I said. "Are you OK? You didn't look great when you arrived."

"Sorry, we were stuck in traffic and I've been in the car with Philomena for the last two and a half hours. It's a bit much." He was still holding my hand and I didn't ever want him to let go. "Is there somewhere we can go?" he said. "Somewhere quiet."

I was about to tell him to go to the office and I'd follow him in a minute when I realised that most of the Die-Hards were gathered around us, staring.

"What?" I asked, trying to signal at them to go away.

As one, Missy, Bella, Dot and my mother all pointed up. Xander and I followed their fingers with our eyes. We were standing under a huge bunch of mistletoe. I felt my stomach contract and my cheeks heat.

"Well, Ms Taylor," Xander said. "There's only one thing for it."

His arm snaked around my waist and he pulled me towards him, pressing me against his body. He ducked his head, that lock of dark hair falling across his forehead as his lips brushed against mine, gently taking my bottom lip between his. Every nerve ending in my body leaped to attention and I almost forgot anyone else was there as my arms wrapped around his neck, pulling him closer, his tongue against mine – gently at first and then harder as my fingers reached up into his hair. When he stopped everyone around us started cheering and wolf-whistling and my face felt as though it was on fire, but Xander was still holding me close.

"I love it when you blush like that," he whispered in my ear, making me blush all over again.

"Now everybody is here," Trixie called above the ruckus, "we can begin the quadrille."

Philomena bustled over to us. "Darling," she said, pressing me to her bosom. "I have something for you." She turned to Xander. "Give her the envelope," she said bossily.

Xander took a white envelope out of the inside pocket of his tailcoat and handed it to me.

"Now," Philomena said. "You have a read of that while I dance with Xander."

I noticed that Philomena didn't call him Alex. I also noticed the look of abject horror that briefly crossed his face when his first dance partner was announced.

Philomena looked at us both before dragging Xander away. "Such beautiful people," she said. "You're going to have the most gorgeous babies." I felt myself blush again and an indecipherable look flashed across Xander's face.

The envelope contained my contract of employment with Bloom & Cuthbert, laying out all the terms and conditions, benefits and surprisingly good pay packet. I needed to look over it properly of course but for now I just held it to my chest and smiled to myself. It was really happening, the future that I never thought would come was finally here.

Be brave, Meg.

"What's that you've got there?" My father had suddenly appeared at my elbow.

"Oh, it's my contract," I said, showing him.

"I'm really proud of you, Megan," he said. "I know what a big step this is for you."

"It's the right time," I said.

"I know, but it can't be easy."

"I'm not sure if anything worth doing is easy," I replied.

"Anyway, your mother sent me over here. As that Bloom woman has commandeered Xander for the quadrille I wondered if you'd like to dance with me?"

I looked at him for a moment and he grinned at me. "That would be lovely, Dad," I said.

Unsurprisingly the quadrille soon got out of hand, mostly because Philomena had no idea what she was doing and the whole thing quickly descended into a cross between line dancing and the Charleston.

"That's quite enough," Trixie's clipped tones bit through the party atmosphere. "Can we please try again with those people who know what they're doing?"

"Looks like I'm in trouble," Philomena said as she left the dance floor to get another drink. Mum replaced me as Dad's partner and Xander took my arm and drew me towards him.

"That was an experience I don't ever want to repeat," he said. When I glanced up at him he looked seasick.

We danced the quadrille that we'd been dancing for weeks. I messed most of it up but Xander managed to cover for me. He'd clearly been practising without me, whatever he'd said about having forgotten it all, although he had always had an innate lightness in the way he moved. It must be that 'float like a butterfly' thing that boxers seem to have.

Afterwards, when all the party guests had applauded and then wanted Trixie to teach them, I was taken aside by Fred Bishop, who I hadn't seen properly in years.

"I hope you won't hold all this against me," he said.

"All what?" I asked.

He waved a hand at the shop around us. "Buying this place, developing it. I am sorry it won't be a bookshop anymore but…"

"Bookshops don't make any money," I sighed. It was true. We'd been struggling for longer than any of us were willing to admit and I hated the fact that Taylor's was about to become a statistic but it was obvious that all of us – me, Mum, Missy, even Colin – wanted different things. If my burning ambition was to keep the bookshop going then maybe I could have done something to save it. But heartbreaking as the next few weeks were going to be, I knew it was the right thing. "I'm not going to hold that against you," I said.

Fred nodded. "Your mum said you might be looking for a flat."

"Yes, I was hoping you'd help me with that."

"I'll even give you mates' rates."

"I should bloody well think so." I laughed.

When I looked around for Xander he was deep in conversation with Colin, which I hoped wasn't going to escalate. Rather than disturb them I did the rounds with the guests, topping up wine glasses and wishing everyone a merry Christmas. Nearly an hour had passed before I felt Xander's touch on my elbow, that familiar tingle of electricity.

"Everything all right?" I asked. "How's Colin?"

"I haven't had a go at him, if that's what you mean," he said with a smile. "I just wanted to reassure him that it was OK, that I wasn't going to drag his name through the mud."

"I must say, you're being much more understanding about this than you were when you thought it was me who blabbed to the papers," I said with a nudge.

"You will never know how sorry I am about that. I was hurting and it made me think about Mum all over again and I shouldn't have taken any of that out on you."

"I know," I said. I knew that our argument had been about so much more than Ruby Bell.

"It would have come out eventually and, as Philomena keeps telling me, it will only improve sales."

"Thank you for being kind to Colin."

Xander shrugged. "He's young. We all do dumb things when we're young. Well, I certainly did!"

I saw Philomena heading towards us again.

"Can we find that quiet place to talk now?" he asked. "I have to be back in London for Christmas lunch and I don't really want to share you with everyone here for the whole evening."

"Come with me," I said, gently leading him away from Philomena, around the back of one of the bookcases and into the office, locking the door behind us. There was only the desk left in here now so I sat on it and Xander came to stand in front of me, his hands on my shoulders, his thighs pressing against my knees.

"This is like that book you lent me," he said.

"*The Devil in Winter*?" I asked.

He nodded, his eyes not leaving mine. "With you in these skirts and me in this tailcoat, we could re-enact a few scenes from it."

"So you did like it?"

"I told you I didn't hate it."

"Which bits did you like best?" I asked.

He bent towards me, his lips close to my ear. "The filthy bits," he whispered. I could hear the smile on his breath and the hairs on the back of my neck stood up as he kissed the spot just below my ear and then pulled away, his hands sliding down my arms and his fingers entwining with mine.

"I want to make this work, Megan," he said softly. "I know that hasn't quite been the impression I've given over the last week – as I said I'm not very good at this – but as soon as I got back to London on Friday, I knew I'd made a mistake. All I wanted was to be back here with you."

"Your brother was right about you," I said.

"He's looking forward to meeting you. All my noisy siblings are." He smiled. "Good luck with that."

I rested my forehead against him, breathing in the scent of him. I could hardly believe he was here. I could hardly bear the tension between us, the anticipation, the need. "Is Philomena going back to London with you tonight?" I asked.

"No, thank God." He laughed. "She's staying in York for Christmas. Did she not tell you?"

"No."

"She wants to spend some time with you and pick up some bargains in your Boxing Day sale."

"Lucky me," I said, wishing it was Xander who was spending Christmas in York.

"I'll be back after Christmas," he said, kissing my hair. "I'll come up to York every weekend if you want me to."

I sat back a little, looking up at him. "You don't have to do that. We can take this slowly."

"I want to be with you," he replied. "And I hope you want to be with me. The rest we can work out as we go along." He held my gaze again and it almost took my breath away. "I'll do anything I have to do to make this work."

When he'd first talked about that when we were snowed in Graydon Hall – when he'd told me that anyone worthy of me would wait until I was ready – I'd known then he was talking about himself but hadn't wanted to acknowledge it, too scared to even consider the possibility. Meeting Xander had changed my life in so many ways.

I squeezed his fingers between mine. "I'm not going to pretend that I'm not scared," I said quietly, hardly able to look at him. "But I am ready, Xander – I want to be with you."

He let go of my fingers then, cupping my face in his hands instead. He smiled at me. "I told you that the people I care about call me Alex."

"And you care about me." It wasn't a question, I already knew it was true – just as I knew that he was fussy about what sort of tea he drank and which restaurants he would eat in, just as I knew that he was a good cook (which was just as well considering how bad my family were in the kitchen), that he acted snobby and uppity when he was anxious and shy, and that he was often hopeless at trying to talk about how he was feeling, that he was better at writing things down. There was so much I didn't know about him too, but I wanted to get to know all of it. And I wanted to share my life with him.

His thumbs gently stroked my face. "Of course I care about you," he said. "I'm scared too you know, but…" He paused, and I heard the hitch in his breath. "I love you, Megan."

My heart turned over at that. I hadn't realised how much I'd needed to hear him say it, to know that this was something real, the next step in the complex, sad, funny, terrifying adventure that was life.

I touched his face, my hand trailing over his jawline, his incredible cheekbones and into his hair. "I love you too," I said. "But I don't know if I'll ever get used to calling you Alex."

He shrugged, bending down to kiss me.

"We can work on that," he said.

Epilogue

One year later

R eader, I married him.

We'd started slowly, tentatively, both of us so used to being alone and nervous of letting someone else into our respective worlds. But a long-distance relationship means you spend a lot of time on trains or motorways and that gives you the space you need to rethink your priorities.

And it turned out our priorities were each other.

I left Bella and Norm in early March and moved into a beautiful three-bedroomed flat near the Minster that Fred Bishop had found for me. Judging by the size of it and the clearly reduced rent, he'd done me a lot more than mates' rates.

He shrugged when I mentioned it. "It's the least I could do," he said.

The first time that Xander (I never did get used to calling him Alex, much to the amusement of his siblings) saw the flat, he spent a lot of time looking at the smallest bedroom and reminding me how tired he was growing of

London. The first time he stayed after I moved in, he set his laptop up in that smallest bedroom, bought an extra bag of dog food for Gus and didn't go back to London for ten days. The second time he stayed, he bought a desk, ostensibly pretending it was for me and then putting it in the smallest bedroom rather than the room I used as an office. The third time he stayed, he brought four boxes of books with him. The fourth time he stayed, he and Gus moved in for good.

Xander and I quickly learned to tolerate each other's quirks and habits. He stopped trying to tidy up the stacks of books that lay all over the flat and I tried to ignore the punchbag in the hallway – although recently he has been teaching me how to box. Goodness knows I need the exercise now I'm sitting on my bum in front of my laptop all day instead of running around a bookshop.

As for work, it's been better even than I'd dreamed it would be. I've met the most brilliant people, eaten lunch in some of the fanciest places and been to book fairs and launches all over Europe. But what I love the most is being at home and getting to read romance novels all day, while Xander is across the hallway writing his next masterpiece. I already have four new authors on my books, two of whom I think I'm about to finalise book deals for. I hadn't realised how much I'd missed working with books and book people until I started doing it again.

Meanwhile my parents found a beautiful apartment in Barcelona and whenever I FaceTime Mum she seems happier than I've seen her for years.

"Living with Dad again seems to suit you," I said.

"Cohabiting doesn't seem to be doing too badly for

you," she replied. "You're glowing, Megan. I'm so happy for you."

Missy had arrived at her parents' house in January and was still there in December – once again her plans of travelling had turned into another epic failure.

"It turns out my parents are really nice people," she said. "And a lot of my old friends still live locally." Bryn had spent the summer with her in Connecticut and she was coming back to York for New Year to see me and Bella, although we both suspected she was actually coming to see Bryn.

In July, Xander had asked me to marry him. It had been hot summer's night and we'd been lying in bed with the windows open and the fan on full blast, both unable to sleep. He'd rolled over to look at me.

"How would you feel about seeing what married life is like again?" he'd said.

I'd always wondered how I'd feel if somebody asked me to marry them again. I had never expected it to feel so right and I'd never expected to hear myself say yes without any qualms or guilt. We got married at York Register Office on a Monday morning six weeks later. As we'd both been married before we'd just wanted something quiet and simple, but we were never going to get away with that with Xander's noisy siblings, nephews, nieces and Philomena Bloom involved. They all clubbed together to organise a party afterwards. Bella and Norm were witnesses, my parents flew over from Spain, and Dot and Trixie brought John and Stan, who had both survived the test of time. Missy insisted on attending via Skype and Gus wore a spotted bow tie and acted as ring bearer.

Joe's parents understandably declined my invitation

but sent a huge bunch of flowers with a card made out to 'Megan and Alexander'. We'd kept in touch all year and I'd seen them a few times when I'd been in London. I knew how hard it must have been for them to watch me moving on like that, but they were nothing but supportive.

I still think about Joe often and Xander understands that my memories of Joe will always be part of our life together, just as his memories of his parents will be. I was still racked by waves of guilt whenever I remembered the day Joe died, the day I was at the coffee machine instead of by his side, but I've started seeing a therapist and things feel easier now, lighter, as though I can live alongside my feelings instead of buried under them.

The bookshop has become a designer boutique. At first, I was furious and refused to even look at it, but I've come around over the last few months. I've even bought Xander a coat from there for Christmas.

The Die-Hard Romantics Book Club still meets every week at Dot's house. There are only four of us now and we keep saying we need some new recruits, but none of us ever seem to do much about it. We know each other so well and have so much fun together that it would be strange for anyone else to join us now.

As for Ruby Bell, her latest novel, the first book that I'd edited after my four-year hiatus, came out to much publicity in the spring and became an instant best-seller. Ruby, sadly, has decided not to write any more books but I've heard a rumour that a debut crime writer called Alexander Tennant is launching his first book next summer. I couldn't possibly tell you who that is the pen-name of but I do know that Tennant was Xander's mum's maiden name.

And so another year has turned, a year in which I've taken huge risks and ended up happy in a way I never thought I would be again. We're spending Christmas with Xander's family, my first experience of a big family Christmas. Xander and I have set up a code word for when I need a break to decompress from them all – but I'm actually really looking forward to it. I love being part of his family and some days I can't believe how much my life has changed in the last year. I'd spent so long trying to control everything, so long not leaving the bookshop, that I'd forgotten what living felt like.

There has never really been any certainty in life – I learned that the day that Joe was first diagnosed. But I know something now that I didn't realise then. We can't spend our lives hiding away from the things that will hurt us because we will never find the things that bring us joy, that bring us companionship, that bring us love. And I've learned that when life brings us lower than we ever thought possible we come out the other side of that armed with a resilience that allows us to live life and love harder than ever before.

Xander Stone taught me that.

Megan and Xander's Playlist

These are the songs I was listening to when I was inside Megan and Xander's heads.

1. 'Hello, Goodbye' – The Beatles
2. 'Ghosts' – Laura Marling
3. 'Wages Day' – Deacon Blue
4. 'Nothing Ever Happens' – Del Amitri
5. 'Step Into My Office, Baby' – Belle & Sebastian
6. 'The Boxer' – Simon & Garfunkel
7. 'What Katie Did' – The Libertines
8. 'How Men Are' – Aztec Camera
9. 'Dear Rosemary' – Foo Fighters
10. 'Everything is Awful' – The Decemberists
11. 'Born to Run' – Bruce Springsteen
12. 'East of the Sun' – A-ha
13. 'Universally Speaking' – Red Hot Chili Peppers
14. 'Home' – Foo Fighters

The Die-Hard Romantics Book Club's Favourite Books

1. *Persuasion* – Jane Austen
2. *Pride and Prejudice* – Jane Austen
3. *Northanger Abbey* – Jane Austen
4. *The Moonstone* – Wilkie Collins
5. *A Christmas Gone Perfectly Wrong* – Cecilia Grant
6. *Snowdrift and Other Stories* – Georgette Heyer
7. *The Devil in Winter* – Lisa Kleypas
8. *Me Before You* – JoJo Moyes
9. *The Lady Most Willing* – Julia Quinn, Eloisa James and Connie Brockway
10. *Love Story* – Erich Segal
11. *Oliver's Story* – Erich Segal
12. *One Day in December* – Josie Silver
13. *Maybe This Christmas* – Jennifer Snow

Xander's Favourite Books

1. *The New York Trilogy* – Paul Auster
2. *Medium Raw* – Anthony Bordain
3. *The Luminaries* – Eleanor Catton

4. *Great Expectations* – Charles Dickens
5. *Enduring Love* – Ian McEwan
6. *The Life and Opinions of Tristram Shandy,
   Gentleman* – Laurence Sterne

Acknowledgements

If somebody had told me at the beginning of 2020 that over the next fourteen months I'd write three books in three lockdowns, I wouldn't have believed them. And yet, here we are. *A Bookshop Christmas* was written during UK Lockdown 3.0 (Tokyo Drift) and I finished the third draft on day 362 of shielding, four days before I got my first vaccine. It has been quite the year but spending part of it in an imaginary bookshop set in a York where Coronavirus never existed has been a soothing balm.

My thanks to my agents Julie Fergusson and Lina Langlee (neither of whom are anything like Philomena Bloom), to Lydia Mason and Thorne Ryan for helping me wrangle my story into shape, to Josephine Gibbons for the copy edits, to Lisa Brewster for another gorgeous cover and everyone else at Aria/Head of Zeus for everything they do to make our books the best they can be.

A Jane Austen Christmas by Maria Grace was an invaluable and amusing guide to Regency festivities – particularly when it came to food and recipes, some of which honestly sounded disgusting!

Thank you to Natalie Sellers for her in-depth knowledge of Porsches and their inability to drive in snow, to Sarah

Bennett for her regular and invaluable synopsis assistance and to my husband for reading an early draft and helping me redevelop Xander's story arc.

Another lockdown book meant another book without seeing my cheerleaders – Nat, Max, Sarah, Rachael, Rachel and Kate. Thank God for WhatsApp, eh?

Thank you to all the reviewers, bloggers and readers who have helped me make this crazy storytelling my job. I can't believe we've done this six times already!

And finally, I can't write acknowledgements to a book about a bookshop without thanking all the booksellers out there who put our books in the hands of the readers they know will love them and who have had such a challenging time after a year of shop closures, lockdowns and furloughs.

About the Author

RACHEL BURTON has a degree in Classics and another in English Literature, and fell into a career in law by mistake. She has spent most of her life between Cambridge and London but now lives in Yorkshire with her husband and their three cats. She loves yoga, ice hockey, tea, The Beatles, dresses with pockets and very tall romantic heroes. You can find her on Twitter and Instagram as @RachelBWriter or follow her blog at rachelburtonwrites.com. She is always happy to talk books, writing, music, cats and how the weather in Yorkshire is rubbish. She is mostly dreaming of her next holiday....

Hello from Aria

We hope you enjoyed this book! If you did let us know, we'd love to hear from you.

We are Aria, a dynamic digital-first fiction imprint from award-winning independent publishers Head of Zeus. At heart, we're committed to publishing fantastic commercial fiction – from romance and sagas to crime, thrillers and historical fiction. Visit us online and discover a community of like-minded fiction fans!

We're also on the look out for tomorrow's superstar authors. So, if you're a budding writer looking for a publisher, we'd love to hear from you. You can submit your book online at ariafiction.com/ we-want-read-your-book

You can find us at:
Email: aria@headofzeus.com
Website: www.ariafiction.com
Submissions: www.ariafiction.com/ we-want-read-your-book

[f] @ariafiction
[twitter] @Aria_Fiction
[instagram] @ariafiction